THE LAW

He was new to this town but the marshal had seen it many times before, this hurry and bustle. He had seen it over cattle, over land, over silver and gold.

Wherever it seemed that money might quickly be had, there men thronged.

Some were good men, builders, men of iron.

The strong, the brave, the true.

But they were not alone, for here also were the scum.

The cheats, the gamblers, the good-for-nothings.

The men who robbed, who destroyed, who lived by deceit or treachery. And here also were those who felt that strength or gun skill made them the law—their own law. And these were often the most dangerous.

And it was for these that he was here.

The marshal looked over the gathering mob. He spoke loudly:

"Those of you who deserve hanging will get it."

Bantam Books by Louis L'Amour
Ask your bookseller for the books you have missed.

NOVELS

BENDIGO SHAFTER
BORDEN CHANTRY
BRIONNE
THE BROKEN GUN
THE BURNING HILLS
THE CALIFORNIOS
CALLAGHEN
CATLOW
CHANCY
THE CHEROKEE TRAIL
COMSTOCK LODE
CONAGHER
CROSSFIRE TRAIL
DARK CANYON
DOWN THE LONG HILLS
THE EMPTY LAND
FAIR BLOWS THE WIND
FALLON
THE FERGUSON RIFLE
THE FIRST FAST DRAW
FLINT
GUNS OF THE TIMBERLANDS
HANGING WOMAN CREEK
THE HAUNTED MESA
HELLER WITH A GUN
THE HIGH GRADERS
HIGH LONESOME
HONDO
HOW THE WEST WAS WON
THE IRON MARSHAL
THE KEY-LOCK MAN
KID RODELO
KILKENNY
KILLOE
KILRONE
KIOWA TRAIL
LAST OF THE BREED
LAST STAND AT PAPAGO
    WELLS
THE LONESOME GODS
THE MAN CALLED NOON
THE MAN FROM SKIBBEREEN
THE MAN FROM THE
    BROKEN HILLS
MATAGORDA
MILO TALON
THE MOUNTAIN VALLEY WAR

NORTH TO THE RAILS
OVER ON THE DRY SIDE
PASSIN' THROUGH
THE PROVING TRAIL
THE QUICK AND THE DEAD
RADIGAN
REILLY'S LUCK
THE RIDER OF LOST CREEK
RIVERS WEST
THE SHADOW RIDERS
SHALAKO
SHOWDOWN AT YELLOW
    BUTTE
SILVER CANYON
SITKA
SON OF A WANTED MAN
TAGGART
THE TALL STRANGER
TO TAME A LAND
TUCKER
UNDER THE SWEETWATER
    RIM
UTAH BLAINE
THE WALKING DRUM
WESTWARD THE TIDE
WHERE THE LONG GRASS
    BLOWS

SHORT STORY COLLECTIONS

BOWDRIE
BOWDRIE'S LAW
BUCKSKIN RUN
DUTCHMAN'S FLAT
THE HILLS OF HOMICIDE
LAW OF THE DESERT BORN
LONG RIDE HOME
LONIGAN
NIGHT OVER THE
    SOLOMONS
THE OUTLAWS OF MESQUITE
THE RIDER OF THE RUBY
    HILLS
RIDING FOR THE BRAND
THE STRONG SHALL LIVE
THE TRAIL TO CRAZY MAN
WAR PARTY

WEST FROM SINGAPORE
YONDERING

SACKETT TITLES

SACKETT'S LAND
TO THE FAR BLUE
    MOUNTAINS
THE WARRIOR'S PATH
JUBAL SACKETT
RIDE THE RIVER
THE DAYBREAKERS
SACKETT
LANDO
MOJAVE CROSSING
MUSTANG MAN
THE LONELY MEN
GALLOWAY
TREASURE MOUNTAIN
LONELY ON THE MOUNTAIN
RIDE THE DARK TRAIL
THE SACKETT BRAND
THE SKY-LINERS

THE HOPALONG CASSIDY NOVELS

THE RUSTLERS OF WEST
    FORK
THE TRAIL TO SEVEN PINES
THE RIDERS OF HIGH ROCK

NONFICTION

EDUCATION OF A
    WANDERING MAN
FRONTIER
THE SACKETT COMPANION:
    A Personal Guide to the
    Sackett Novels
A TRAIL OF MEMORIES:
    The Quotations of Louis
    L'Amour, compiled by
    Angelique L'Amour

POETRY

SMOKE FROM THIS ALTAR

LAW OF THE DESERT BORN

The Only Authorized Edition

LOUIS L'AMOUR

BANTAM BOOKS

NEW YORK • TORONTO • LONDON • SYDNEY • AUCKLAND

This is a collection of Louis L'Amour short stories that have been collected and revised by the author with additional newly written material. It is the only authorized edition of these stories.

LAW OF THE DESERT BORN
A Bantam Book / August 1983
6 printings through January 1989

PRINTING HISTORY
The stories contained in this volume were previously published in slightly different form.

ISBN 0-553-24133-8

Published simultaneously in the United States and Canada

Bantam Books are published by Bantam Books, a division of Bantam Doubleday Dell Publishing Group, Inc. Its trademark, consisting of the words "Bantam Books" and the portrayal of a rooster, is Registered in U.S. Patent and Trademark Office and in other countries. Marca Registrada. Bantam Books, 1540 Broadway, New York, New York 10036.

PRINTED IN THE UNITED STATES OF AMERICA

KR   15 14

**To my loyal readers, who
will know how to read a brand.**

CONTENTS

FOREWORD

LAW OF THE DESERT BORN is the latest collection of short stories I have been putting together in a carefully planned series published by Bantam Books to offer my readers the products of my earlier years as a writer. Like the previous collections, WAR PARTY, THE STRONG SHALL LIVE, BUCKSKIN RUN, and BOWDRIE these are frontier stories. As I have been trying to do in recent collections, I have also included special new notes between the stories. In many cases these are historical notes to illustrate the background of the stories and the society from which they derived.

After so many years legends have grown up, and debunkers with no actual knowledge of western history have made statements accepted by some as the truth. We do not have to imagine what happened in the West; we know. It is well documented in newspaper accounts as well as diaries and memoirs of the time by people who were present.

In several instances I have included some of my personal experiences traveling around the kind of country I've written about, an approach I enjoyed taking for some of the notes in the first collection of some of my non-frontier stories, YONDERING.

My own travels have not only taken me over all kinds of country but down some pretty mean streets as well. Part of those latter experiences prompted me to write some detective stories for the pulp magazines. Those of my readers who have only been exposed to my frontier stories might find this surprising but over the years I have tried to bring to all kinds of fiction the best storytelling I'm capable of, and these detective stories have a lot of action and colorful backgrounds in a period style similar to the stories of Hammett and Chandler.

I mention this because I have been putting together my first collection of some of those early detective stories, THE HILLS OF HOMICIDE, at the same time I have been completing LAW OF THE DESERT BORN. It is unusual to publish two collections so close together but I have worked very hard to do so because, as I have announced on the back cover of this book, I have become aware that a publisher I am in no way associated with has announced publication of two completely unauthorized editions bearing these two titles. Those two books are completely unauthorized editions of some of the same stories that I have collected here. I had absolutely nothing to do with the putting together of the unauthorized editions of these two titles; in fact, for the first time in my career I went to court to try to protect the very rights I have struggled to gain over the years—to have my work published *only* as I see fit in the way I feel best serves my readers. The court ruled that since the copyrights in some of my stories had not been properly renewed, this other publisher could publish the original magazine versions in unauthorized collections.

Imagine, this other publisher did not even have enough respect for me to tell me which of my stories they were planning to publish!

The authors of the copyright law were attempting to protect a writer's property rights to his work, and protected him for twenty-eight years after which he had a year to renew the copyright for another twenty-eight. Unfortunately, when the stories I recently went to court to try to protect were coming due for renewal, it was at a time when every day's work was important if I was to earn a living for myself and my family, and some of the copyrights, in a very few of the stories, were not properly renewed.

In determining the meaning of any law one has to ask: What was the intent of the lawmakers? The intent here was obvious: They intended to protect a writer's rights to the work he had produced, not to open a gate to any interloper who might choose to rush in and try to profit from the hard work of someone else.

The new copyright law indicates understanding of the problem. A writer's work is now automatically protected for his lifetime plus fifty years.

So that my readers will not be deprived of the authorized, proper presentation of my stories, I have worked around the clock to get ready this collection of frontier stories plus THE HILLS OF HOMICIDE collection of detective fiction which contain not only my revised versions of the stories in the unauthorized books but several additional stories, plus the aforementioned notes of interest.

I have a very good and satisfying sense of my readers from the letters I receive and the personal contact I have had with many of them through the years: As far as I am concerned—and I'm confident, as far as my fans are concerned—any unauthorized editions of *any* of my fiction does not exist. I feel so strongly about this fact that should any of my readers, during one of my upcom-

ing public appearances, bring me a copy of any unauthorized copy of a book with my name on it, I will refuse to
sign it under any circumstances.

Louis L'Amour
Los Angeles, California
July 1983

LAW OF THE
DESERT BORN

Shad Marone crawled out of the water swearing and slid into the mesquite. Suddenly, for the first time since the chase began, he was mad. He was mad clear through. "The hell with it!" He got to his feet, his eyes blazing. "I've run far enough! If they cross Black River, they're askin' for it!"

For three days he had been on the dodge, using every stratagem known to men of the desert, but they clung to him like leeches. That was what came of killing a sheriff's brother, and the fact that he killed in self-defense wasn't going to help a bit. Especially when the killer was Shad Marone.

That was what you could expect when you were the last man of the losing side in a cattle war. All his friends were gone now but Madge.

The best people of Puerto de Luna hadn't been the toughest in this scrap, and they had lost. And Shad Marone, who had been one of the toughest, had lost with them. His guns hadn't been enough to outweigh those of the other faction.

Of course, he admitted to himself, those on his side hadn't been angels. He'd branded a few head of calves himself from time to time, and when cash was short, he had often run a few steers over the border. But hadn't they all?

Truman and Dykes had been good men, but Dykes had been killed at the start, and Truman had fought like a gentleman, and that wasn't any way to win in the Black River country.

Since then, there had been few peaceful days for Shad Marone.

After they'd elected Clyde Bowman sheriff, he knew they were out to get him. Bowman hated him, and Bowman had been one of the worst of them in the cattle war.

The trouble was, Shad was a gunfighter, and they all knew it. Bowman was fast with a gun and in a fight could hold his own. Also, he was smart enough to leave Shad Marone strictly alone. So they just waited, watched, and planned.

Shad had taken their dislike as a matter of course. It took tough men to settle a tough country, and if they started shooting, somebody got hurt. Well, he wasn't getting hurt. There had been too much shooting to suit him.

He wanted to leave Puerto de Luna, but Madge was still living on the old place, and he didn't want to leave her there alone. So he stayed on, knowing it couldn't last.

Then Jud Bowman rode into town. Shad was thoughtful when he heard that. Jud was notoriously quarrelsome and was said to have twelve notches on his gun. Shad had a feeling that Jud hadn't come to Puerto de Luna by accident.

Jud hadn't been in town two days before the grapevine had the story that if Clyde and Lopez were afraid to run Marone out of town, he wasn't.

Jud Bowman might have done it, too, if it hadn't been for Tips. Tips Hogan had been tending bar in Puerto de Luna for a long time. He'd come over the trail as wagon boss for Shad's old man, something everyone had forgotten but Shad and Tips himself.

Tips saw the gun in Bowman's lap, and he gave Marone a warning. It was just a word, through unmoving lips, while he mopped the bar.

After a moment, Shad turned, his glass in his left hand, and he saw the way Bowman was sitting and how the tabletop would conceal a gun in his lap. Even then, when he knew they had set things up to kill him, he hadn't wanted trouble. He decided to get out while the getting was good. Then he saw Slade near the door and Henderson across the room.

He was boxed. They weren't gambling this time. Tips Hogan knew what was likely to happen, and he was working his way down the bar.

Marone took it easy. He knew it was coming, and it wasn't a new thing. That was his biggest advantage, he thought. He had been in more fights than any of them. He didn't want any more trouble, but if he got out of this, it would be right behind a six-gun. The back door was barred and the window closed.

Jud Bowman looked up suddenly. He had a great shock of blond, coarse hair, and under bushy brows his eyes glinted. "What's this about you threatenin' to kill me, Marone?"

So that was their excuse. He had not threatened Bowman, scarcely knew him, in fact, but this was the way to put him in the wrong, to give them the plea of self-defense.

He let his eyes turn to Bowman, saw the tensity in the man's face. A denial, and there would be shooting. Jud's right-hand fingertips rested on the table's edge. He had only to drop a hand and fire.

"Huh?" Shad said stupidly, as though startled from a daydream. He took a step toward the table, his face puzzled. "Wha'd you say? I didn't get it."

They had planned it all very carefully. Marone would deny, Bowman would claim he'd been called a liar; there would be a killing. They were tense, all three of them set to draw.

"Huh?" Shad repeated blankly.

They were caught flat-footed. After all, you couldn't shoot a man in cold blood. You couldn't shoot a man who was half-asleep. Most of the men in the saloon were against Marone, but they would never stand for murder.

They were poised for action, and nothing happened. Shad blinked at them. "Sorry," he said, "I must've been dreamin'. I didn't hear you."

Bowman glanced around uncertainly, wetting his lips with his tongue. "I said I heard you threatened to kill me," he repeated. It sounded lame, and he knew it, but Shad's response had been unexpected. What happened then was even more unexpected.

Marone's left hand shot out, and before anyone could move, the table was spun from in front of Bowman. Everyone saw the naked gun lying in his lap.

Every man in the saloon knew that Jud Bowman, for all his reputation, had been afraid to shoot it out with an even break. It would have been murder.

Taken by surprise, Bowman blinked foolishly. Then his wits came back. Blood rushed to his face. He grabbed the gun. "Why, you . . . !"

Then Shad Marone shot him. Shad shot him through the belly, and before the other two could act, he wheeled, not toward the door, but to the closed window. He battered it with his shoulder and went right on through. Outside, he hit the ground on his hands but came up in a lunging run. Then he was in the saddle and on his way.

There were men in the saloon who would tell the

truth—two at least, although neither had much use for him. But Marone knew that with Clyde Bowman as sheriff he would never be brought to trial. He would be killed "evading arrest."

For three days, he fled, and during that time, they were never more than an hour behind him. Then, at Forked Tree, they closed in. He got away, but they clipped his horse. The roan stayed on his feet, giving all he had, as horses always had given for Shad Marone, and then died on the riverbank, still trying with his last breath.

Marone took time to cache his saddle and bridle, then started on afoot. He made the river, and they thought that would stop him, for he couldn't swim a stroke. But he found a drift log, and with his guns riding high, he shoved off. Using the current and his own kicking, he got to the other bank, considerably downstream.

The thing that bothered him was the way they clung to his trail. Bowman wasn't the man to follow as little trail as he left. Yet the man hung to him like an Apache.

Apache!

Why hadn't he thought of that? It would be Lopez following that trail, not Bowman. Bowman was a bulldog, but Lopez was wily as a fox and bloodthirsty as a weasel.

Shad got to his feet and shook the water from him like a dog. He was a big, rawboned, sun-browned man. His shirt was half torn away, and a bandolier of cartridges was slung across his shoulder and chest. His six-gun was on his hip, his rifle in his hand.

He poured the water out of his boots. Well, he was through playing now. If they wanted a trail, he'd see that they got one.

Lopez was the one who worried him. He could shake the others, but Lopez was one of the men who had built this country. He was ugly, he killed freely and often, he was absolutely ruthless, but he had nerve.

9

You had to hand it to him. The man wasn't honest, and he was too quick to kill, but it had taken men like him to tame this wild, lonely land. It was a land that didn't tame easy.

Well, what they'd get now would be death for them all. Even Lopez. This was something he'd been saving.

Grimly he turned up the steep, little-used path from the river. They thought they had him at the river. And they would think they had him again at the lava beds.

Waterless, treeless, and desolate, the lava beds were believed to harbor no life of any kind. Only sand and great, jagged rocks—rocks shaped like flame—grotesque, barren, awful. More than seventy miles long, never less than thirty miles wide, so rough a pair of shoes wouldn't last five miles and footing next to impossible for horses.

On the edge of the lava, Shad Marone sat down and pulled off his boots. Tying their strings, he hung them to his belt. Then he pulled out a pair of moccasins he always carried and slipped them on. Pliable and easy on his feet, they would give to the rough rock and would last many times as long in this terrain as boots. He got up and walked into the lava beds.

The bare lava caught the fierce heat and threw it back in his face. A trickle of sweat started down his cheek. He knew the desert, knew how to live in the heat, and he did not try to hurry. That would be fatal. Far ahead of him was a massive tower of rock jutting up like a church steeple from a tiny village. He headed that way, walking steadily. He made no attempt to cover his trail, no attempt to lose his pursuers. He knew where he was going.

An hour passed, and then another. It was slow going. The rock tower had come abreast of him and then fallen behind. Once he saw the trail of some tiny creature, perhaps a horned frog.

Once, when he climbed a steep declivity, he glanced back. They were still coming. They hadn't quit.

Lopez—that was like Lopez. He wouldn't quit. Shad smiled then, but his eyes were without humor. All right, they wanted to kill him bad enough to try the lava beds. They would have to learn the hard way— learn when they could never profit from the lesson.

He kept working north, using the shade carefully. There was little of it, only here and there in the lee of a rock. But each time he stopped, he cooled off a little. So far he hadn't taken a drink.

After the third hour, he washed his lips and rinsed his mouth. Twice, after that, he took only a spoonful of water and rinsed his mouth before swallowing.

Occasionally, he stopped and looked around to get his bearings. He smiled grimly when he thought of Bowman. The sheriff was a heavy man. Davis would be there, too. Lopez was lean and wiry. He would last. He would be hard to kill.

By his last count, there were eight left. Four had turned back at the lava beds. He gained a little.

At three in the afternoon, he finally stopped. It was a nice piece of shade and would grow better as the hours went on. The ground was low, and in one corner there was a pocket. He dug with his hands until the ground became damp. Then he lay back on the sand and went to sleep.

He wasn't worried. Too many years he had been awakening at the hour he wished, his senses alert to danger. He was an hour ahead of them, at least. He would need this rest he was going to get. What lay ahead would take everything he had. He knew that.

Their feet would be punishing them cruelly now. Three of them still had their horses, leading them.

He rested his full hour, then got up. He had cut it very thin. Through a space in the rocks, he could see them, not three hundred yards away. Lopez, as he had suspected, was in the lead. How easy to pick them off now! But no, he would not kill again. Let their own anxiety to kill him kill them.

11

Within a hundred yards, he had put two jumbled piles of boulders between himself and his pursuers. A little farther then, and he stopped.

Before him was a steep slide of shale, near the edge of a great basin. Standing where he did, he could see, far away in the distance, a purple haze over the mountains. Between there was nothing but a great white expanse, shimmering with heat.

He slid down the shale and brought up at the bottom. He was now, he knew, seventy feet below sea level. He started away, and at every step, dry, powdery dust lifted in clouds. It caked in his nostrils, filmed his eyelashes, and covered his clothes with whitish, alkaline dust. Far across the Sink, and scarcely discernible from the crest behind him, was the Window in the Rock. He headed for it, walking steadily. It was ten miles if you walked straight across.

"So far that Navajo was right," Shad told himself. "An' he said to make it before dark . . . or else!"

Shad Marone's lips were dry and cracked. After a mile, he stopped, tilting his canteen until he could get his finger into the water, then carefully moistened his lips. Just a drop then, inside his mouth.

All these men were desertwise. None of them, excepting perhaps Lopez, would know about the Sink. They would need water. They would have to know where to find it. By day they could follow his trail, but after darkness fell . . . ?

And then, the Navajo had said, the wind would begin to blow. Shad looked at the dry, powdery stuff under him. He could imagine what a smothering, stifling horror this would be if the wind blew. Then, no man could live.

Heat waves danced a queer rigadoon across the lower sky, and heat lifted, beating against his face from the hot white dust beneath his feet. Always it was over a man's shoe tops, sometimes almost knee-deep. Far away, the mountains were a purple line that seemed to waver vaguely in the afternoon sun. He walked on, heading by instinct rather than sight for the Window.

Dust arose in a slow, choking cloud. It came up from his feet in little puffs, like white smoke. He stumbled, then got his feet right, and kept on. Walking in this was like dragging yourself through heavy mud. The dust pulled at his feet. His pace was slow.

Thirst gathered in his throat, and his mouth seemed filled with something thick and clotted. His tongue was swollen, his lips cracked and swollen. He could not seem to swallow.

He could not make three miles an hour. Darkness would reach him before he made the other side. But he would be close. Close enough. Luckily, at this season, the light stayed long in the sky.

After a long time, he stopped and looked back. Yes, they were coming. But there was not one dust cloud. There were several. Through red-rimmed, sun-squinted eyes, he watched. They were straggling. Every straggler would die. He knew that. Well, they had asked for it.

Dust covered his clothing, and only his gun he kept clean. Every half hour he stopped and wiped it as clean as he could. Twice he pulled a knotted string through the barrel.

Finally, he used the last of his water. Every half hour he had been wetting his lips. He did not throw the canteen away, but slung it back upon his hip. He would need it later, when he got to the Nest. His feet felt very heavy, his legs seemed to belong to an automaton. Head down, he slogged wearily on. In an hour he made two miles.

There is a time when human nature seems able to stand no more. There is a time when every iota of strength seems burned away. This was the fourth day of the chase. Four days without a hot meal, four days of riding, walking, running. Now this. He had only to stop, they would come up with him, and it would be over.

The thought of how easy it would be to quit came to him. He considered the thought. But he did not consider quitting. He could no more have stopped than a bee could stop making honey. Life was ahead, and he had to live. It was a matter only of survival now. The man with the greatest urge to live would be the one to survive.

Those men behind him were going to die. They were going to die for three reasons. First, he alone knew where there was water, and at the right time he would lose them.

Second, he was in the lead, and after dark they would have no trail, and if they lived through the night, there would be no trail left in the morning.

Third, at night, at this season, the wind always blew, and their eyes and mouths and ears would fill with soft, white filmy dust, and if they lay down, they would be buried by the sifting, swirling dust.

They would die then, every manjack of them.

They had it coming. Bowman deserved it; so did Davis and Gardner. Lopez most of all. They were all there; he had seen them. Lopez was a killer. The man's father had been Spanish and Irish, his mother an Apache.

Without Lopez, he would have shaken them off long before. Shad Marone tried to laugh, but the sound was only a choking grunt. Well, they had followed Lopez to their death, all of them. Aside from Lopez, they were weak sisters.

He looked back again. He was gaining on them now. The first dust cloud was farther behind, and the distance between the others was growing wider. It was a shame Lopez had to die, at that. The man was tough and had plenty of trail savvy.

Shad Marone moved on. From somewhere within him he called forth a new burst of strength. His eyes watched the sun. While there was light, they had a chance. What would they think in Puerto de Luna when eight men did not come back?

Marone looked at the sun, and it was low, scarcely above the purple mountains. They seemed close now. He lengthened his stride again. The Navajo had told him how his people once had been pursued by Apaches, and had led the whole Apache war party into the Sink. There they had been caught by darkness, and none were ever seen again according to the Indian's story.

Shad stumbled then and fell. Dust lifted thickly about him, clogging his nostrils. Slowly, like a groggy fighter, he got his knees under him, and using his rifle for a staff, pushed himself to his feet.

He started on, driven by some blind, brute desire for life. When he fell again, he could feel rocks under his hands. He pulled himself up.

He climbed the steep, winding path toward the Window in the Rock. Below the far corner of the Window was the Nest. And in the Nest, there was water. Or so the Navajo had told him.

When he was halfway up the trail, he turned and looked back over the Sink. Far away, he could see the dust clouds. Four of them. One larger than the others. Probably there were two men together.

"Still coming," he muttered grimly, "and Lopez leading them!"

Lopez, damn his soul!

The little devil had guts, though; you had to give him that. Suddenly, Marone found himself almost wishing Lopez would win through. The man was like a wolf. A killer wolf. But he had guts. And it wasn't just the honest men who had built up this country to what it was today.

Maybe, without the killers and rustlers and badmen, the West would never have been won so soon. Shad Marone remembered some of them: wild, dangerous men, who went into country where nobody else dared venture. They killed and robbed to live, but they stayed there.

It took iron men for that: men like Lopez, who was a mongrel of the Santa Fe Trail. Lopez had drunk water from a buffalo track many a time. *Well, so have I,* Shad told himself.

Shad Marone took out his six-shooter and wiped it free of dust. Only then did he start up the trail.

He found the Nest, a hollow among the rocks, sheltered from the wind. The Window loomed above him now, immense, gigantic. Shad stumbled, running, into the Nest. He dropped his rifle and lunged for the water hole, throwing himself on the ground to drink. Then he stared, unbelieving.

Empty!

The earth was dry and parched where the water had been, but only cracked earth remained.

He couldn't believe it. It couldn't be! It couldn't . . . ! Marone came to his feet, glaring wildly about. His eyes were red rimmed, his face heat flushed above the black whiskers, now filmed with gray dust.

He tried to laugh. Lopez dying down below there, he dying up here! The hard men of the West, the tough men! He sneered at himself. Both of them now would die, he at the water hole, Lopez down there in the cloying, clogging dust!

He shook his head. Through the flame-sheathed torment of his brain, there came a cool ray of sanity.

There had been water here. The Indian had been right. The cracked earth showed that. But where?

Perhaps a dry season. . . . But no; it had not been a dry season. Certainly no dryer than any other year at this time.

He stared across the place where the pool had been. Rocks and a few rock cedar and some heaped-up rocks from a small slide. He stumbled across and began clawing at the rocks, pulling, tearing. Suddenly, a trickle of water burst through! He got hold of one big rock and in a mad frenzy, tore it from its place. The water shot through then, so suddenly he was knocked to his knees.

He scrambled out of the depression, splashing in the water. Then, lying on his face, he drank, long and greedily.

Finally, he rolled away and lay still, panting. Dimly, he was conscious of the wind blowing. He crawled to the water again and bathed his face, washing away the dirt and grime. Then, careful as always, he filled his canteen from the fresh water bubbling up from the spring.

If he only had some coffee. . . . But he'd left his food in his saddlebags.

Well, Madge would be all right now. He could go back to her. After this, they wouldn't bother him. He would take her away. They would go to the Blue Mountains in Oregon. He had always liked that country.

The wind was blowing more heavily now, and he could smell the dust. That Navajo hadn't lied. It would be hell down in the Sink. He was above it now and almost a mile away.

He stared down into the darkness, wondering how far Lopez had been able to get. The others didn't matter; they were weak sisters who lived on the strength of better men. If they didn't die there, they would die elsewhere, and the West could spare them. He got to his feet.

Lopez would hate to die. The ranch he had built so carefully in a piece of the wildest, roughest country was going good. It took a man with guts to settle where he had and make it pay. Shad Marone rubbed the stubble on his jaw. "That last thirty head of his cows I rustled for him brought the best price I ever got!" he remembered thoughtfully. "Too bad there ain't more like him!"

Well, after this night, there would be one less. There wouldn't be anything to guide Lopez down there now.

A man caught in a thick whirlpool of dust would have no landmarks; there would be nothing to get him out except blind instinct. The Navajos had been clever, leading the Apaches into a trap like that. Odd, that Lopez's mother had been an Apache, too.

Just the same, Marone thought, he had nerve. He'd shot his way up from the bottom until he had one of the best ranches.

Shad Marone began to pick up some dead cedar. He gathered some needles for kindling and in a few minutes had a fire going.

Marone took another drink. Somehow, he felt restless. He got up and walked to the edge of the Nest. How far had Lopez come? Suppose . . . Marone gripped his pistol.

Suddenly, he started down the mountain. "The hell with it!" he muttered.

A stone rattled.

Shad Marone froze, gun in hand.

Lopez, a gray shadow, weaving in the vague light from the cliff, had a gun in his hand. For a full minute, they stared at each other.

Marone spoke first. "Looks like a dead heat," he said.

Lopez said, "How'd you know about that water hole?"

"Navajo told me," Shad replied, watching Lopez like a cat. "You don't look so bad," he added. "Have a full canteen?"

"No. I'd have been a goner. But my mother was an Apache. A bunch of them got caught in the Sink once. That never happened twice to no Apache. They found this water hole then, and one down below. I made the one below, an' then I was finished. She was a dry hole. But then water began to run in from a crack in the rock."

"Yeah?" Marone looked at him again. "You got any coffee?"

"Sure."

"Well," Shad said as he holstered his gun, "I've got a fire."

18

Author's Note:
THE SYCAMORE WILD AREA

After World War II, while living in Los Angeles, I would occasionally make up a backpack and head for the wild country, usually in Arizona.

One of my favorite places was what is called The Sycamore Wild Area in Sycamore Canyon. In those days there was a branch line railroad that ran from Clarkdale to Drake and the train crew would drop you off anywhere along the line and pick you up on the way back whenever you showed up. The train was known as the Verde-Mix.

The land was rough, wild, and beautiful. There were deer, mountain lion, and occasional bear, some beautiful springs and running streams all with nobody around to bother you. Usually I would spend three or four days hiking lonely canyons, climbing mountains, or wandering in the forests, sleeping under the stars or in caves that had sheltered Indians or outlaws in their time.

There were stories of ghosts, lost mines, horse thieves, and ancient Indians. Some of them I heard from Jim Roberts when he was a peace officer in Clarkdale. I first ran into him when I was doing assessment work in a mining claim not far from Jerome. Roberts was a survivor of the Tonto Basin War and we talked about it several times as I had known Tom Pickett who was also involved.

RIDING ON

"Good cowboys never run; they just ride away."
—Old Saying

The riders moved forward in a body. "Strike a match, Reb!" Nathan Embree's voice trembled with triumph. "We finally got one; I heard him fall."

Reb Farrell slid from the saddle. "I see him! He's right over here!" A match whispered on his jeans and the light flared.

All necks craned forward. The man on the ground had a bullet through his head, but his face was placid. It was a face seamed with care and years that had not been kind. The face of a man tired of the struggle of living. It was the face of Reb Farrell's father.

Numb with horror, Reb stared down at the man he had killed, the man who had fought to give him some little education and a sense of honor, who had fought so hard and lost, and who now was dead, killed by the son he had loved.

"My God!" Dave Barbot's exclamation was low. "Not Jim Farrell! It can't be!"

Nathan Embree's own shock changed to sudden, bitter fury. "So that was it? So that was why you couldn't find any rustlers for me, Reb? Maybe this explains how they always knew when an' where to strike! Maybe this explains why they were always one jump ahead of us!"

Reb Farrell stared unbelievingly at the body, shocked as much by his father's presence here as by the feeling that he himself had shot him. He did not hear the words of Nathan Embree. He did not hear Dave Barbot's refusal to agree.

"You don't believe that, Nathan!" Dave's voice was sharp. "Reb fought them harder than anybody. He's recovered two herds for you."

"Uh-huh." There was cold certainty in Nathan Embree's voice. "Why did he find 'em when nobody else could? Maybe it was because he knew where to look? When did this rustling start? Right after I made him foreman, wasn't it?"

Reb Farrell looked up. "What was that? What did you say, Nathan?"

Nathan Embree was a just man, but he was also hard and merciless. The moon had emerged from under a cloud and showed him the face of his young foreman.

"You're fired, Reb! Fired! Get your gear an' get off the place. I can't prove anything against you, but if you're still in the country within twenty-four hours, we'll hunt you down an' you'll hang."

Astonishment held Reb speechless for a full minute and then, as the riders began to turn their horses to ride away, he found his voice. "You accusin' me of rustlin', Nathan?" His eyes seemed to flare. "I won't take that from no man. Don't call me a rustler unless you're willing to grab iron."

Embree turned on him. "Yes," he said contemptuously,

"you would try something like that. Dare me into a gunfight so you could kill me. Oh, we all know you're a gunfighter, Reb, but now that you've killed your own father by your too free use of a gun, you should have some sense in that head of yours."

Reb Farrell stared, unable to believe what he heard. Embree himself had shouted at him to fire when they heard the rush of hoofs, and he had shot at the silhouette of a man in the saddle.

"Either you figured your father was safely away from here, or thought you could miss in the dark an' nobody the wiser. Well, you're finished here. You've got just twenty-four hours!"

Bitterness mounted within Reb Farrell. "You mean I don't get a chance to look into this? You'd condemn me an' my father without a trial?"

"Trial?" Nathan Embree was beside himself with fury. "We catch the rustlers movin' a herd. You shoot an' one falls, an' it's your father. What more evidence would anybody need? By rights you should be hangin', an' it's only because of my daughter that you ain't! But get out, an' don't ever show your face around my place!"

Wheeling his horse, he led the group away, and only Dave Barbot lingered. "Sorry, Reb," he said softly. "I'm really sorry."

Alone in the darkness, Reb Farrell stood beside the body of his father and listened to the sound of their retreating hoofs.

Like a man walking in his sleep, he caught up his own horse and then his father's. He loaded the body across the saddle and started for home, riding slowly, his head hanging, devoid of thought. It was the end of everything for him—the job on the ranch he loved, Laura, everything.

The old cabin where he had spent his boyhood was dark and silent. Dismounting, Reb went inside and lighted a lamp. Without waiting for daylight he got some loose boards and knocked together a crude coffin, lining it with an old poncho. Sodden with grief, he went to the green place under the trees and there beside the grave of his mother, who had died when he was a child, he buried his father.

Although he had eaten nothing since morning, Reb had no thought of food. Slowly, he looked around the cabin that had been his home. What should he take with him? Though men may die, the living must continue to live, and he must think of food, bedding, ammunition, guns.

Guns . . . his father's fine old Sharps .50, the new Winchester .44 which his father had . . .

The Winchester was gone!

Reb felt a tingle of excitement go through him. The Sharps was in its place on the rack, but the new Winchester was gone! And there had been no scabbard on the saddle of his father's horse. Knowing his father, Reb was certain he would never have gone out at night without taking a rifle, and that meant the Sharps. Despite the fact that Reb had made him a present of the Winchester, his father had kept it on the rack and continued to carry his familiar old buffalo gun.

Aware of something wrong, Reb stood stock-still in the middle of the cabin. Suddenly, he thought of his father's carefully hoarded cache of money. A few hundred dollars only, it had been his insurance against illness or old age. Reb dropped on his knees and slid the board from its grooves in the floor. The money was gone!

Slowly Reb got to his feet. There had been no money in his father's pockets. And his father had worn a pistol. That in itself was strange, for Jim Farrell had not worn a belt gun in years. Three things were wrong—the missing Winchester, the missing money, and the presence of a belt gun on his father. But what could it all mean?

Looking around the cabin, Reb suddenly noticed

the coffeepot on the stove and going to it, lifted the lid. There were grounds in the pot. Either somebody else had made that coffee and left the pot or Jim Farrell had been drawn from his fire while making coffee, for Jim had habits of neatness acquired from years of living with his meticulous wife. He never left a pot on the stove and never left a dish unwashed.

As he packed the remaining food the conviction grew in Reb Farrell's mind that either his father had been somehow alarmed and left the cabin or he had been taken from it by force.

And why the belt gun? His father's right wrist had been weak for years, not up to swinging the heavy Colt. Suppose . . . suppose he had not put that belt on himself? Suppose somebody else had put it on for him? But why? And who?

It was daylight when Reb Farrell finally left the cabin. He took with him two packhorses and four head of saddle stock aside from the horse he himself rode. There were Rocking F cattle around that belonged to him, but they would have to wait.

Reb struck for the hills above Indian Creek. Of one thing he was certain. He was not leaving the country until he discovered exactly what had happened. He knew his father had never done anything dishonest. There had been too many times in the past when he might have profited without anyone the wiser, but Jim Farrell had not taken one single thing that did not belong to him.

As Reb rode up the narrowing canyon he thought the matter over. His father had no enemies. A kindly man, he never had trouble with anyone. Therefore, if his cabin had been looted it had been by chance thieves. Or . . . the thought came to him suddenly . . . enemies of Reb's!

But who were his enemies? Aside from a few fistfights at dances, none of which led to enmity, Reb had no enemies.

Except . . . except the rustlers themselves. Reb had found and recovered two herds of stolen cattle, and he had upon several occasions trailed the rustlers for miles. In fact, he had been the only man they had reason to fear. Suppose they had chosen this way to strike at him?

Skirting South Peak, Reb Farrell rode into a narrow canyon, and circling into the back of the canyon, he dismounted near an old corral he had built years ago, and turned in his horses. Then he switched saddles from the animal he had been riding to a long-legged zebra dun. There was plenty of grass in the corral, growing rich and green, and a small stream flowed through one corner of it.

There was no cabin, but the deep overhang of a cliff provided all the shelter he needed, and the firs growing before it would keep his fire from reflecting by night and would dissipate his smoke by day. Reb had no intention of leaving the country.

The dun was a fast and tough horse, one whose staying power and heart he had tested before this. In the saddle, he headed for town. First, he had to see Laura Embree.

Palo Seco was resting when he rode into town. There were lights in the two saloons and in a few scattered houses. One of these was Nathan Embree's townhouse. Knowing well the hard-headedness of his former boss, Reb dismounted in the cottonwoods some fifty yards from the house and walked up along the rail fence surrounding the Embree garden. Easing into the yard, he glanced through the window.

Laura was alone at the piano. Swiftly, he mounted the porch and tapped gently on the door. A second time he tapped, and then the music stopped. He heard the sound of steps and the door opened.

"Reb!" Laura's hand went to her lips and her eyes widened. "If Father finds you here, you'll be killed!"

"Maybe. But I had to see you." His eyes searched her face. "Where do you stand, Laura? Do you believe I was a rustler?"

"No." There was the merest flicker of hesitation. "No, I don't. But your father—"

"Then you do believe he was? A kind old man like him? Never took a dishonest dime in his life!"

"But Reb, you . . . you shot and he . . . you killed him! He was riding with them!" she protested.

"No," he said quietly, "maybe nobody else will believe me but I know he was dead before he ever reached that herd! Dead or close to it!"

Laura drew back a little. "I'm sorry, Reb, but you'd better go."

"Laura!" Reb protested. "Listen to me!" She made a move to close the door and he put his hand against it. "I tell you it's the truth! When I left your father, I rode home and found Dad's new Winchester was gone. Someone had stolen that gun! I know Dad hadn't taken it himself because he never used it, still favoring his old Sharps. An' somebody had strapped a gun on him— Dad hasn't used a pistol in years. His right wrist is too weak!"

"I'm sorry, Reb." Laura's face had grown stiff. "It just won't do. It's hard to believe that you were a cattle thief, but I don't see what else I can believe. Now if you'll take your foot out of that door, I'll—"

"Laura?" It was Nathan Embree's voice. "Who's there? Who you talkin' to?"

Reb withdrew his hand. "All right," he said quietly, "but if it's the last thing I do, I'll—"

The door closed in his face, and he stood staring at it, his world collapsing around him.

27

Laura, too! Stunned, he turned away and walked back to the dun.

One hand on the pommel, Reb Farrell hesitated, scowling. All right, he had to begin somewhere. He knew his father was not a rustler. He knew his father had not been out there willingly. So then, as long as he knew it, there was a chance to prove himself right.

One other person, perhaps several others, knew the truth also. The rustlers knew he had been framed.

But who was doing the rustling? The most likely person was Lon Melchor over on Tank Mesa. Melchor had rustled cattle before but had always been too slick to be caught at it. But somehow he could not believe that Lon would kill his father. They had been on opposite sides of the fence, but they had always been friendly. Anyway, it was a place to start.

Hard riding put him on Lon's place shortly after midnight. All was dark and still. Swinging down from the dun's saddle, Reb moved swiftly along the sidehill toward the cabin. There was something about the feel of the night that he did not like. Hesitating, he tried to resolve the feeling into something concrete and definite.

He moved up to the corner of the house. The door was standing open, which was unusual for the night was cool. Straining his ears he could hear hoarse breathing but no other sound.

He spoke softly, "Lon!"

All was still. He stepped into the door of the cabin and pushed the door shut, listening. Again he spoke the old rustler's name, but again there was no sound. Then he took a chance and struck a match.

Lon Melchor was sprawled on the floor, lying in a stupor, his shirt stained with blood!

Reb dropped to his knees and made a quick examination of the old man, and then he began to work swiftly. He got a fire going and put water on the stove. Then he put a pillow under the old man's head and stretched him out easier, rolling him onto a blanket which he placed on the floor. When the water was hot he bathed the wound, a nasty gunshot high on the left side, and only when he had the wound bandaged did he turn to look around.

Lon's gun lay on the floor, and picking it up, Reb saw it had been fired three times. His rifle was nowhere about and was probably on his horse. Slipping out of the door, Reb looked about until he found the horse. The saddle was wet with blood where the old man had bled. Lon stripped the saddle from the horse and turned him into the corral. There was water in the trough, and he forked some hay to the horses, then returned to the cabin.

Lon's eyes were open. "Reb!" he gasped. "You seen 'em? Them rustlers, I mean?"

"Who were they, Lon? Did they shoot you?"

"Yep," he stared up at the younger man, his misery showing in his face. "It's my fault, too. I knowed Joe Banta was a bad—"

"Joe *who*?" Reb Farrell leaned over the bunk. "Did you say Joe *Banta*?"

"Yep. He come in here wantin' a hideout, maybe three weeks ago. I knowed he was a plumb bad hombre, but I let him stay on. Fact is, I couldn't have drove him away. Then he did leave, but he came back with a bunch of hard cases. They started for the herd, and I raised hob. Joe, he turned right on me and shot, then he let me drop an' left me.

"I got into the saddle, how I'll never know." The old man's voice was weak. "I started for your place, but I never made it. Your old man found me. He got me back in the saddle, but when I told him what was up, he took off to tackle them rustlers by his ownself."

"They got him, Lon. They killed him." Briefly, Reb explained all that had taken place. The old man was angry.

"Nathan Embree always was a pigheaded fool!" he snorted. He grabbed Reb's hand. "Get you some men, son. I know where he'll go. He'll head for the old hideout at Burro Springs. You got to follow Dark Canyon to get there. Right up the canyon through all them boulders. He'll have the cattle there where he can get 'em over the Border easy. He can sell that herd to the minin' camps easy as pie."

Reb hesitated, but the old man waved him on. "Don't mind me. I'll get along."

Reb wheeled and ran to the door. There was no time to go for help, and there was a chance he might be shot if he did go back.

Day was just breaking in the east when he first found the opening into Dark Canyon and rode down from the lip of the mesa into the deep, shadowy green recesses of this oasis in the desert. Long suspected as a possible hangout for rustlers, the canyon had been searched several times in the past year, but searchers had always been stopped by the seemingly impassable jumble of boulders, some of them so close together there seemed no way through. Moreover, the place was exceedingly dangerous. If caught in the canyon bottom during a heavy rain, a man would have small chance of escaping the roaring flood which came down the canyon.

Now Reb knew there was a way through those boulders. He rode now with extreme caution, pausing often to study the canyon ahead of him, and then pushing on. Soon the huge boulders that had hitherto blocked all progress in the ancient river bed were before him. He searched for a way between them, but try as he might, he could find none that would allow the passage of a horse or cow. Yet, with Lon Melchor's statement to urge him on, he persisted, and it was finally a mark on the canyon wall that tipped him off. It was such a mark that might have been made by the brushing of a stirrup. Riding close to the wall, ducking his head because of the overhang, Reb suddenly saw the opening, barely wide enough to allow for passage. He rode through, then paused in the deep shadow.

The canyon appeared to be nothing but a jumble of boulders for some distance ahead. After a careful study of the rocks and walls, he rode on, then turned up a narrow path that showed at one side of the canyon. It was a little-used trail, probably made by wandering cattle or wild horses. It led him into the broken rock of the shattered canyon wall, and then onto a green-topped mesa. Crossing this, he paused under some trees and looked down. Below him the canyon widened out into a long, green, and well-watered valley of some five hundred acres. Two huts and a long bunkhouse were against the wall of the canyon below him. There was a stable and some corrals, and scattered over the canyon, several hundred head of cattle were feeding.

As he watched, two men came from the long building and strolled toward the corrals. They walked as men do who have enjoyed a good meal and are in no hurry to go to work. One of them was Joe Banta.

Banta had never been known to operate in this part of the country, and Nathan Embree would have been the first to scoff at such an idea. Yet here he was, and in plain sight. He was a stocky man of considerable breadth and little height, a swarthy fellow with a battered gray hat. Even from a distance, Reb could recognize him without trouble. When the two men turned around, Reb recognized the second as Ike Goodrich, a small-time outlaw and occasional cowhand who had once worked for Embree.

Two hours of waiting and watching while his horse cropped grass contentedly gave Reb Farrell the knowledge that at least four men were below. Aside from Banta and Ike, there was the cook, whom Reb had seen come to the door to throw out some water, and a thin, redheaded fellow who walked with a slight limp and appeared to favor that leg considerably as though it had been recently injured. This man went to the corral and saddled four horses.

There was no time to go for help. It would take hours to get out and hours to get back. Even if he could convince somebody of the truth of his story, by the time they returned, the cattle would be gone, for obviously there was another way out of the canyon, probably the route that led over the Border.

Leading his horse, Reb left the mesa top and made his way slowly down a back trail into a deep draw that opened on the valley. Leaving his horse in the brush, Reb walked down the canyon, rifle in hand. From the mouth he looked out over the valley. The nearest corral was not twenty yards away, the back of the nearest shack about the same distance. The stable and the other corrals formed an open corner with the corral near which he stood. He was facing north, the stable faced west, and the houses faced north as he did. The redhead was standing in front of the stable, tightening a saddle girth.

Reb walked out of the canyon mouth and strolled along the corral bars until he was facing the man in front of the stable. Nobody else was in sight.

"All right, Red!" His voice was low but strong enough. "Unloose your gun belts and turn around! One wrong move and you die!"

Red turned slowly, his hands wide. His face was tight with surprise. "Where'd you come from?" he demanded.

"Unloose your belt, Red! *Quick!*"

Red's hands went to the buckle, then he hurled himself to one side and grabbed his gun. Reb's Winchester barked and the redhead kept falling, the gun slipping from his fingers and sliding along the earth a foot from the outstretched hand.

A chair slammed over inside the house and Goodrich jumped into the doorway. Reb was waiting for him and fired. The shot burned Ike on the neck, cutting along that side nearest the cabin. Goodrich jerked away from the pain and fell out of the door.

From the window a bullet slammed near Reb, and he ducked and ran. Goodrich grabbed his gun and rolled over on his face. Reb chanced a running shot and saw the bullet kick dirt in Ike's eyes. While the gunman swore and grabbed at his eyes, Reb dropped his rifle, grabbed a gun, and lunged through the door. He took a chance, gambling that Joe Banta would be expecting nothing of the kind. Banta wheeled as Reb came through the door and both men fired at once and both missed. It was close range, but both were moving. Reb grabbed the edge of the table to stop his forward movement and fired again. Banta jerked hard and his shot went wild. Then Reb jumped at him, clubbing with his six-gun barrel. Banta went down to his hands and knees. He was starting to get up when Reb hit him a second time.

Wheeling, he sprang to the door. Goodrich was crawling for the rifle Reb had dropped, and Reb put a bullet in the ground before him. Goodrich stopped, and glared at the doorway. "You'll suffer for this. If I live a thousand years, I'll never forget it!"

A board creaked and Reb looked up. The cook was facing him across a double-barrelled shotgun.

"Drop it!" he said, his eyes bright with satisfaction. "Drop it or I'll cut you in two!"

Reb Farrell's gun was level and he did not hesitate. "You fire," he said, "and I'll kill you. You'll get me, but I'll take you with me. Now go ahead and shoot, because I'll not miss at this range!"

The cook stared, gulped and his eyes shifted. He didn't like the situation even a little. That Reb would not surrender in the face of the scattergun was something of which he had never dreamed. Now it was quite obvious that while he would kill Reb, the bullet from the pistol would unquestionably kill him. And he was not ready to die.

"Shoot," Reb said, "or drop it!"

"Go ahead!" Ike shouted. "Shoot, you greasy fool!"

The cook's eyes wavered. "Yeah," he sneered, "a lot you care what happens to me." His eyes swung back to Reb and the six-gun was unwavering. "Never was much of a poker player. I reckon you got me. I'd rather be alive an' in jail then dead on this ground." He bent over and placed the shotgun carefully on the ground and took a step back. "Hope you'll recall that when the trial comes."

Quickly, Reb gathered up the loose weapons, tied the hands of Ike and the cook, and bandaged Banta's wounds. The redhead was dead. The .44 from Reb's Winchester had cut into the center of his chest at an angle from right to left and had drilled the redhead right through the heart.

It was noon on the following day when Reb Farrell rode down the street of Palo Seco. Doors began to open and people stepped out to look at the procession. Joe Banta, the cook, and Ike Goodrich, followed by the horse carrying the body of Red, and behind them all, his rifle across his saddle, was Reb Farrell.

Nathan Embree stepped from the saloon and stopped. Laura was standing at the door of the post office, her face suddenly white.

"Embree," Reb's voice rang loud in the street, "here's your rustlers. You'll find your cattle in Dark Canyon, all fat an' sassy. This here, in case you don't know him, is Joe Banta. My Dad tried to stop 'em, but they killed him. Then they figured I'd be more apt to get wise to 'em than a fathead like you, so they carried my Dad's body out there and when I shot, they dropped the body an' ran, figurin' I'd think I killed my own father, an' you'd think I was a rustler. Isn't that right, Banta?"

The rustler shrugged. "You got me. Why should I lie? Sure, it's right, just like I told you. Embree was no trouble for us. I made inquiries around. Folks all allowed that without you, Embree couldn't catch a frog in a rain barrel!"

Embree's face was red. "I guess I owe you an apology," he said stiffly, "but you'll admit that I had reason . . ."

Reb Farrell looked at him. "Reason to doubt a man who had worked hard for you for years? Reason to doubt an old man who had harmed nobody? Embree, I'm ridin' out of this country, but I hope this teaches you a lesson. Next time don't be so quick to judge."

Reb moved on, then drew up. Dave Barbot was standing on the walk.

"Dave, you were the only one who gave me a kind word. Understand you're in the market for some cows? Well, between Dad an' me we had maybe four hundred head."

"I'd say a few more," Dave said. "You aim to sell?"

"To you the price is one thousand dollars and the care of my Dad's grave so long as you live."

"A thousand?" Barbot was incredulous. "They are worth twice that!"

"You heard my price. How about it?"

"Sure," Dave said. "I'd be a fool to pass it up."

"All right, then. Have the money when I come back from the jail."

Laura stood before the post office, her face white, her teeth touching her lip. Suddenly Reb felt sorry for her, yet he knew now that she had never loved him. He glanced at her and gravely tipped his hat.

"Reb!" She put out a hand as if to hold him back.

He drew up. "I'm ridin' on, Laura. I'm not blamin' you, nor anybody. I figure you never knew me real well or you'd never have been so quick to doubt. There's a lot of country west of here I've never seen. That's the way I'll ride."

Barbot was waiting in front of the bank when Reb drew up. Reb told him about the horses in the corral at the lone cabin. "Pick 'em up, Dave. They are yours."

"Sure, I was goin' to speak about that. You gave me a

flat price an' no time nor reason to argue. Well, I'm doin' the same by you. Down in the livery barn corral there's a horse you'll know. My palouse stallion. You always fancied that horse. Well, he's yours. Throw your saddle over him an' take this one for a packhorse."

A door slammed up the street and Reb looked up. An old man stood on the edge of the porch, leaning against the awning post. It was Lon Melchor.

"Me, all right. I ain't so strong right now, son, but I aim to be. I'd have to ride a mite easy the first few days, because I lost a sight of blood, but if you'll have me, son, I'll trail along."

He waved a hand at the town. "Folks here don't cotton to me. I want to see a new country."

Reb Farrell's heart warmed to the old rustler. "Get up in your saddle, Lon. We're headin' west for the Blue River country, out Arizona way."

The old man crawled painfully into the saddle and faced around. His face was white and strained, but his lips smiled and there was even humor in his eyes. "Let's go, son! The Blues it is!"

The sun was high and the mountains in the west were far and purple. The air smelled fresh, and there was the tang of sagebrush in the air, and far off in his memory there was a smell of pines, which he soon would be smelling once more.

The palouse stallion stepped out, tugging the bit.

Author's Note:
DIAMOND CANYON

Often when I would get the urge to wander, I would take a backpack and go to Peach Springs and hike some of the branch canyons that open into the Grand Canyon. Many years ago when people wished to see the Grand Canyon before any other places had been set up, the best view was from the old Diamond Creek Hotel in Diamond Canyon. By the time I got into that part of the country, the hotel was ancient history and there was nothing left but the site. There were trails nearby that lead down to the river, others that lead up Diamond Canyon, or some up to Meriwitica Canyon.

Not being much of a camp cook, I usually carried nuts, raisins, and a couple of small cans that could be opened easily. I did carry a small coffeepot and coffee. Several times I ate with the Indians who knew friends of mine from Kingman, Oakland, or Williams. I never wanted to bother with cooking.

It was an easy, lazy time. I never had a set schedule to follow; no one was waiting for me or expected me. When I got tired of sleeping on the ground I would head for the highway, often hitching a ride with an Indian in his pickup. Then I would take a bus or a train ride back to Los Angeles and hole up for another long stretch of writing.

Several times I slept in Indian ruins, old cliff dwellings long abandoned by the Anasazi and their neighbors. There were ghosts around of course. Once a bear came along down the path past a ruin in which I was camped. He could not see me but he caught my scent and sniffed around, hesitated and then went about his business. It was the right decision for both of us.

THE BLACK ROCK
COFFIN MAKERS

The Five-Thousand-Dollar Fake

Jim Gatlin had been up the creek and over the mountains, and more than once had been on both ends of a six-shooter. Lean and tall, with shoulders wide for his height and a face like saddle leather, he was, at the moment, doing a workmanlike job of demolishing the last of a thick steak and picking off isolated beans that had escaped his initial attack. He was a thousand miles from home and knew nobody in the town of Tucker.

He glanced up as the door opened and saw a short, thick-bodied man. The man gave one startled look at Jim and ducked back out of sight. Gatlin blinked in surprise, then shrugged and filled his coffee cup from the pot standing on the restaurant table.

Puzzled, he listened to the rapidly receding pound of a horse's hoofs, then rolled a smoke, sitting back with a contented sigh. Two hundred and fifty-odd miles to the north was the herd he had drifted northwest from Texas. The money the cattle had brought was in the belt around his waist and his pants pockets. Nothing remained now but to return to Texas, bank the profit, and pick up a new herd.

The outer door opened again, and a tall girl entered the restaurant. Turning right, she started for the door leading to the hotel. She stopped abruptly as though his presence had only then registered. She turned, and her eyes widened in alarm. Swiftly, she crossed the room to him. "Are you insane?" she whispered. "Sitting here like that when the town is full of Wing Cary's hands? They know you're coming and have been watching for you for days!"

Gatlin looked up, smiling. "Ma'am, you've sure got the wrong man, although if a girl as pretty as you is worried about him, he sure is a lucky fellow. I'm a stranger here. I never saw the place until an hour ago!"

She stepped back, puzzled, and then the door slammed open once more, and a man stepped into the room. He was as tall as Jim, but thinner, and his dark eyes were angry. "Get away from him, Lisa! I'm killin' him—right now!"

The man's hand flashed for a gun, and Gatlin dove sidewise to the floor, drawing as he fell. A gun roared in the room; then Gatlin fired twice.

The tall man caught himself, jerking his left arm against his ribs, his face twisted as he gasped for breath. Then he wilted slowly to the floor, his gun sliding from his fingers.

Gatlin got to his feet, staring at the stranger. He swung his eyes to the girl staring at him. "Who is that hombre?" he snapped. "What's this all about? Who did he think I was?"

"You—you're not—you aren't Jim Walker?" Her voice was high, amazed.

"Walker?" He shook his head. "I'm sure as hell not. The name is Gatlin. I'm just driftin' through."

There was a rush of feet in the street outside. She caught his hand. "Come! Come quickly! They won't listen to you! They'll kill you! All the Cary outfit are in town!"

She ran beside him, dodging into the hotel, and then swiftly down a hall. As the front door burst open, they plunged out the back and into the alley behind the building. Unerringly, she led him to the left and then opened the back door of another building and drew him inside. Silently, she closed the door and stood close beside him, panting in the darkness.

Shouts and curses rang from the building next door. A door banged, and men charged up and down outside. Jim was still holding his gun, but now he withdrew the empty shells and fed two into the cylinder to replace those fired. He slipped a sixth into the usually empty chamber. "What is this place?" he whispered. "Will they come here?"

"It's a law office," she whispered. "I work here part-time, and I left the door open myself. They'll not think of this place." Stealthily, she lifted the bar and dropped it into place. "Better sit down. They'll be searching the streets for some time."

He found the desk and seated himself on the corner, well out of line with the windows. He could see only the vaguest outline of her face. His first impression of moments before was strong enough for him to remember she was pretty. The gray eyes were wide and clear, her figure rounded yet slim. What is this?" he repeated. "What was he gunnin' for me for?"

"It wasn't you. He thought you were Jim Walker, of the XY. If you aren't actually him, you look enough like him to be a brother, a twin brother."

"Where is he? What goes on here? Who was that hombre who tried to gun me down?"

She paused, and seemed to be thinking, and he had the idea she was still uncertain whether to believe him or not. "The man you killed was Bill Trout. He was the

41

badman of Paradise country and *segundo* on Wing Cary's Flying C spread. Jim Walker called him a thief and a murderer in talking to Cary, and Trout threatened to shoot him on sight. Walker hasn't been seen since, and that was four days ago, so everybody believed Walker had skipped the country. Nobody blamed him much."

"What's it all about?" Gatlin inquired.

"North of here, up beyond Black Rock, is Alder Creek country, with some rich bottom hay land lying in several corners of the mountains. This is dry country, but that Alder Creek area has springs and some small streams flowing down out of the hills. The streams flow into the desert and die there, so the water is good only for the man who controls the range."

"And that was Walker?"

"No, up until three weeks ago, it was old Dave Butler. Then Dave was thrown from his horse and killed, and when they read his will, he had left the property to be sold at auction and the money to be paid to his nephew and niece back in New York. However, the joker was, he stipulated that Jim Walker was to get the ranch if he would bid ten thousand cash and forty thousand on his note, payable in six years."

"In other words, he wanted Walker to have the property?" Jim asked. "He got first chance at it?"

"That's right. And I was to get second chance. If Jim didn't want to make the bid, I could have it for the same price. If neither of us wanted it, the ranch was to go on public auction, and that means that Cary and Horwick would get it. They have the money, and nobody around here could outbid them."

The street outside was growing quieter as the excitement of the chase died down. "I think," Lisa continued, "that Uncle Dave wanted Jim to have the property because Jim did so much to develop it. Jim was foreman of the XY acting for Dave. Then, Uncle Dave knew my father and liked me, and he knew I loved the ranch, so he wanted me to have second chance, but I don't have the money, and they all know it. Jim had some of it, and he could get the rest. I think that was the real trouble behind his trouble with Trout. I believe Wing deliberately set Trout to kill him, and Jim's statements about Bill were a result of the pushing around Bill Trout had given him."

The pattern was not unfamiliar, and Gatlin could easily appreciate the situation. Water was gold in this country of sparse grass. To a cattleman, such a ranch as Lisa described could be second to none, with plenty of water and grass and good hay meadows. Suddenly, she caught his arm. Men were talking outside the door.

"Looks like he got plumb away, Wing. Old Ben swears there was nobody in the room with him but that Lisa Cochrane, an' she never threw that gun, but how Jim Walker ever beat Trout is more'n I can see. Why, Bill was the fastest man around here unless it's you or me."

"That wasn't Walker, Pete. It couldn't have been!"

"Ben swears it was, an' Woody Hammer busted right through the door in front of him. Said it was Jim, all right."

Wing Cary's voice was irritable. "I tell you, it couldn't have been!" he flared. "Jim Walker never saw the day he dared face Trout with a gun," he added. "I've seen Walker draw an' he never was fast."

"Maybe he wasn't," Pete Chasin agreed dryly, "but Trout's dead, ain't he?"

"Three days left," Cary said. "Lisa Cochrane hasn't the money, and it doesn't look like Walker will even be bidding. Let it ride, Pete. I don't think we need to worry about anything. Even if that was Walker, an' I'd take an oath it wasn't, he's gone for good now. All we have to do is sit tight."

The two moved off, and Jim Gatlin, staring at the girl in the semidarkness, saw her lips were pressed tight. His eyes had grown accustomed to the dim light, and he could see around the small office. It was a simple room with a desk, chair, and filing cabinets. Well-filled bookcases lined the walls.

He got to his feet. "I've got to get my gear out of that hotel," he said, "and my horse."

"You're leaving?" she asked.

Jim glanced at her in surprise. "Why, sure! Why stay here in a fight that's not my own? I've already killed one man, and if I stay, I'll have to kill more or be killed myself. There's nothing here for me."

"Did you notice something?" she asked suddenly. "Wing Cary seemed very sure that Jim Walker wasn't coming back, that you weren't he."

Gatlin frowned. He had noticed it, and it had him wondering. "He did sound mighty sure. Like he might *know* Walker wasn't coming back."

They were silent in the dark office, yet each knew what the other was thinking. Jim Walker was dead. Pete Chasin had not known it. Neither, obviously, had Bill Trout.

"What happens to you then?" Gatlin asked suddenly. "You lose the ranch?"

She shrugged. "I never had it, and never really thought I would have it, only . . . well, if Jim had lived . . . I mean, if Jim got the ranch we'd have made out. We were very close, like brother and sister. Now I don't know what I can do."

"You haven't any people?"

"None that I know of." Her head came up suddenly. "Oh, it isn't myself I'm thinking of; it's all the old hands, the ranch itself. Uncle Dave hated Cary, and so do his men. Now he'll get the ranch, and they'll all be fired, and he'll ruin the place! That's what he's wanted all along."

Gatlin shifted his feet. "Tough," he said, "mighty tough."

He opened the door slightly. "Thanks," he said, "for getting me out of there." She didn't reply, so after a

44

moment, he stepped out of the door and drew it gently to behind him.

There was no time to lose. He must be out of town by daylight and with miles behind him. There was no sense getting mixed up in somebody else's fight, for all he'd get out of it would be a bellyful of lead. There was nothing he could do to help. He moved swiftly, and within a matter of minutes was in his hotel room. Apparently, searching for Jim Walker, they hadn't considered his room in the hotel, so Gatlin got his duffel together, stuffed it into his saddlebags, and picked up his rifle. With utmost care, he eased down the back stairs and into the alley.

The streets were once more dark and still. What had become of the Flying C hands, he didn't know, but none were visible. Staying on back streets, he made his way carefully to the livery barn, but there his chance of cover grew less, for he must enter the wide door with a light glowing over it.

After listening, he stepped out and, head down, walked through the door. Turning, he hurried to the stall where his powerful black waited. It was the work of only a few minutes to saddle up. He led the horse out of the stall and caught up the bridle. As his hand grasped the pommel, a voice stopped him.

"Lightin' out?"

It was Pete Chasin's voice. Slowly, he released his grip on the pommel and turned slightly. The man was hidden in a stall. "Why not?" Gatlin asked. "I'm not goin' to be a shootin' gallery for nobody. This ain't my range, an' I'm slopin' out of here for Texas. I'm no trouble hunter."

He heard Chasin's chuckle. "Don't reckon you are. But it seems a shame not to make the most of your chance. What if I offered you five thousand to stay? Five thousand, in cash?"

"Five thousand?" Gatlin blinked. That was half as much as he had in his belt, and the ten thousand he carried had taken much hard work and bargaining to get. Buying a herd, chancing the long drive.

"What would I have to do?" he demanded.

Chasin came out of the stall. "Be yourself," he said, "just be yourself—but let folks think you're Jim Walker. Then you buy a ranch here . . . I'll give you the money, an' then you hit the trail."

Chasin was trying to double-cross Cary! To get the ranch for himself!

Gatlin hesitated. "That's a lot of money, but these boys toss a lot of lead. I might not live to spend the dough."

"I'll hide you out." Chasin argued. "I've got a cabin in the hills. I'd hide you out with four or five of my boys to stand guard. You'd be safe enough. Then you could come down, put your money on the line, an' sign the papers."

"Suppose they want Walker's signature checked?"

"Jim Walker never signed more'n three, four papers in his life. He left no signatures hereabouts. I've took pains to be sure."

Five thousand because he looked like a man. It was easy money, and he'd be throwing a monkey wrench into Wing Cary's plans. Cary, a man he'd decided he disliked. "Sounds like a deal," he said. "Let's go!"

The cabin on the north slope of Bartlett Peak was well hidden, and there was plenty of grub. Pete Chasin left him there with two men to guard him and two more standing by on the trail toward town. All through the following day, Jim Gatlin loafed, smoking cigarettes and talking idly with the two men. Hab Johnson was a big, unshaven hombre with a sullen face and a surly manner. He talked little, and then only to growl. Pink Stabineau was a wide-chested, flat-faced jasper with an agreeable grin.

Gatlin had a clear idea of his own situation. He could use five thousand, but he knew Chasin never intended him to leave the country with it and doubted if he would last an hour after the ranch was transferred to Chasin himself. Yet Gatlin had been around the rough country, and he knew a trick or two of his own. Several times he thought of Lisa Cochrane, but avoided that angle as much as he could.

After all, she had no chance to get the ranch, and Walker was probably dead. That left it between Cary and Chasin. The unknown Horwick of whom he had heard mention was around, too, but he seemed to stand with Cary in everything.

Yet Gatlin was restless and irritable, and he kept remembering the girl beside him in the darkness and her regrets at breaking up the old outfit. Jim Gatlin had been a hand who rode for the brand; he knew what it meant to have a ranch sold out from under a bunch of old hands. The home that had been theirs gone, the friends drifting apart never to meet again, everything changed.

He finished breakfast on the morning of the second day, then walked out of the cabin with his saddle. Hab Johnson looked up sharply. "Where you goin'?" he demanded.

"Ridin'," Gatlin said briefly, "an' don't worry. I'll be back."

Johnson chewed a stem of grass, his hard eyes on Jim's. "You ain't goin' nowheres. The boss said to watch you an' keep you here. Here you stay."

Gatlin dropped his saddle. "You aren't keepin' me nowheres, Hab," he said flatly. "I've had enough sittin' around. I aim to see a little of this country."

"I reckon not." Hab got to his feet. "You may be a fast hand with a gun, but you ain't gittin' both of us, and you ain't so foolish as to try." He waved a big hand. "Now you go back an' set down."

"I started for a ride," Jim said quietly, "an' a ride I'm takin'." He stooped to pick up the saddle and saw Hab's boots as the big man started for him. Jim had lifted the saddle clear of the ground, and now he hurled it,

47

suddenly, in Hab's path. The big man stumbled and hit the ground on his hands and knees, then started up.

As he came up halfway, Jim slugged him. Hab tottered, fighting for balance, and Gatlin moved in, striking swiftly with a volley of lefts and rights to the head. Hab went down and hit hard, then came up with a lunge, but Gatlin dropped him again. Blood dripped from smashed lips and a cut on his cheekbone.

Gatlin stepped back, working his fingers. His hard eyes flicked to Pink Stabineau, who was smoking quietly, resting on one elbow, looking faintly amused. "You stoppin' me?" Gatlin demanded.

Pink grinned. "Me? Now where did you get an idea like that? Take your ride. Hab's just too persnickety about things. Anyway, he's always wantin' to slug somebody. Now maybe he'll be quiet for a spell."

There was a dim trail running northwest from the cabin and Gatlin took it, letting his horse choose his own gait. The black was a powerful animal, not only good on a trail but an excellent roping horse, and he moved out eagerly, liking the new country. When he had gone scarcely more than two miles, he skirted the edge of a high meadow with plenty of grass, then left the trail and turned off along a bench of the mountain, riding due north.

Suddenly, the mountain fell away before him, and below, in a long finger of grass, he saw the silver line of a creek, and nestled against a shoulder of the mountain, he discerned roofs among the trees. Pausing, Jim rolled a smoke and studied the lie of the land. Northward, for all of ten miles, there was good range. Dry, but not so bad as over the mountain, and in the spring and early summer it would be good grazing land. He had looked at too much range not to detect, from the colors of the valley before him, some of the varieties of grass and brush. Northwest, the range stretched away through a wide gap in the mountains, and he seemed to distinguish a deeper green in the distance.

Old Dave Butler had chosen well, and his XY had been well handled, Gatlin could see as he rode nearer. Tanks had been built to catch some of the overflow from the mountains and to prevent the washing of valuable range. The old man, and evidently Jim Walker, had worked hard to build this ranch into something. Even while wanting money for his relatives in the East, Butler had tried to ensure that the work would be continued after his death. Walker would continue it, and so would Lisa Cochrane.

The Kill-Branded Pardner

All morning he rode, and well into the afternoon, studying the range but avoiding the buildings. Once, glancing back, he saw a group of horsemen riding swiftly out of the mountains from which he had come and heading for the XY. Reining in, he watched from a vantage point among some huge boulders. Men wouldn't ride that fast without adequate reason.

Morosely, he turned and started back along the way he had come, thinking more and more of Lisa. Five thousand was a lot of money, but what he was doing was not dishonest, and so far he had played the game straight. Still, why think of that? In a few days, he'd have the money in his pocket and be headed for Texas. He turned on the brow of the hill and glanced back, carried away despite himself by the beauty of the wide sweep of range.

Pushing on, he skirted around and came toward the cabin from the town trail. He was riding with his mind

far away when the black snorted violently and shied.
Jim drew up, staring at the man who lay sprawled in
the trail. It was the cowhand Pete Chasin had left on
guard there. He'd been shot through the stomach, and a
horse had been ridden over him.

Swinging down, a quick check showed the man was
dead. Jim grabbed up the reins and sprang into the
saddle. Sliding a six-gun from its holster, he pushed
forward, riding cautiously. The tracks told him that a
party of twelve horsemen had come this way.

He heard the wind in the trees, the distant cry of an
eagle, but nothing more. He rode out into the clearing
before the cabin and drew up. Another man had died
here. It wasn't Stabineau or Hab Johnson, but the
other guard, who must have retreated to this point for
aid.

Gun in hand, Gatlin pushed the door open and looked
into the cabin. Everything was smashed, yet when he
swung down and went in, he found his own gear intact,
under the overturned bed. He threw his bedroll on his
horse and loaded up his saddlebags. He jacked a shell
into the chamber of the Winchester and was about to
mount up when he heard a muffled cry.

Turning, he stared around, then detected a faint stir
among the leaves of a mountain mahogany. Warily, he
walked over and stepped around the bush.

Pink Stabineau, his face pale and his shirt dark with
blood, lay sprawled on the ground. Curiously, there was
still a faint touch of humor in his eyes when he looked
up at Gatlin. "Got me," he said finally. "It was that
damned Hab. He sold us out . . . to Wing Cary. The
damn dirty—!"

Jim dropped to his knees and gently unbuttoned the
man's shirt. The wound was low down on the left side,
and although he seemed to have lost much blood, there
was a chance. Working swiftly, he built a fire, heated
water, and bathed and then dressed the wound. From
time to time, Pink talked, telling him much of what he

suspected, that Cary would hunt Chasin down now and kill him.

"If they fight," Jim asked, "who'll win?"

Stabineau grinned wryly. "Cary . . . he's tough, an' cold as ice. Pete's too jumpy. He's fast, but mark my words, if they face each other, he'll shoot too fast and miss his first shot. Wing won't miss!

"But it won't come to that. Wing's a cinch player. He'll chase him down an' the bunch will gun him to death. Wing's bloodthirsty."

Leaving food and a canteen of water beside the wounded man and giving him two blankets, Jim Gatlin mounted. His deal was off then. The thought left him with a distinct feeling of relief. He had never liked any part of it, and he found himself without sympathy for Pete Chasin. The man had attempted a double cross and failed.

Well, the road was open again now, and there was nothing between him and Texas but the miles. Yet he hesitated, and then turned his horse toward the XY. He rode swiftly, and at sundown was at the ranch. He watched it for a time, and saw several hands working around, yet there seemed little activity. No doubt they were waiting to see what was to happen.

Suddenly, a sorrel horse started out from the ranch and swung into the trail toward town. Jim Gatlin squinted his eyes against the fading glare of the sun and saw the rider was a woman. That would be Lisa Cochrane. Suddenly, he swung the black and, touching spurs to the horse, raced down the mountains to intercept her.

Until that moment, he had been uncertain as to the proper course, but now he knew. Yet for all his speed, his eyes were alert and watchful, for he realized the risk he ran. Wing Cary would be quick to discover that as long as he was around and alive, there was danger, and even now the rancher might have his men out, scouring the country for him. Certainly, there were plausible reasons enough, for it could be claimed that he had joined with Chasin in a plot to get the ranch by appearing as Jim Walker.

Lisa's eyes widened when she saw him. "I thought you'd be gone by now. There's a posse after you!"

"You mean some of Cary's men?" he corrected.

"I mean a posse. Wing has men on your trail, too, but they lost you somehow. He claims that you were tied up in a plan with Pete Chasin to get the ranch, and that you killed Jim Walker!"

"That *I* did?" His eyes searched her face. "You mean he actually claims that?"

She nodded, watching him. "He says that story about your being here was all nonsense, that you actually came on purpose, that you an' Chasin rigged it that way! You'll have to admit it looks funny, you arriving right at this time and looking just like Jim."

"What if it does?" he demanded impatiently. "I never heard of Jim Walker until you mentioned him to me, and I never heard of the town of Tucker until a few hours before I met you."

"You'd best go, then," she warned. "They're all over the country. Sheriff Eaton would take you in, but Wing wouldn't, nor any of his boys. They'll kill you on sight."

"Yeah," he agreed. "I can see that." Nevertheless, he didn't stir, but continued to roll a cigarette. She sat still, watching him curiously. Finally, he looked up. "I'm in a fight," he admitted, "and not one I asked for. Cary is making this a mighty personal thing, ma'am, an' I reckon I ain't even figurin' on leavin'." He struck a match. "You got any chance of gettin' the ranch?"

"How could I? I have no money!"

"Supposin'," he suggested, squinting an eye against the smoke, "you had a pardner—with ten thousand dollars?"

Lisa shook her head. "Things like that don't happen," she said. "They just don't."

"I've got ten thousand dollars on me," Gatlin volunteered, "an' I've been pushed into this whether I like it or not. I say we ride into Tucker now an' we see this boss of yours, the lawyer. I figure he could get the deal all set up for us tomorrow. Are you game?"

"You—you really have that much?" She looked doubtfully at his shabby range clothes. "It's honest money?"

"I drove cattle to Montana," he said. "That was my piece of it. Let's go."

"Not so fast!" The words rapped out sharply. "I'll take that money, an' take it now! Woody, get that girl!"

For reply Jim slapped the spurs to the black and, at the same instant, slapped the sorrel a ringing blow. The horses sprang off together in a dead run. Behind them, a rifle shot rang out, and Jim felt the bullet clip past his skull. "Keep goin'!" he yelled. "Ride!"

At a dead run, they swung down the trail, and then Jim saw a side trail he had noticed on his left. He jerked his head at the girl and grabbed at her bridle. It was too dark to see the gesture, but she felt the tug and turned the sorrel after him, mounting swiftly up the steep side hill under the trees. There the soft needles made it impossible for their horses' hoofs to be heard, and Jim led the way, pushing on under the pines.

That it would be only a minute or so before Cary discovered his error was certain, but each minute counted. A wall lifted on their right, and they rode on, keeping in the intense darkness close under it, but then another wall appeared on their left, and they were boxed in. Behind them they heard a yell, distant now, but indication enough their trail had been found. Boulders and slabs of rock loomed before them, but the black horse turned down a slight incline and worked his way around the rocks. From time to time, they spoke to each other to keep together, but he kept moving, knowing that Wing Cary would be close behind.

The canyon walls seemed to be drawing closer, and the boulders grew larger and larger. Somewhere Jim heard water running, and the night air was cool and slightly damp on his face. He could smell pine, so he knew that there were trees about and they had not ridden completely out of them. Yet Jim was becoming worried, for the canyon walls towered above them, and obviously there was no break. If this turned out to be a box canyon, they were bottled up. One man could hold this canyon corked with no trouble at all.

The black began to climb and in a few minutes walked out on a flat of grassy land. The moon was rising, but as yet there was no light in this deep canyon.

Lisa rode up beside him. "Jim"—it was the first time she had ever called him by name—"I'm afraid we're in for it now. Unless I'm mistaken, this is a box canyon. I've never been up here, but I've heard of it, and there's no way out."

"I was afraid of that." The black horse stopped as he spoke, and he heard water falling ahead. He urged the horse forward, but he refused to obey. Jim swung down into the darkness. "Pool," he said. "We'll find some place to hole up and wait for daylight."

They found a group of boulders and seated themselves among them, stripping the saddles from their horses and picketing them on a small patch of grass behind the boulders. Then, for a long time, they talked, the casual talk of two people finding out about each other. Jim talked of his early life on the Neuces, of his first trip into Mexico after horses when he was fourteen, and how they were attacked by Apaches. There had been three Indian fights that trip, two south of the border and one north of it.

He had no idea when sleep took him, but he awakened with a start to find the sky growing gray and to see Lisa Cochrane sleeping on the grass six feet away. She looked strangely young, with her face relaxed and her lips slightly parted. A dark tendril of hair had blown across her cheek. He turned away and walked out to the horses. The grass was thick and rich there.

He studied their position with care and found they were on a terrace separated from the end wall of the canyon only by the pool, at least an acre of clear, cold water into which a small fall poured from the cliff above. There were a few trees, and some of the scattered boulders they had encountered the previous night. The canyon on which they had come was a wild jumble of boulders and brush surmounted on either side by cliffs that lifted nearly three hundred feet. While escape might be impossible if Wing Cary attempted, as he surely would, to guard the opening, their own position was secure, too, for one man with a rifle might stand off an army from the terrace.

After he had watered the horses, he built a fire and put water on for coffee. Seeing some trout in the pool, he tried his luck, and from the enthusiasm with which they went for his bait, the pool could never have been fished before, or not in a long time. Lisa came from behind the boulders just as the coffee came to a boil. "What is this? A picnic?" she asked brightly.

He grinned, touching his unshaven jaw. "With this beard?" He studied her a minute. "You'd never guess you'd spent the night on horseback or sleeping at the end of a canyon," he said. Then his eyes sobered. "Can you handle a rifle? I mean, well enough to stand off Cary's boys if they tried to come up here?"

She turned quickly and glanced down the canyon. The nearest boulders to the terrace edge were sixty yards away, and the approach even that close would not be easy. "I think so," she said. "What are you thinking of?"

He gestured at the cliff. "I've been studyin' that. With a mite of luck, a man might make it up there."

Her face paled. "It isn't worth it. We're whipped, and we might as well admit it. All we can do now is sit still and wait until the ranch is sold."

"No," he said positively. "I'm goin' out of here if I

55

have to blast my way out. They've made a personal matter out of this, now, and"—he glanced at her—"I sort of have a feeling you should have that ranch. Lookin' at it yesterday, I just couldn't imagine it without you. You lived there, didn't you?"

"Most of my life. My folks were friends of Uncle Dave's, and after they were killed, I stayed on with him."

"Did he leave you anything?" he asked.

She shook her head. "I . . . I think he expected me to marry Jim. . . . He always wanted it that way, but we never felt like that about each other, and yet Jim told me after Uncle Dave died that I was to consider the place my home, if he got it."

As they ate, he listened to her talk while he studied the cliff. It wasn't going to be easy, and yet it could be done.

A shout rang out from the rocks behind them, and they both moved to the boulders, but there was nobody in sight. A voice yelled again that Jim spotted as that of Wing Cary. He shouted a reply, and Wing yelled back, "We'll let Lisa come out if she wants, an' you, too, if you come with your hands up!"

Lisa shook her head, so Gatlin shouted back, "We like it here! Plenty of water, plenty of grub! If you want us, you'll have to come an' get us!"

In the silence that followed, Lisa said, "*He* can't stay, not if he attends the auction."

Jim turned swiftly. "Take the rifle. If they start to come, shoot an' shoot to kill! I'm going to take a chance!"

Keeping out of sight behind the worn gray boulders, Gatlin worked his way swiftly along the edge of the pool toward the cliff face. As he felt his way along the rocky edge, he stared down into the water. That pool was deep, from the looks of it. And that was something to remember.

At the cliff face, he stared up. It looked even easier

than he thought, and at one time and another, he had climbed worse faces. However, once he was well up the face, he would be within sight of the watchers below . . . or would he?

Hell's Chimney

He put a hand up and started working his way to a four-inch ledge that projected from the face of the rock and slanted sharply upward. There were occasional clumps of brush growing from the rock, and they would offer some security. A rifle shot rang out behind him, then a half dozen more, farther off. Lisa had fired at something and had been answered from down the canyon.

The ledge was steep, but there were good handholds, and he worked his way along it more swiftly than he would have believed possible. His clothing blended well with the rock, and by refraining from any sudden movements, there was a chance that he could make it.

When almost two hundred feet up the face, he paused, resting on a narrow ledge, partly concealed by an outcropping. He looked up, but the wall was sheer. Beyond, there was a chimney, but almost too wide for climbing, and the walls looked slick as a blue clay sidehill. Yet study the cliff as he would, he could see no other point where he might climb farther. Worse, part of that chimney was exposed to fire from below.

If they saw him, he was through. He'd be stuck, with no chance of evading their fire. Yet he knew he'd take the chance. Squatting on the ledge, he pulled off his boots, and running a loop of piggin' string through their loops, he slung them from his neck. Slipping thongs over his guns, he got into the chimney and braced his back against one side, then lifted his feet, first his left, then his right, against the opposite wall.

Whether Lisa was watching or not, he didn't know, but almost at that instant she began firing. The chimney was, at this point, all of six feet deep and wide enough to allow for climbing, but very risky climbing. His palms flat against the slippery wall, he began to inch himself upward, working his stocking feet up the opposite wall. Slowly, every movement a danger, his breath coming slow, his eyes riveted on his feet, he began to work his way higher.

Sweat poured down his face and smarted in his eyes, and he could feel it trickling down his stomach under his wool shirt. Before he was halfway up, his breath was coming in great gasps, and his muscles were weary with the strain of opposing their strength against the walls to keep from falling. Then, miraculously, the chimney narrowed a little, and climbing was easier.

He glanced up. Not over twenty feet to go. His heart bounded, and he renewed his effort. A foot slipped, and he felt an agonizing moment when fear throttled him and he seemed about to fall. To fall meant to bound from that ledge and go down, down into that deep green pool at the foot of the cliff, a fall of nearly three hundred feet.

Something smacked against the wall near him and from below there was a shout. Then Lisa opened fire, desperately, he knew, to give him covering fire. Another shot splashed splinters in his face and he struggled wildly, sweat pouring from him, to get up those last few feet. Suddenly, the rattle of fire ceased and then opened up again. He risked a quick glance and saw Lisa Cochrane running out in the open, and as she ran, she halted and fired.

She was risking her life, making her death or capture inevitable, to save him.

Suddenly, a breath of air was against his cheek, and he hunched himself higher, his head reaching the top of the cliff. Another shot rang out and howled off the edge of the rock beside him. Then his hands were on the edge, and he rolled over on solid ground, trembling in every limb.

There was no time to waste. He got to his feet, staggering, and stared around. He was on the very top of the mountain, and Tucker lay far away to the south. He seated himself and got his boots on, then slipped the thongs from his guns. Walking as swiftly as his still-trembling muscles would allow, he started south.

There was a creek, he remembered, that flowed down into the flatlands from somewhere near there, an intermittent stream, but with a canyon that offered an easy outlet to the plain below. Studying the terrain, he saw a break in the rocky plateau that might be it and started down the steep mountainside through the cedar, toward that break.

A horse was what he needed most. With a good horse under him, he might make it. He had a good lead, for they must come around the mountain, a good ten miles by the quickest trail. That ten miles might get him to town before they could catch him, to town and to the lawyer who would make the bid for them, even if Eaton had him in jail by that time. Suddenly, remembering how Lisa had run out into the open, risking her life to protect him, he realized he would willingly give his own to save her.

He stopped, mopping his face with a handkerchief. The canyon broke away before him, and he dropped into it, sliding and climbing to the bottom. When he reached the bottom, he started off toward the flat country at a swinging stride. A half hour later, his shirt dark with sweat, the canyon suddenly spread wide into the flat country. Dust hung in the air, and he slowed down, hearing voices.

"Give 'em a blow." It was a man's voice speaking. "Hear any more shootin'?"

"Not me." The second voice was thin and nasal. "Reckon it was my ears mistakin' themselves."

"Let's go, Eaton," another voice said. "It's too hot here. I'm pinin' for some o' that good XY well water!"

Gatlin pushed his way forward. "Hold it, sheriff! You huntin' me?"

Sheriff Eaton was a tall, gray-haired man with a handlebar mustache and keen blue eyes. "If you're Gatlin, an' from the looks of you, you must be, I sure am! How come you're so all-fired anxious to get caught?"

Gatlin explained swiftly. "Lisa Cochrane's back there, an' they got her," he finished. "Sheriff, I'd be mighty pleased if you'd send a few men after her, or go yourself an' let the rest of them go to Tucker with me."

Eaton studied him. "What you want in Tucker?"

"To bid that ranch in for Lisa Cochrane," he said flatly. "Sheriff, that girl saved my bacon back there, an' I'm a grateful man! You get me to town to get that money in Lawyer Ashton's hands, an' I'll go to jail!"

Eaton rolled his chaw in his lean jaws. "Dave Butler come over the Cut-Off with me, seen this ranch, then, an' would have it no other way but that he come back here to settle. I reckon I know what he wanted." He turned. "Doc, you'll git none of that XY water today! Take this man to Ashton, then put him in jail! An' make her fast!"

Doc was a lean, saturnine man with a lantern jaw and cold eyes. He glanced at Gatlin, then nodded. "If you say so, sheriff. I sure was hopin' for some o' that good XY water, though. Come on, pardner."

They wheeled their horses and started for Tucker, Doc turning from the trail to cross the desert through a thick tangle of cedar and sagebrush. "Mite quicker thisaway. Ain't nobody ever rides it, an' she's some rough."

It was high noon, and the sun was blazing. Doc led off, casting only an occasional glance back at Gatlin. Jim was puzzled, for the man made no show of guarding him. Was he deliberately offering him the chance to make a break? It looked it, but Jim wasn't having any. His one idea was to get to Tucker, see Ashton, and get his money down. They rode on, pushing through the dancing heat waves, no breeze stirring the air, and the sun turning the bowl into a baking oven.

Doc slowed the pace a little. "Hosses won't stand it." he commented, then glanced at Gatlin. "I reckon you're honest. You had a chance for a break an' didn't take it." He grinned wryly. "Not that you'd have got far. This here ol' rifle o' mine sure shoots where I aim it at."

"I've nothin' to run from," Gatlin replied. "What I've said was true. My bein' in Tucker was strictly accidental."

The next half mile they rode side by side, entering now into a devil's playground of boulders and arroyos. Doc's hand went out, and Jim drew up. Buzzards roosted in a tree not far off the trail, a half dozen of the great birds. "Somethin' dead," Doc said. "Let's have a look."

Two hundred yards farther and they drew up. What had been a dappled gray horse lay in a saucerlike depression among the cedars. Buzzards lifted from it, flapping their great wings. Doc's eyes glinted, and he spat. "Jim Walker's mare," he said, "an' his saddle."

They pushed on, circling the dead horse. Gatlin pointed. "Look," he said, "he wasn't killed. He was crawlin' away."

"Yeah"—Doc was grim—"but not far. Look at the blood he was losin'."

They got down from their horses, their faces grim. Both men knew what they'd find, and neither man was looking forward to the moment. Doc slid his rifle from the scabbard. "Jim Walker was by way o' bein' a friend o' mine," he said. "I take his goin' right hard."

The trail was easy. Twice the wounded man had obviously lain still for a long time. They found torn cloth where he had ripped up his shirt to bandage a wound. They walked on until they saw the gray rocks and the foot of the low bluff. It was a cul-de-sac.

"Wait a minute," Gatlin said. "Look at this." He indicated the tracks of a man who had walked up the trail. He had stopped there, and there was blood on the sage, spattered blood. The faces of the men hardened, for the deeper impression of one foot, the way the step was taken, and the spattered blood told but one thing. The killer had walked up and kicked the wounded man.

They had little farther to go. The wounded man had nerve, and nothing had stopped him. He was backed up under a clump of brush that grew from the side of the bluff, and he lay on his face. That was an indication to these men that Walker had been conscious for some time, that he had sought a place where the buzzards couldn't get at him.

Doc turned, and his gray white eyes were icy. "Step your boot beside that track," he said, his rifle partly lifted.

Jim Gatlin stared back at the man and felt cold and empty inside. At that moment, familiar with danger as he was, he was glad he wasn't the killer. He stepped over to the tracks and made a print beside them. His boot was almost an inch shorter and of a different type.

"Didn't figger so," Doc said. "But I aimed to make sure."

"On the wall there," Gatlin said. "He scratched somethin'."

Both men bent over. It was plain, scratched with an edge of whitish rock on the slate of a small slab, *Cary done* . . . and no more.

Doc straightened. "He can wait a few hours more. Let's get to town."

*   *   *

Tucker's street was more crowded than usual when they rode up to Ashton's office and swung down. Jim Gatlin pulled open the door and stepped in. The tall, gray-haired man behind the desk looked up. "You're Ashton?" Gatlin demanded.

At the answering nod, he opened his shirt and unbuckled his money belt. "There's ten thousand there. Bid in the XY for Cochrane an' Gatlin."

Ashton's eyes sparkled with sudden satisfaction. "You're her partner?" he asked. "You're putting up the money? It's a fine thing you're doing, man."

"I'm a partner only in name. My gun backs the brand, that's all. She may need a gun behind her for a little while, an' I've got it."

He turned to Doc, but the man was gone. Briefly, Gatlin explained what they had found and added, "Wing Cary's headed for town now."

"Headed for town?" Ashton's head jerked around. "He's here. Came in about twenty minutes ago!"

Jim Gatlin spun on his heel and strode from the office. On the street, pulling his hat brim low against the glare, he stared left, then right. There were men on the street, but they were drifting inside now. There was no sign of the man called Doc or of Cary.

Gatlin's heels were sharp and hard on the boardwalk. He moved swiftly, his hands swinging alongside his guns. His hard brown face was cool, and his lips were tight. At the Barrelhouse, he paused, put up his left hand, and stepped in. All faces turned toward him, but none was that of Cary. "Seen Wing Cary?" he demanded. "He murdered Jim Walker."

Nobody replied, and then an oldish man turned his head and jerked it down the street. "He's gettin' his hair cut, right next to the livery barn. Waitin' for the auction to start up."

Gatlin stepped back through the door. A dark figure, hunched near the blacksmith shop, jerked back from sight. Jim hesitated, alert to danger, then quickly pushed on..

The red and white barber pole marked the frame building. Jim opened the door and stepped in. A sleeping man snored with his mouth open, his back to the street wall. The bald barber looked up, swallowed, and stepped back.

Wing Cary sat in the chair, his hair half-trimmed, the white cloth draped around him. The opening door and sudden silence made him look up. "You, is it?" he said.

"It's me. We found Jim Walker. He marked your name, Cary, as his killer."

Cary's lips tightened, and suddenly a gun bellowed, and something slammed Jim Gatlin in the shoulder and spun him like a top, smashing him sidewise into the door. That first shot saved him from the second. Wing Cary had held a gun in his lap and fired through the white cloth. There was sneering triumph in his eyes, and as though time stood still, Jim Gatlin saw the smoldering of the black-rimmed circles of the holes in the cloth.

He never remembered firing, but suddenly Cary's body jerked sharply, and Jim felt the gun buck in his hand. He fired again then, and Wing's face twisted and his gun exploded into the floor, narrowly missing his own foot.

Wing started to get up, and Gatlin fired the third time, the shot nicking Wing's ear and smashing a shaving cup, spattering lather. The barber was on his knees in one corner, holding a chair in front of him. The sleeping man had dived through the window, glass and all.

Men came running, and Jim leaned back against the door. One of the men was Doc, and he saw Sheriff Eaton, and then Lisa tore them aside and ran to him. "Oh, you're hurt! You've been shot! You've . . . !"

His feet gave away slowly, and he slid down the door to the floor. Wing Cary still sat in the barbershop, his hair half-clipped.

Doc stepped in and glanced at him, then at the barber. "You can't charge him for it, Tony. You never finished!"

Author's Note:
BODIE

There was a time when a man with a few drinks under his belt who wished to impress people would proclaim himself a "Badman from Bodie!"

Bodie, California, was a rich camp, and a tough one. On one day in 1880 they had three shootings and two stage holdups, and the town was just getting warmed up. Another man noted six shootings in one week and made no mention of various knifings, cuttings, or other passages of arms.

In approximately three years, from 1879 to 1881, miners took something over $30 million in gold from the mines of Bodie. Laundrymen were getting rich panning out the dirt they washed from miners' clothing.

It is reported that Rough-and-Tumble Jack, Bodie's first badman, was explaining how tough he was when someone saw fit to challenge him. He and his antagonist went outside and opened fire on each other at point-blank range. Rough-and-Tumble Jack staggered back into the saloon, but his opponent, with one arm broken, reloaded his gun by holding it between his knees and then went back into the saloon and finished the job. Jack became one of the first to bed down in Bodie's Boot Hill.

Much of the town still remains, although a fire in 1932 swept away many of its buildings.

DESERT DEATH SONG

When Jim Morton rode up to the fire, three unshaven men huddled there warming themselves and drinking hot coffee. Morton recognized Chuck Benson from the Slash Five. The other men were strangers.

"Howdy, Chuck!" Morton said. "He still in there?"

"Sure is!" Benson told him. "An' it don't look like he's figurin' on comin' out."

"I don't reckon to blame him. Must be a hundred men scattered about."

"Nigher two hundred, but you know Nat Bodine. Shakin' him out of these hills is going to be tougher'n shaking a possum out of a tree."

The man with the black beard stubble looked up sourly. "He wouldn't last long if they'd let us go in after him! I'd sure roust him out of there fast enough!"

Morton eyed the man with distaste. "You think so. That means you don't know Bodine. Goin' in after him is like sendin' a houn' dog down a hole after a badger. That man knows these hills, every crack an' crevice. He can hide places an Apache would pass up."

The black-bearded man stared sullenly. He had thick lips and small, heavy-lidded eyes. "Sounds like maybe you're a friend of his'n. Maybe when we get him, you should hang alongside of him."

Somehow the long rifle over Morton's saddlebows shifted to stare warningly at the man, although Morton made no perceptible movement. "That ain't a handy way to talk, stranger," Morton said casually. "Ever'body in these hills knows Nat, an' most of us been right friendly with him one time or another. I ain't takin' up with him, but I reckon there's worse men in this posse than he is."

"Meanin'?" The big man's hand lay on his thigh.

"Meanin' anything you like." Morton was a Tennessee mountain man before he came west, and gun talk was not strange to him. "You call it your ownself." The long rifle was pointed between the big man's eyes, and Morton was building a cigarette with his hands only inches away from the trigger.

"Forget it!" Benson interrupted. "What you two got to fight about? Blackie, this here's Jim Morton. He's lion hunter for the Lazy S."

Blackie's mind underwent a rapid readjustment. This tall, lazy stranger wasn't the soft-headed drink of water he had thought him, for everybody knew about Morton. A dead shot with rifle and pistol, he was known to favor the former, even in fairly close combat. He had been known to go up trees after mountain lions, and once, when three hardcase rustlers had tried to steal his horses, the three had ended up in Boot Hill.

"How about it, Jim?" Chuck asked. "You know Nat. Where'd you think he'd be?"

Morton squinted and drew on his cigarette. "Ain't no figurin' him. I know him, an' I've hunted along of him. He's almighty knowin' when it comes to wild country. Moves like a cat an' got eyes like a turkey buzzard." He glanced at Chuck. "What's he done? I heard some talk down to the Slash Five, but nobody seemed to have it clear."

"Stage robbed yestiddy. Pete Daley of the Diamond D was ridin' it, an' he swore the robber was Nat. When they went to arrest him, Nat shot the sheriff."

"Kill him?"

"No. But he's bad off, an' like to die. Nat only fired once, an' the bullet took Larrabee too high."

"Don't sound reasonable," Morton said slowly. "Nat ain't one to miss somethin' he aims to kill. You say Pete Daley was there?"

"Yeah. He's the on'y one saw it."

"How about this robber? Was he masked?"

"Uh-huh, an' packin' a Winchester .44 an' two tied-down guns. Big black-haired man, the driver said. He didn't know Bodine, but Pete identified him."

Morton eyed Benson. "I shouldn't wonder," he said, and Chuck flushed.

Each knew what the other was thinking. Pete Daly had never liked Bodine. Nat married the girl Pete wanted, even though it was generally figured Pete never had a look-in with her, anyway, but Daley had worn his hatred like a badge ever since. Mary Callahan had been a pretty girl, but a quiet one, and Daley had been sure he'd win her.

But Bodine had come down from the hills and changed all that. He was a tall man with broad shoulders, dark hair, and a quiet face. He was a good-looking man, even a handsome man, some said. Men liked him, and women too, but the men liked him best because he left their women alone. That was more than could be said for Daley, who lacked Bodine's good looks but made up for it with money.

Bodine had bought a place near town and drilled a good well. He seemed to have money, and that puzzled people, so hints began to get around that he had been rustling as well as robbing stages. There were those, like Jim Morton, who believed most of the stories were started by Daley, but no matter where they originated, they got around.

Hanging Bodine for killing the sheriff—the fact that he was still alive was overlooked and considered merely a technical question, anyway—was the problem before the posse. It was a self-elected posse, inspired to some extent by Daley and given a semiofficial status by the presence of Burt Stoval, Larrabee's jailer.

Yet, to hang a man, he must first be caught, and Bodine had lost himself in that broken, rugged country known as Powder Basin. It was a region of some ten square miles backed against an even rougher and uglier patch of waterless desert, but the basin was bad enough itself.

Fractured with gorges and humped with fir-clad hogbacks, it was a maze where the juniper region merged into the fir and spruce and where the canyons were liberally overgrown with manzanita. There were at least two cliff dwellings in the area and a ghost mining town of some dozen ramshackle structures, tumbled in and wind worried.

"All I can say," Morton said finally, "is that I don't envy those who corner him—when they do and if they do."

Blackie wanted no issue with Morton, yet he was still sore. He looked up. "What do you mean, *if* we do? We'll get him!"

Morton took his cigarette from his lips. "Want a suggestion, friend? When he's cornered, don't you be the one to go in after him."

Four hours later, when the sun was moving toward noon, the net had been drawn tighter, and Nat Bodine lay on his stomach in the sparse grass on the crest of a hogback and studied the terrain below.

There were many hiding places, but the last thing he wanted was to be cornered and forced to fight it out. Until the last moment, he wanted freedom of movement.

Among the searchers were friends of his, men with whom he rode and hunted, men he had admired and liked. Now they believed him wrong; they believed him a killer, and they were hunting him down.

They were searching the canyons with care, so he had chosen the last spot they would examine, a bald hill with only the foot-high grass for cover. His vantage point was excellent, and he had watched with appreciation the care with which they searched the canyon below him.

Bodine scooped another handful of dust and rubbed it along his rifle barrel. He knew how far a glint of sunlight from a Winchester can be seen, and men in that posse were Indian fighters and hunters.

No matter how he considered it, his chances were slim. He was a better woodsman than any of them, unless it was Jim Morton. Yet that was not enough. He was going to need food and water. Sooner or later, they would get the bright idea of watching the water holes, and after that. . . .

It was almost twenty-four hours since he had eaten, and he would soon have to refill his canteen.

Pete Daley was behind this, of course. Trust Pete not to tell the true story of what happened. Pete had accused him of the holdup right to his face when they had met him on the street. The accusation had been sudden, and Nat's reply had been prompt. He'd called Daley a liar, and Daley moved a hand for his gun. The sheriff sprang to stop them and took Nat's bullet. The people who rushed to the scene saw only the sheriff on the ground, Daley with no gun drawn and Nat gripping his six-shooter. Yet it was not that of which he thought now. He thought of Mary.

What would she be thinking now? They had been married so short a time and had been happy despite the fact that he was still learning how to live in civilization and with a woman. It was a mighty different thing, living with a girl like Mary.

Did she doubt him now? Would she, too, believe he had held up the stage and then killed the sheriff? As he lay in the grass, he could find nothing on which to build hope.

Hemmed in on three sides, with the waterless mountains and desert behind him, the end seemed inevitable. Thoughtfully, he shook his canteen. It was nearly empty. Only a little water sloshed weakly in the bottom. Yet he must last the afternoon through, and by night he could try the water hole at Mesquite Springs, no more than a half mile away.

The sun was hot, and he lay very still, knowing that only the faint breeze should stir the grass where he lay if he were not to be seen.

Below him, he heard men's voices and from time to time could distinguish a word or even sentence. They were cursing the heat, but their search was not relaxed. Twice men mounted the hill and passed near him. One man stopped for several minutes, not more than a dozen yards away, but Nat held himself still and waited. Finally, the man moved on, mopping sweat from his face. When the sun was gone, he wormed his way off the crest and into the manzanita. It took him over an hour to get within striking distance of Mesquite Springs. He stopped just in time. His nostrils caught the faint fragrance of tobacco smoke.

Lying in the darkness, he listened, and after a moment heard a stone rattle, then the faint *chink* of metal on stone.

When he was far enough away, he got to his feet and worked his way through the night toward Stone Cup, a spring two miles beyond. He moved more warily now, knowing they were watching the water holes.

The stars were out, sharp and clear, when he snaked his way through the reeds toward the cup. Deliberately, he chose the route where the overflow from the Stone Cup kept the earth soggy and high grown with reeds and dank grass. There would be no chance of a watcher waiting there on the wet ground, nor would the wet grass rustle. He moved close, but there, too, men waited.

He lay still in the darkness, listening. Soon he picked out three men, two back in the shadows of the rock shelf, one over under the brush but not more than four feet from the small pool's edge.

There was no chance to get a canteen filled there, for the watchers were too wide-awake. Yet he might manage a drink.

He slid his knife from his pocket and opened it carefully. He cut several reeds, allowing no sound. When he had them cut, he joined them and reached them toward the water. Lying on his stomach within only a few feet of the pool and no farther from the nearest watcher, he sucked on the reeds until the water started flowing. He drank for a long time, then drank again, the trickle doing little, at first, to assuage his thrist. After a while, he felt better.

He started to withdraw the reeds, then grinned and let them lay. With care, he worked his way back from the cup and got to his feet. His shirt was muddy and wet, and with the wind against his body, he felt almost cold. With the water holes watched, there would be no chance to fill his canteen, and the day would be blazing hot. There might be an unwatched hole, but the chance of that was slight, and if he spent the night in fruitless search of water, he would exhaust his strength and lose the sleep he needed. Returning like a deer to a resting place near a ridge, he bedded down in a clump of manzanita. His rifle cradled in his arm, he was almost instantly asleep.

Dawn was breaking when he awakened, and his nostrils caught a whiff of wood smoke. His pursuers were at their breakfasts. By now they would have found his reeds, and he grinned at the thought of their anger at having had him so near without knowing. Morton, he reflected, would appreciate that. Yet they would all know he was short of water.

LOUIS L'AMOUR

Worming his way through the brush, he found a trail that followed just below the crest and moved steadily along in the partial shade, angling toward a towering hogback.

Later, from well up on the hogback, he saw three horsemen walking their animals down the ridge where he had rested the previous day. Two more were working up a canyon, and wherever he looked, they seemed to be closing in. He abandoned the canteen, for it banged against brush and could be heard too easily. He moved back, going from one cluster of boulders to another, then pausing short of the ridge itself.

The only route that lay open was behind him, into the desert, and that way they were sure he would not go. The hogback on which he lay was the highest ground in miles, and before him the jagged scars of three canyons running off the hogback stretched their ugly length into the rocky, brush-blanketed terrain. Up those three canyons, groups of searchers were working. Another group had cut down from the north and come between him and the desert ghost town.

The far-flung skirmishing line was well disposed, and Nat could find it in himself to admire their skill. These were his brand of men, and they understood their task. Knowing them as he did, he knew how relentless they could be. The country behind him was open. It would not be open long. They were sure he would fight it out rather than risk dying of thirst in the desert. They were wrong.

Nat Bodine learned that himself, suddenly. Had he been asked, he would have accepted their solution, yet now he saw that he could not give up.

The desert was the true Powder Basin. The Indians had called it the Place of No Water, and he had explored deep into it in past years and found nothing. While the distance across was less than twenty miles, a man must travel twice that or more, up and down and around, if he would cross it, and his sense of direction must be perfect. Yet, with water and time, a man might cross it.

76

But Nat Bodine had neither. Moreover, if he went into the desert, they would soon send word and have men waiting on the other side. He was fairly trapped, and yet he knew that he would die in that waste alone before he surrendered to be lynched. Nor could he hope to fight off this posse for long. Carefully, he got to his feet and worked his way to the crest. Behind him lay the vast red maw of the desert. He nestled among the boulders and watched the men below. They were coming carefully, still several yards away. Cradling his Winchester against his cheek, he drew a bead on a rock ahead of the nearest man and fired.

Instantly, the searchers vanished. Where a dozen men had been in sight, there was nobody now. He chuckled. "That made 'em eat dirt!" he said. "Now they won't be so anxious."

The crossing of the crest was dangerous, but he made it and hesitated there, surveying the scene before him. Far away to the horizon stretched the desert. Before him, the mountain broke sharply away in a series of sheer precipices and ragged chasms, and he scowled as he stared down at them, for it seemed no descent could be possible from there.

Chuck Benson and Jim Morton crouched in the lee of a stone wall and stared up at the ridge from which the shot had come. "He didn't shoot to kill," Morton said, "or he'd have had one of us. He's that good."

"What's on his mind?" Benson demanded. "He's stuck now. I know that ridge, an' the only way down is the way he went up."

"Let's move in," Blackie protested. "There's cover enough."

"You don't know Nat. He's never caught until you see him down. I know the man. He'll climb cliffs that would stop a hossfly."

Pete Daley and Burt Stoval moved up to join them, peering at the ridge before them through the concealing leaves. The ridge was a gigantic hogback almost a thousand feet higher than the plateau on which they waited. On the far side, it fell away to the desert, dropping almost two thousand feet in no more than two hundred yards, and most of the drop in broken cliffs.

Daley's eyes were hard with satisfaction. "We got him now!" he said triumphantly. "He'll never get off that ridge! We've only to wait a little, then move in on him. He's out of water, too!"

Morton looked with distaste at Daley. "You seem powerful anxious to get him, Pete. Maybe the sheriff ain't dead yet. Maybe he won't die. Maybe his story of the shootin' will be different."

Daley turned on Morton, his dislike evident. "Your opinion's of no account, Morton. I was there, and I saw it. As for Larrabee, if he ain't dead, he soon will be. If you don't like this job, why don't you leave?"

Jim Morton stroked his chin calmly. "Because I aim to be here if you get Bodine," he said, "an' I personally figure to see he gets a fair shake. Furthermore, Daley, I'm not beholdin' to you, no way, an' I ain't scared of you. Howsoever, I figure you've got a long way to go before you get Bodine."

High on the ridge, flat on his stomach among the rocks, Bodine was not so sure. He mopped sweat from his brow and studied again the broken cliff beneath him. There seemed to be a vaguely possible route, but at the thought of it, his mouth turned dry and his stomach, empty.

A certain bulge in the rock looked as though it might afford handholds, although some of the rock was loose, and he couldn't see below the bulge where it might become smooth. Once over that projection, getting back would be difficult if not impossible. Nevertheless, he determined to try.

Using his belt for a rifle strap, he slung the Winchester over his back, then turned his face to the rock and slid feet first over the bulge, feeling with his toes for a hold. If he fell from here, he could not drop less than two hundred feet, although close in there was a narrow ledge only sixty feet down.

Using simple pull holds and working down with his feet, Bodine got well out over the bulge. Taking a good grip, he turned his head and searched the rock below him. On his left, the rock was cracked deeply, with the portion of the face to which he clung projecting several inches farther into space than the other side of the crack. Shifting his left foot carefully, he stepped into the crack, which afforded a good jam hold. Shifting his left hand, he took a pull grip, pulling away from himself with the left fingers until he could swing his body to the left and get a grip on the edge of the crack with his right fingers. Then, lying back, his feet braced against the projecting far edge of the crack and pulling toward himself with his hands, he worked his way down, step by step and grip by grip, for all of twenty feet. There the crack widened into a chimney, far too wide to be climbed with a lie back, its inner sides slick and smooth from the scouring action of wind and water.

Working his way into the chimney, he braced his feet against one wall and his back against the other, and by pushing against the two walls and shifting his feet carefully, he worked his way down until he was well past the sixty-foot ledge. The chimney ended in a small cavernlike hollow in the rock, and he sat there, catching his breath.

Nat ran his fingers through his hair and mopped sweat from his brow. Anyway—he grinned at the thought—they wouldn't follow him down here!

Carefully, he studied the cliff below him, then to the right and left. To escape his present position, he must make a traverse of the rock face, working his way gradually down. For all of forty feet of climb, he would be exposed to a dangerous fall or to a shot from above if they had dared the ridge. Yet there were precarious handholds and some inch-wide ledges for his feet.

When he had his breath, he moved out, clinging to the rock face and carefully working across it and down. Sliding down a steep slab, he crawled out on a knife-edge ridge of rock and, straddling it, worked his way along until he could climb down a farther face, hand over hand. Landing on a wide ledge, he stood there, his chest heaving, staring back up at the ridge. No one was yet in sight, and there was a chance that he was making good his escape. At the same time, his mouth was dry, and the effort expended in descending had increased his thirst. Unslinging his rifle, he completed the descent without trouble, emerging at last upon the desert below.

Heat lifted against his face in a stifling wave. Loosening the buttons of his shirt, he pushed back his hat and stared up at the towering height of the mountain, and even as he looked up, he saw men appear on the ridge. Lifting his hat, he waved to them.

Benson was the first man on that ridge, and involuntarily he drew back from the edge of the cliff, catching his breath at the awful depth below. Pete Daley, Burt Stoval, and Jim Morton moved up beside him, and then the others. It was Morton who spotted Bodine first.

"What did I tell you?" he snapped. "He's down there on the desert!"

Daley's face hardened. "Why, the dirty—"

Benson stared. "You got to hand it to him!" he said. "I'd sooner chance a shootout with all of us than try that alone."

A bearded man on their left spat and swore softly.

"Well, boys, this does it! I'm quittin! No man that game deserves to hang! I'd say, let him go!"

Pete Daley turned angrily but changed his mind when he saw the big man and the way he wore his gun. Pete was no fool. Some men could be bullied, and it was a wise man who knew which and when. "I'm not quitting," he said flatly. "Let's get the boys, Chuck. We'll get our horses and be around there in a couple of hours. He won't get far on foot."

Nat Bodine turned and started off into the desert with a long swinging stride. His skin felt hot, and the air was close and stifling, yet his only chance was to get across this stretch and work into the hills at a point where they could not find him.

All this time, Mary was in the back of his mind, her presence always near, always alive. Where was she now? And what was she doing? Had she been told?

Nat Bodine had emerged upon the desert at the mouth of a boulder-strewn canyon slashed deep into the rocky flank of the mountain itself. From the mouth of the canyon there extended a wide fan of rock, coarse gravel, sand and silt flushed down from the mountain by torrential rains. On his right, the edge of the fan of sand was broken by the deep scar of another wash, cut at some later date when the water had found some crevice in the rock to give it an unexpected hold. It was toward this wash that Bodine walked.

Clambering down the slide, he walked along the bottom. Working his way among the boulders, he made his way toward the shimmering basin that marked the extreme low level of the desert. Here, dancing with heat waves and seeming from a distance to be a vast blue lake, was one of those dry lakes that collect the muddy runoff from the mountains. Yet as he drew closer, he discovered he had been mistaken in his hope that it was a *playa* of the dry type. Wells sunk in the dry type of *playa* often produce fresh cool water, and occasionally at shallow depths. This, however, was a pasty, water-surfaced *salinas*, and water found there would be salty and worse than none at all. Moreover, there was danger that he might break through the crust beneath the dry, powdery dust and into the slime below.

The *playa* was such that it demanded a wide detour from his path, and the heat there was even more intense than on the mountain. Walking steadily, dust rising at each footfall, Bodine turned left along the desert, skirting the *playa*. Beyond it, he could see the edge of a rocky escarpment, and this rocky ledge stretched for miles toward the far mountain range bordering the desert.

Yet the escarpment must be attained as soon as possible, for knowing as he was in desert ways and lore, Nat understood in such terrain there was always a possibility of stumbling on one of those desert tanks, or *tinajas*, which contain the purest water any wanderer of the dry lands could hope to find. Yet he knew how difficult these were to find, for hollowed by some sudden cascade or scooped by wind, they are often filled to the brim with gravel or sand and must be scooped out to obtain the water in the bottom.

Nat Bodine paused, shading his eyes toward the end of the *playa*. It was not much farther. His mouth was powder dry now, and he could swallow only with an effort.

He was no longer perspiring. He walked as in a daze, concerned only with escaping the basin of the *playa*, and it was with relief that he stumbled over a stone and fell headlong. Clumsily, he got to his feet, blinking away the dust and pushing on through the rocks. He crawled to the top of the escarpment through a deep crack in the rock and then walked on over the dark surface.

It was some ancient flow of lava, crumbling to ruin now, with here and there a broken blister of it. In each of them, he searched for water, but they were dry. At this hour, he would see no coyote, but he watched for tracks, knowing the wary and wily desert wolves knew where water could be found.

The horizon seemed no nearer, nor had the peaks begun to show their lines of age or the shapes into which the wind had carved them. Yet the sun was lower now, its rays level and blasting as the searing flames of a furnace. Bodine plodded on, walking toward the night, hoping for it, praying for it. Once he paused abruptly at a thin whine of sound across the sun-blasted air.

Waiting, he listened, searching the air about him with eyes suddenly alert, but he did not hear the sound again for several minutes, and when he did hear it, there was no mistaking it. His eyes caught the dark movement, striking straight away from him on a course diagonal with his own.

A bee!

Nat changed his course abruptly, choosing a landmark on a line with the course of the bee, and then followed on. Minutes later, he saw a second bee, and altered his course to conform with it. The direction was almost the same, and he knew that water could be found by watching converging lines of bees. He could afford to miss no chance, and he noted the bees were flying deeper *into* the desert, not away from it.

Darkness found him suddenly. At the moment, the horizon range had grown darker, its crest tinted with old rose and gold, slashed with the deep fire of crimson, and then it was night, and a coyote was yapping myriad calls at the stars.

In the coolness, he might make many miles by pushing on, and he might also miss his only chance at water. He hesitated; then his weariness conformed with his judgment, and he slumped down against a boulder and dropped his chin on his chest. The coyote voiced a shrill complaint, then satisfied with the echo against the rocks, ceased his yapping and began to hunt. He scented the man smell and skirted wide around, going about his business.

There were six men in the little cavalcade at the base of the cliff, searching for tracks. The rider found them there. Jim Morton calmly sitting his horse and watching with interested eyes but lending no aid to the men who tracked his friend, and there were Pete Daley, Blackie, Chuck Benson, and Burt Stoval. Farther along were other groups of riders.

The man worked a hard-ridden horse, and he was yelling before he reached them. He raced up and slid his horse to a stop, gasping, "Call it off! It wasn't him!"

"What?" Daley burst out. "What did you say?"

"I said . . . it wa'n't Bodine! We got our outlaw this mornin' out east of town! Mary Bodine spotted a man hidin' in the brush below Wenzel's place, an' she come down to town. It was him, all right. He had the loot on him, an' the stage driver identified him!"

Pete Daley stared, his little eyes tightening. "What about the sheriff?" he demanded.

"He's pullin' through." The rider stared at Daley. "He said it was his fault he got shot. His an' your'n. He said if you'd kept your fool mouth shut, nothin' would have happened, an' that he was another fool for not lettin' you get leaded down like you deserved!"

Daley's face flushed, and he looked around angrily like a man badly treated. "All right, Benson. We'll go home."

"Wait a minute." Jim Morton crossed his hands on the saddle horn. "What about Nat? He's out there in the desert, an' he thinks he's still a hunted man. He's got no water. Far's we know, he may be dead by now."

Daley's face was hard. "He'll make out. My time's too valuable to chase around in the desert after a no-account hunter."

"It wasn't too valuable when you had an excuse to kill him," Morton said flatly.

"I'll ride with you, Morton," Benson offered.

Daley turned on him, his face dark. "You do an' you'll hunt you a job!"

Benson spat. "I quit workin' for you ten minutes ago. I never did like coyotes."

He sat his horse, staring hard at Daley, waiting to see if he would draw, but the rancher merely stared back until his eyes fell. He turned his horse.

"If I were you," Morton suggested, "I'd sell out an' get out. This country don't cotton to your type, Pete."

Morton started his horse. "Who's comin'?"

"We all are." It was Blackie who spoke. "But we better fly some white. I don't want that salty Injun shootin' at me!"

It was near sundown of the second day of their search and the fourth since the holdup, when they found him. Benson had a shirt tied to his rifle barrel, and they took turns carrying it.

They had given up hope the day before, knowing he was out of water and knowing the country he was in.

The cavalcade of riders was almost abreast of a shoulder of sandstone outcropping when a voice spoke out of the rocks. "You huntin' me?"

Jim Morton felt relief flood through him. "Huntin' you peaceful," he said. "They got their outlaw, an' Larrabee owes you no grudge."

His face burned red from the desert sun, his eyes squinting at them, Nat Bodine swung his long body down over the rocks. "Glad to hear that," he said. "I was some worried about Mary."

"She's all right." Morton stared at him. "What did you do for water?"

"Found some. Neatest *tinaja* in all this desert."

The men swung down, and Benson almost stepped on a small, red-spotted toad.

"Watch that, Chuck. That's the boy who saved my life."

"That toad?" Blackie was incredulous. "How d' you mean?"

"That kind of toad never gets far from water. You only find them near some permanent seepage or spring. I was all in, down on my hands and knees, when I heard him cheeping.

"It's a noise like a cricket, and I'd been hearing it some time before I remembered that a Yaqui had told me about these frogs. I hunted and found him, so I knew there had to be water close by. I'd followed the bees for a day and a half, always this way, and then I lost them. While I was studyin' the lay of the land, I saw another bee, an' then another. All headin' for this bunch of sand rock. But it was the toad that stopped me."

They had a horse for him, and he mounted up. Blackie stared at him. "You better thank that Morton," he said dryly. "He was the only one was sure you were in the clear."

"No, there was another," Morton said. "Mary was sure. She said you were no outlaw and that you'd live. She said you'd live through anything." Morton bit off a chew, then glanced again at Nat. "They were wonderin' where you make your money, Nat."

"Me?" Bodine looked up, grinning. "Minin' turquoise. I found me a place where the Indians worked. I been cuttin' it out an' shippin' it East." He stooped and picked up the toad, and put him carefully in the saddlebag.

"That toad," he said emphatically, "goes home to Mary an' me. Our place is green an' mighty pretty, an' right on the edge of the desert, but with plenty of water. This toad has got him a good home from here on, and I mean a good home!"

Author's Note:
THE TONTO BASIN

Bounded on the north by the 2,000-foot Mogollon Rim (pronounced Muggy Own by westerners), the Tonto Basin is a green and lovely area of pine forest, grassy meadows, running streams, and occasional springs. To the old-timers, much of what was referred to as the Tonto Basin actually lay outside of it, but it served to specify the locality.

It was the scene of several Indian battles, including those General Crook led against the Apaches, but it is better known for the Tonto Basin War between the Tewksberry and Graham factions.

This is often referred to as a war between cattlemen and sheepmen, and certainly that was one element involved, but the Grahams and Tewksberrys had trouble before sheep entered the picture. The number of people killed varies with the information available to the teller, but probably twenty-six men were killed during the war, and more likely twice that number. The father of the Blevins boys disappeared during the fighting and was probably killed. At one point, the fighting became so bitter that if a man saw a stranger, he shot him. The idea was that if he wasn't on my side, he had to be on the other or he wouldn't be there. Tom Horn was briefly involved.

Zane Grey had a cabin in the Basin.

RIDE, YOU TONTO RAIDERS!

The Seventh Man

The rain, which had been falling steadily for three days, had turned the trail into a sloppy river of mud. Peering through the slanting downpour, Mathurin Sabre cursed himself for the quixotic notion that impelled him to take this special trail to the home of the man that he had gunned down.

Nothing good could come of it, he reflected, yet the thought that the young widow and child might need the money he was carrying had started him upon the long ride from El Paso to the Mogollons. Certainly, neither the bartender nor the hangers-on in the saloon could have been entrusted with that money, and nobody was taking that dangerous ride to the Tonto Basin for fun.

Matt Sabre was no trouble hunter. At various times, he had been many things, most of them associated with violence. By birth and inclination, he was a western man, although much of his adult life had been lived far from his native country. He had been a buffalo hunter, a prospector, and for a short time, a two-gun marshal of a tough cattle town. It was his stubborn refusal either to back up or back down that kept him in constant hot water.

Yet some of his trouble derived from something more than that. It stemmed from a dark and bitter drive toward violence—a drive that lay deep within him. He was aware of this drive and held it in restraint, but at times it welled up, and he went smashing into trouble—a big, rugged, and dangerous man who fought like a Viking gone berserk, except that he fought coldly and shrewdly.

He was a tall man, heavier than he appeared, and his lean, dark face had a slightly patrician look with high cheekbones and green eyes. His eyes were usually quiet and reserved. He had a natural affinity for horses and weapons. He understood them, and they understood him. It had been love of a good horse that brought him to his first act of violence.

He had been buffalo hunting with his uncle and had interfered with another hunter who was beating his horse. At sixteen, a buffalo hunter was a man and expected to stand as one. Matt Sabre stood his ground and shot it out, killing his first man. Had it rested there, all would have been well, but two of the dead man's friends had come hunting Sabre. Failing to find him, they had beaten his ailing uncle and stolen the horses. Matt Sabre trailed them to Mobeetie and killed them both in the street, taking his horses home.

Then he left the country, to prospect in Mexico, fight a revolution in Central America, and join the Foreign Legion in Morocco, from which he deserted after two years. Returning to Texas, he drove a trail herd up to Dodge, then took a job as marshal of a town. Six months later, in El Paso, he became engaged in an altercation with Billy Curtin, and Curtin called him a liar and went for his gun.

With that incredible speed that was so much a part of him, Matt drew his gun and fired. Curtin hit the floor. An hour later, he was summoned to the dying man's hotel room.

Billy Curtin, his dark, tumbled hair against a folded blanket, his face drawn and deathly white, was dying. They told him outside the door that Curtin might live an hour or even two. He could not live longer.

Tall, straight, and quiet, Sabre walked into the room and stood by the dying man's bed. Curtin held a packet wrapped in oilskin. "Five thousand dollars," he whispered. "Take it to my wife—to Jenny, on the Pivotrock, in the Mogollons. She's in—in—trouble."

It was a curious thing that this dying man should place a trust in the hands of the man who had killed him. Sabre stared down at him, frowning a little.

"Why me?" he asked. "You trust me with this? And why should I do it?"

"You—you're a gentleman. I trust—you help her, will you? I—I was a hot—headed fool. Worried—impatient. It wasn't your fault."

The reckless light was gone from the blue eyes, and the light that remained was fading.

"I'll do it, Curtin. You've my word—you've got the word of Matt Sabre."

For an instant, then, the blue eyes blazed wide and sharp with knowledge. "You—Sabre?"

Matt nodded, but the light had faded, and Billy Curtin had bunched his herd.

It had been a rough and bitter trip, but there was little farther to go. West of El Paso there had been a brush with marauding Apaches. In Silver City, two strangely familiar riders had followed him into a saloon and started a brawl. Yet Matt was too wise in the ways of thieves to be caught by so obvious a trick, and he had slipped away in the darkness after shooting out the light.

The roan slipped now on the muddy trail, scrambled up and moved on through the trees. Suddenly, in the rain-darkened dusk, there was one light, then another.

"Yellowjacket," Matt said with a sigh of relief. "That means a good bed for us, boy. A good bed and a good feed."

Yellowjacket was a jumping-off place. It was a stage station and a saloon, a livery stable and a ramshackle hotel. It was a cluster of 'dobe residences and some false-fronted stores. It bunched its buildings in a corner of Copper Creek.

It was Galusha Reed's town, and Reed owned the Yellowjacket Saloon and the Rincon Mine. Sid Trumbull was town marshal, and he ran the place for Reed. Wherever Reed rode, Tony Sikes was close by, and there were some who said that Reed in turn was owned by Prince McCarran, who owned the big PM brand in the Tonto Basin country.

Matt Sabre stabled his horse and turned to the slope-shouldered liveryman. "Give him a bait of corn. Another in the morning."

"Corn?" Simpson shook his head. "We've no corn."

"You have corn for the freighters' stock and corn for the stage horses. Give my horse corn."

Sabre had a sharp ring of authority in his voice, and before he realized it, Simpson was giving the big roan his corn. He thought about it and stared after Sabre. The tall rider was walking away, a light, long step, easy and free, on the balls of his feet. And he carried two guns, low hung and tied down.

Simpson stared, then shrugged. "A bad one," he muttered. "Wish he'd kill Sid Trumbull!"

Matt Sabre pushed into the door of the Yellowjacket and dropped his saddlebags to the floor. Then he strode to the bar. "What have you got, man? Anything but rye?"

"What's the matter? Ain't rye good enough for you?" Hobbs was sore himself. No man should work so many hours on feet like his.

"Have you brandy? Or some Irish whiskey?"

Hobbs stared. "Mister, where do you think you are? New York?"

"That's all right, Hobbs. I like a man who knows what he likes. Give him some of my cognac."

Matt Sabre turned and glanced at the speaker. He was a tall man, immaculate in black broadcloth, with blond hair slightly wavy and a rosy complexion. He might have been thirty or older. He wore a pistol on his left side, high up.

"Thanks," Sabre said briefly. "There's nothing better than cognac on a wet night."

"My name is McCarran. I run the PM outfit, east of here. Northeast, to be exact."

Sabre nodded. "My name is Sabre. I run no outfit, but I'm looking for one. Where's the Pivotrock?"

He was a good poker player, men said. His eyes were fast from using guns, and so he saw the sudden glint and the quick caution in Prince McCarran's eyes.

"The Pivotrock? Why, that's a stream over in the Mogollons. There's an outfit over there, all right. A one-horse affair. Why do you ask?"

Sabre cut him off short. "Business with them."

"I see. Well, you'll find it a lonely ride. There's trouble up that way now, some sort of a cattle war."

Matt Sabre tasted his drink. It was good cognac. In fact, it was the best, and he had found none west of New Orleans.

McCarran, his name was. He knew something, too. Curtin had asked him to help his widow. Was the Pivotrock outfit in the war? He decided against asking McCarran, and they talked quietly of the rain and of cattle, then of cognac. "You never acquired a taste for cognac in the West. May I ask where?"

"Paris," Sabre replied, "Marseilles, Fez, and Marrakesh."

"You've been around, then. Well, that's not uncommon." The blond man pointed toward a heavy-shouldered young man who slept with his head on his arms. "See that chap? Calls himself Camp Gordon. He's a Cambridge man, quotes the classics when he's drunk—which is over half the time—and is one of the best cowhands in the country when he's sober.

"Keys over there, playing the piano, studied in Weimar. He knew Strauss, in Vienna, before he wrote 'The Blue Danube.' There's all sorts of men in the West, from belted earls and remittance men to vagabond scum from all corners of the world. They are here a few weeks, and they talk the lingo like veterans. Some of the biggest ranches in the West are owned by Englishmen."

Prince McCarran talked to him a few minutes longer, but he learned nothing. Sabre was not evasive, but somehow he gave out no information about himself or his mission. McCarran walked away very thoughtfully. Later, after Matt Sabre was gone, Sid Trumbull came in.

"Sabre?" Trumbull shook his head. "Never heard of him. Keys might know. He knows about ever'body. What's he want on the Pivotrock?"

Lying on his back in bed, Matt Sabre stared up into the darkness and listened to the rain on the window and on the roof. It rattled hard, skeleton fingers against the glass, and he turned restlessly in his bed, frowning as he recalled that quick, guarded expression in the eyes of Prince McCarran.

Who was McCarran, and what did he know? Had Curtin's request that he help his wife been merely the natural request of a dying man, or had he felt that there was a definite need of help? Was something wrong here?

He went to sleep vowing to deliver the money and ride away. Yet even as his eyes closed the last time, he knew he would not do it if there was trouble.

It was still raining, but no longer pouring, when he awakened. He dressed swiftly and checked his guns, his mind taking up his problems where they had been left the previous night.

Camp Gordon, his face puffy from too much drinking and too sound a sleep, staggered down the stairs after him. He grinned woefully at Sabre. "I guess I really hung one on last night," he said. "What I need is to get out of town."

They ate breakfast together, and Gordon's eyes sharpened suddenly at Matt's query of directions to the Pivotrock. "You'll not want to go there, man. Since Curtin ran out they've got their backs to the wall. They are through! Leave it to Galusha Reed for that."

"What's the trouble?"

"Reed claims title to the Pivotrock. Bill Curtin's old man bought it from a Mex who had it from a land grant. Then he made a deal with the Apaches, which seemed to cinch his title. Trouble was, Galusha Reed shows up with a prior claim. He says Fernandez had no grant. That his man Sonoma had a prior one. Old Man Curtin was killed when he fell from his buckboard, and young Billy couldn't stand the gaff. He blew town after Tony Sikes buffaloed him."

"What about his wife?"

Gordon shook his head, then shrugged. Doubt and worry struggled on his face. "She's a fine girl, Jenny Curtin is. The salt of the earth. It's too bad Curtin hadn't a tenth of her nerve. She'll stick, and she swears she'll fight."

"Has she any men?"

"Two. An old man who was with her father-in-law

and a half-breed Apache they call Rado. It used to be Silerado."

Thinking it over, Sabre decided there was much left to be explained. Where had the five thousand dollars come from? Had Billy really run out, or had he gone away to get money to put up a battle? And how did he get it?

"I'm going out." Sabre got to his feet. "I'll have a talk with her."

"Don't take a job there. She hasn't a chance!" Gordon said grimly. "You'd do well to stay away."

"I like fights when one side doesn't have a chance," Matt replied lightly. "Maybe I will ask for a job. A man's got to die sometime, and what better time than fighting when the odds are against him?"

"I like to win," Gordon said flatly. "I like at least a chance."

Matt Sabre leaned over the table, aware that Prince McCarran had moved up behind Gordon, and that a big man with a star was standing near him. "If I decide to go to work for her"—Sabre's voice was easy, confident—"then you'd better join us. Our side will win."

"Look here, you!" The man wearing the star, Sid Trumbull, stepped forward. "You either stay in town or get down the trail! There's trouble enough in the Mogollons. Stay out of there."

Matt looked up. "You're telling me?" His voice cracked like a whip. "You're town marshal, Trumbull, not a United States marshal or a sheriff, and if you were a sheriff, it wouldn't matter. It is out of this county. Now suppose you back up and don't step into conversations unless you're invited."

Trumbull's head lowered, and his face flushed red. Then he stepped around the table, his eyes narrow and mean. "Listen, you!" His voice was thick with fury. "No two-by-twice cowpoke tells me—!"

"Trumbull"—Sabre spoke evenly—"you're asking for it. You aren't acting in line of duty now. You're picking trouble, and the fact that you're marshal won't protect you."

"Protect me?" His fury exploded. "Protect me? Why, you—!"

Trumbull lunged around the table, but Matt side-stepped swiftly and kicked a chair into the marshal's path. Enraged, Sid Trumbull had no chance to avoid it and fell headlong, bloodying his palms on the slivery floor.

Kicking the chair away, he lunged to his feet, and Matt stood facing him, smiling. Camp Gordon was grinning, and Hobbs was leaning his forearms on the bar, watching with relish.

Trumbull stared at his torn palms, then lifted his eyes to Sabre's. Then he started forward, and suddenly, in midstride, his hand swept for his gun.

Sabre palmed his Colt, and the gun barked even as it lifted. Stunned, Sid Trumbull stared at his numbed hand. His gun had been knocked spinning, and the .44 slug, hitting the trigger guard, had gone by to rip off the end of Sid's little finger. Dumbly, he stared at the slow drip of blood.

Prince McCarran and Gordon were only two of those who stared, not at the marshal, but at Matt Sabre.

"You throw that gun mighty fast, stranger," McCarran said. "Who are you, anyway? There aren't a half-dozen men in the country who can throw a gun that fast. I know most of them by sight."

Sabre's eyes glinted coldly. "No? Well, you know another one now. Call it seven men." He spun on his heel and strode from the room. All eyes followed him.

Coyote Trouble

Matt Sabre's roan headed up Shirt Tail Creek, crossed Bloody Basin and Skeleton Ridge, and made the Verde in the vicinity of the hot springs. He bedded down that night in a corner of a cliff near Hardscrabble Creek. It was late when he turned in, and he had lit no fire.

He had chosen his position well, for behind him the cliff towered, and on his left there was a steep hillside that sloped away toward Hardscrabble Creek. He was almost at the foot of Hardscrabble Mesa, with the rising ground of Deadman Mesa before him. The ground in front sloped away to the creek, and there was plenty of dry wood. The overhang of the cliff protected it from the rain.

Matt Sabre came suddenly awake. For an instant, he lay very still. The sky had cleared, and as he lay on his side, he could see the stars. He judged that it was past midnight. Why he had awakened he could not guess, but he saw that the roan was nearer, and the big gelding had his head up and ears pricked.

"Careful, boy!" Sabre warned.

Sliding out of his bedroll, he drew on his boots and got to his feet. Feeling out in the darkness, he drew his Winchester near.

He was sitting in absolute blackness due to the cliff's overhang. He knew the boulders and the clumps of cedar were added concealment. The roan would be lost against the blackness of the cliff, but from where he sat, he could see some thirty yards of the creek bank and some open ground.

There was subdued movement below and whispering voices. Then silence. Leaving his rifle, Sabre belted on his guns and slid quietly out of the overhang and into the cedars.

After a moment, he heard the sound of movement, and then a low voice: "He can't be far! They said he came this way, and he left the main trail after Fossil Creek."

There were two of them. He waited, standing there among the cedars, his eyes hard and his muscles poised and ready. They were fools. Did they think he was that easy?

He had fought Apaches and Kiowas, and he had fought the Tauregs in the Sahara and the Riffs in the Atlas Mountains. He saw them then, saw their dark figures moving up the hill, outlined against the pale gravel of the slope.

That hard, bitter thing inside him broke loose, and he could not stand still. He could not wait. They would find the roan, and then they would not leave until they had him. It was now or never. He stepped out, quickly, silently.

"Looking for somebody?"

They wheeled, and he saw the starlight on a pistol barrel and heard the flat, husky cough of his own gun. One went down, coughing and gasping. The other staggered, then turned and started off in a stumbling run, moaning half in fright, half in pain. He stood there, trying to follow the man, but he lost him in the brush.

He turned back to the fellow on the ground but did not go near him. He circled wide instead, returning to his horse. He quieted his roan, then lay down. In a few minutes, he was dozing.

Daybreak found him standing over the body. The roan was already saddled for the trail. It was one of the two he had seen in Silver City, a lean, dark-faced man with deep lines in his cheeks and a few gray hairs at the temples. There was an old scar, deep and red, over his eye.

Sabre knelt and went through his pockets, taking a few letters and some papers. He stuffed them into his own pockets, then mounted. Riding warily, he started up the creek. He rode with his Winchester across his saddle, ready for whatever came. Nothing did.

The morning drew on, the air warm and still after the rain. A fly buzzed around his ears, and he whipped it away with his hat. The roan had a long-striding, space-eating walk. It moved out swiftly and surely toward the far purple ranges, dipping down through grassy meadows lined with pines and aspens, with here and there the whispering leaves of a tall cottonwood.

It was a land to dream about, a land perfect for the grazing of either cattle or sheep, a land for a man to live in. Ahead and on his left he could see the towering Mogollon Rim, and it was beyond this rim, up on the plateau, that he would find the Pivotrock. He skirted a grove of rustling aspen and looked down a long valley.

For the first time, he saw cattle—fat, contented cattle, fat from the rich grass of these bottomlands. Once, far off, he glimpsed a rider, but he made no effort to draw near, wanting only to find the trail to the Pivotrock.

A wide-mouthed canyon opened from the northeast, and he turned the roan and started up the creek that ran down it. Now he was climbing, and from the look of the country, he would climb nearly three thousand feet to reach the rim. Yet he had been told there was a trail ahead, and he pushed on.

The final eight hundred feet to the rim was by a switchback trail that had him climbing steadily, yet the air on the plateau atop the rim was amazingly fresh and clear. He pushed on, seeing a few scattered cattle, and then he saw a crude wooden sign by the narrow trail. It read:

PIVOTROCK . . . 1 MILE

The house was low and sprawling, lying on a flat-topped knoll with the long barns and sheds built on three sides of a square. The open side faced the rim and the trail up which he was riding. There were cottonwood, pine, and fir backing up the buildings. He could see the late afternoon sunlight glistening on the coats of the saddlestock in the corral.

An old man stepped from the stable with a carbine in his hands. "All right, stranger. You stop where you are. What you want here?"

Matt Sabre grinned. Lifting his hand carefully, he pushed back his flat-brimmed hat. "Huntin' Mrs. Jenny Curtin," he said. "I've got news." He hesitated. "Of her husband."

The carbine muzzle lowered. "Of *him*? What news would there be of him?"

"Not good news," Sabre told him. "He's dead."

Surprisingly, the old man seemed relieved. "Light," he said briefly. "I reckon we figured he was dead. How'd it happen?"

Sabre hesitated. "He picked a fight in a saloon in El Paso, then drew too slow."

"He was never fast." The old man studied him. "My name's Tom Judson. Now, you sure didn't come all the way here from El Paso to tell us Billy was dead. What did you come for?"

"I'll tell Mrs. Curtin that. However, they tell me down the road you've been with her a long time, so you might as well know. I brought her some money. Bill Curtin gave it to me on his death bed; asked me to bring it to her. It's five thousand dollars."

"Five thousand?" Judson stared. "Reckon Bill must have set some store by you to trust you with it. Know him long?"

Sabre shook his head. "Only a few minutes. A dying man hasn't much choice."

A door slammed up at the house, and they both turned. A slender girl was walking toward them, and the sunlight caught the red in her hair. She wore a simple cotton dress, but her figure was trim and neat. Ahead of her dashed a boy who might have been five or six. He lunged at Sabre, then slid to a stop and stared up at him, then at his guns.

"Howdy, old-timer!" Sabre said, smiling. "Where's your spurs?"

The boy was startled and shy. He drew back, surprised at the question. "I—I've got no spurs!"

"What? A cowhand without spurs? We'll have to fix that." He looked up. "How are you, Mrs. Curtin? I'm Mathurin Sabre, Matt for short. I'm afraid I've some bad news for you."

Her face paled a little, but her chin lifted. "Will you come to the house, Mr. Sabre? Tom, put his horse in the corral, will you?"

The living room of the ranchhouse was spacious and cool. There were Navajo rugs upon the floor, and the chairs and the divan were beautifully tanned cowhide. He glanced around appreciatively, enjoying the coolness after his hot ride in the Arizona sun, like the naturalness of this girl, standing in the home she had created.

She faced him abruptly. "Perhaps you'd better tell me now; there's no use pretending or putting a bold face on it when I have to be told."

As quickly and quietly as possible, he explained. When he was finished, her face was white and still. "I—I was afraid of this. When he rode away, I knew he would never come back. You see, he thought—he believed he had failed me, failed his father."

Matt drew the oilskin packet from his pocket. "He sent you this. He said it was five thousand dollars. He said to give it to you."

She took it, staring at the package, and tears welled into her eyes. "Yes." Her voice was so low that Matt scarcely heard it. "He would do this. He probably felt it was all he could do for me, for us. You see"—Jenny Curtin's eyes lifted—"we're in a fight, and a bad one. This is war money.

"I—guess Billy thought—well, he was no fighter himself, and this might help, might compensate. You're probably wondering about all this."

"No," he said. "I'm not. And maybe I'd better go out with the boys now. You'll want to be alone."

"Wait!" Her fingers caught his sleeve. "I want you to know, since you were with him when he died, and you have come all this way to help us. There was no trouble with Billy and me. It was—well, he thought he was a coward. He thought he had failed me.

"We've had trouble with Galusha Reed in Yellowjacket. Tony Sikes picked a fight with Billy. He wanted to kill him, and Billy wouldn't fight. He—he backed down. Everybody said he was a coward, and he ran. He went away."

Matt Sabre frowned thoughtfully, staring at the floor. The boy who picked a fight with him, who dared him, who went for his gun, was no coward. Trying to prove something to himself? Maybe. But no coward.

"Ma'am," he said abruptly, "you're his widow. The mother of his child. There's something you should know. Whatever else he was, I don't know. I never knew him long enough. But that man was no coward. Not even a little bit!

"You see," Matt hesitated, feeling the falseness of his position, not wanting to tell this girl that he had killed her husband, yet not wanting her to think him a coward, "I saw his eyes when he went for his gun. I was there, ma'am, and saw it all. Bill Curtin was no coward."

Hours later, lying in his bunk, he thought of it, and the five thousand was still a mystery. Where had it come from? How had Curtin come by it?

He turned over and after a few minutes went to sleep. The next day, he would be riding.

The sunlight was bright the next morning when he finally rolled out of bed. He bathed and shaved, taking

103

his time, enjoying the sun on his back, and feeling glad he was footloose again. He was in the bunkhouse belting on his guns when he heard the horses. He stepped to the door and glanced out.

Neither the dark-faced Rado nor Judson were about, and there were three riders in the yard. One of them he recognized as a man from Yellowjacket, and the tallest of the riders was Galusha Reed. He was a big man, broad and thick in the body without being fat. His jaw was brutal.

Jenny Curtin came out on the steps. "Ma'am," Reed said abruptly, "we're movin' you off this land. We're goin' to give you ten minutes to pack, an' one of my boys'll hitch the buckboard for you. This here trouble's gone on long enough, an' mine's the prior claim to this land. You're gettin' off!"

Jenny's eyes turned quickly toward the stable, but Reed shook his head. "You needn't look for Judson or the breed. We watched until we seen them away from here, an' some of my boys are coverin' the trail. We're tryin' to get you off here without any trouble."

"You can turn around and leave, Mr. Reed. I'm not going!"

"I reckon you are," Reed said patiently. "We know that your man's dead. We just can't put up with you squattin' on our range."

"This happens to be my range, and I'm staying."

Reed chuckled. "Don't make us put you off, ma'am. Don't make us get rough. Up here"—he waved a casual hand—"we can do anything we want, and nobody the wiser. You're leavin', as of now."

Matt Sabre stepped out of the bunkhouse and took three quick steps toward the riders. He was cool and sure of himself, but he could feel the jumping invitation to trouble surging up inside him. He fought it down and held himself still for an instant. Then he spoke.

"Reed, you're a fat-headed fool and a bully. You ride up here to take advantage of a woman because you think she's helpless. Well, she's not. Now you three turn your horses—turn 'em mighty careful—and start down the trail. And don't you ever set foot on this place again!"

Reed's face went white, then dark with anger. He leaned forward a little. "So you're still here? Well, we'll give you a chance to run. Get goin'!"

Matt Sabre walked forward another step. He could feel the eagerness pushing up inside him, and his eyes held the three men, and he saw the eyes of one widen with apprehension.

"Watch it, boss! Watch it!"

"That's right, Reed. Watch it. You figured to find this girl alone. Well, she's not alone. Furthermore, if she'll take me on as a hand, I'll stay. I'll stay until you're out of the country or dead. You can have it either way you want.

"There's three of you. I like that. That evens us up. If you want to feed buzzards, just edge that hand another half inch toward your gun and you can. That goes for the three of you."

He stepped forward again. He was jumping with it now—that old drive for combat welling up within him. Inside, he was trembling, but his muscles were steady, and his mind was cool and ready. His fingers spread, and he moved forward again.

"Come on, you mangy coyotes! Let's see if you've got the nerve. *Reach!*"

Reed's face was still and cold. His mouth looked pinched, and his eyes were wide. Some sixth sense warned him that this was different. This was death he was looking at, and Galusha Reed suddenly realized he was no gambler when the stakes were so high.

He could see the dark eagerness that was driving this cool man; he could see beyond the coolness on his surface the fierceness of his readiness; inside, he went sick and cold at the thought.

"Boss!" the man at his side whispered hoarsely "Let's get out of here. This man's poison!"

Galusha Reed slowly eased his hand forward to the pommel of the saddle. "So, Jenny, you're hiring gunfighters? Is that the way you want it?"

"I think you hired them first," she replied coolly. "Now you'd better go."

"On the way back," Sabre suggested, "you might stop in Hardscrabble Canyon and pick up the body of one of your killers. He guessed wrong last night."

Reed stared at him. "I don't know what you mean," he flared. "I sent out no killer."

Matt Sabre watched the three men ride down the trail and he frowned. There had been honest doubt in Reed's eyes, but if he had not sent the two men after him, who had? Those men had been in Silver City and El Paso, yet they also knew this country and knew someone in Yellowjacket. Maybe they had not come after him but had first followed Bill Curtin.

He turned and smiled at the girl. "Coyotes," he said, shrugging. "Not much heart in them."

She was staring at him strangely. "You—you'd have killed them, wouldn't you? Why?"

He shrugged. "I don't know. Maybe it's because— well, I don't like to see men take advantage of a woman alone. Anyway"—he smiled—"Reed doesn't impress me as a good citizen."

"He's a dangerous enemy." She came down from the steps. "Did you mean what you said, Mr. Sabre? I mean about staying here and working for me? I need men, although I must tell you that you've small chance of winning, and it's rather a lonely fight."

"Yes, I meant it." Did he mean it? Of course. He remembered the old Chinese proverb: If you save a person's life he becomes your responsibility. That wasn't the case here, but he had killed this girl's husband, and the least he could do would be to stay until she was out of trouble.

Was that all he was thinking of? "I'll stay," he said. "I'll see you through this. I've been fighting all my life, and it would be a shame to stop now. And I've fought for lots less reasons."

Hot Night in Yellowjacket

Throughout the morning, he worked around the place. He worked partly because there was much to be done and partly because he wanted to think.

The horses in the remuda were held on the home place and were in good shape. Also, they were better than the usual ranch horses, for some of them showed a strong Morgan strain. He repaired the latch on the stable door and walked around the place, sizing it up from every angle, studying all the approaches.

With his glasses, he studied the hills and searched the notches and canyons wherever he could see them. Mentally, he formed a map of all that terrain within reach of his glass.

It was midafternoon before Judson and Rado returned, and they had talked with Jenny before he saw them.

"Howdy." Judson was friendly, but his eyes studied Sabre with care. "Miss Jenny tells me you run Reed off. That you're aimin' to stay on here."

"That's right. I'll stay until she's out of trouble, if she'll have me. I don't like being pushed around."

"No, neither do I." Judson was silent for several minutes, and then he turned his eyes on Sabre. "Don't you be gettin' any ideas about Miss Jenny. She's a fine girl."

Matt looked up angrily. "And don't you be getting any ideas," he said coldly. "I'm helping her the same as you are, and we'll work together. As to personal things, leave them alone. I'll only say that when this fight is over, I'm hitting the trail."

"All right," Judson said mildly. "We can use help."

Three days passed smoothly. Matt threw himself into the work of the ranch, and he worked feverishly. Even he could not have said why he worked so desperately hard. He dug postholes and fenced an area in the long meadow near the seeping springs in the bottom.

Then, working with Rado, he rounded up the cattle nearest the rim and pushed them back behind the fence. The grass was thick and deep there and would stand a lot of grazing, for the meadow wound back up the canyon for some distance. He carried a running iron and branded stock wherever he found it required.

As the ranch had been shorthanded for a year, there was much to do. Evenings, he mended gear and worked around the place, and at night he slept soundly. During all this time, he saw nothing of Jenny Curtin.

He saw nothing of her, but she was constantly in his thoughts. He remembered her as he had seen her that first night, standing in the living room of the house, listening to him, her eyes, wide and dark, upon his face. He remembered her facing Galusha Reed and his riders from the steps.

Was he staying on because he believed he owed her a debt or because of her?

Here and there around the ranch, Sabre found small, intangible hints of the sort of man Curtin must have been. Judson had liked him, and so had the half-breed. He had been gentle with horses. He had been thoughtful. Yet he had hated and avoided violence. Slowly, rightly or wrongly Matt could not tell, a picture was forming in his mind of a fine young man who had been totally out of place.

Western birth, but born for peaceful and quiet ways,

he had been thrown into a cattle war and had been aware of his own inadequacy. Matt was thinking of that, and working at a rawhide riata, when Jenny came up.

He had not seen her approach, or he might have avoided her, but she was there beside him before he realized it.

"You're working hard, Mr. Sabre."

"To earn my keep, ma'am. There's a lot to do, I find, and I like to keep busy." He turned the riata and studied it.

"You know, there's something I've been wanting to talk to you about. Maybe it's none of my affair, but young Billy is going to grow up, and he's going to ask questions about his dad. You aren't going to be able to fool him. Maybe you know what this is all about, and maybe I'm mounting on the off-side, but it seems to me that Bill Curtin went to El Paso to get that money for you.

"I think he realized he was no fighting man, and that the best thing he could do was to get that money so he could hire gunfighters. It took nerve to do what he did, and I think he deliberately took what Sikes handed him because he knew that if Sikes killed him, you'd never get that money.

"Maybe along the way to El Paso he began to wonder, and maybe he picked that fight down there with the idea of proving to himself that he did have the nerve to face a gun."

She did not reply, but stood there, watching his fingers work swiftly and evenly, plaiting the leather.

"Yes," she said finally, "I thought of that. Only I can't imagine where he got the money. I hesitate to use it without knowing."

"Don't be foolish," he said irritably. "Use it. Nobody would put it to better use, and you need gun hands."

"But who would work for me?" Her voice was low and bitter. "Galusha Reed has seen to it that no one will."

"Maybe if I rode in, I could find some men." He was thinking of Camp Gordon, the Shakespeare-quoting English cowhand. "I believe I know one man."

"There's a lot to be done. Jud tells me you've been doing the work of three men."

Matt Sabre got to his feet. She stepped back a little, suddenly aware of how tall he was. She was tall for a girl, yet she came no farther than his lips. She drew back a little at the thought. Her eyes dropped to his guns. He always wore them, always low and tied down.

"Judson said you were a fast man with a gun. He said you had the mark of the—of the gunfighter."

"Probably." He found no bitterness at the thought. "I've used guns. Guns and horses; they are about all I've known."

"Where were you in the army? I've watched you walk and ride and you show military training."

"Oh, several places. Africa mostly."

"Africa?" She was amazed. "You've been there?"

He nodded. "Desert and mountain country. Morocco and the Sahara, all the way to Timbuktu and Lake Chad, fighting most of the time." It was growing dark in the shed where they were standing. He moved out into the dusk. A few stars had already appeared, and the red glow that was in the west beyond the rim was fading.

"Tomorrow I'll ride in and have a look around. You'd better keep the other men close by."

Dawn found him well along on the trail to Yellowjacket. It was a long ride, and he skirted the trail most of the time, having no trust in well-traveled ways at such a time. The air was warm and bright, and he noticed a few head of Pivotrock steers that had been overlooked in the rounding up of cattle along the rim.

He rode ready for trouble, his Winchester across his saddlebows, his senses alert. Keeping the roan well back under the trees, he had the benefit of the evergreen needles that formed a thick carpet and muffled the sound of his horse's hoofs.

Yet as he rode, he considered the problem of the land grant. If Jenny were to retain her land and be free of trouble he must look into the background of the grant and see which had the prior and best claim, Fernandez or Sonoma.

Next, he must find out, if possible, where Bill Curtin had obtained that five thousand dollars. Some might think that the fact he had it was enough and that now his wife had it, but it was not enough if Bill had sold any rights to water or land on the ranch or if he had obtained the money in some way that would reflect upon Jenny or her son.

When those things were done, he could ride on about his business, for by that time he would have worked out the problem of Galusha Reed.

In the few days he had been on the Pivotrock, he had come to love the place, and while he had avoided Jenny, he had not avoided young Billy. The youngster had adopted him and had stayed with him hour after hour.

To keep him occupied, Matt had begun teaching him how to plait rawhide, and so, as he mended riatas and repaired bridles, the youngster had sat beside him, working his fingers clumsily through the intricacies of the plaiting.

It was with unease that he recalled his few minutes alone with Jenny. He shifted his seat in the saddle and scowled. It would not do for him to think of her as anything but Curtin's widow. The widow, he reflected bitterly, of the man he had killed.

What would he say when she learned of *that*? He avoided the thought, yet it remained in the back of his mind, and he shook his head, wanting to forget it. Sooner or later, she would know. If he did not finally tell her himself, then he was sure that Reed would let her know.

Avoiding the route by way of Hardscrabble, Matt Sabre turned due south, crossing the eastern end of the mesa and following an old trail across Whiterock and Polles Mesa, crossing the East Verde at Rock Creek. Then he cut through Boardinghouse Canyon to Bullspring, crossing the main stream of the Verde near Tangle Peak. It was a longer way around by a few miles, but Sabre rode with care, watching the country as he traveled. It was very late when he walked his roan into the parched street of Yellowjacket.

He had a hunch and he meant to follow it through. During his nights in the bunkhouse he had talked much with Judson, and from him heard of Pepito Fernandez, a grandson of the man who sold the land to Old Man Curtin.

Swinging down from his horse at the livery stable, he led him inside. Simpson walked over to meet him, his eyes searching Sabre's face. "Man, you've a nerve with you. Reed's wild. He came back to town blazing mad, and Trumbull's telling everybody what you can expect."

Matt smiled at the man. "I expected that. Where do you stand?"

"Well," Simpson said grimly, "I've no liking for Trumbull. He carries himself mighty big around town, and he's not been friendly to me and mine. I reckon, mister, I've rare been so pleased as when you made a fool of him in yonder. It was better than the killing of him, although he's that coming, sure enough."

"Then take care of my horse, will you? And a slip knot to tie him with."

"Sure, and he'll get corn, too. I reckon any horse you ride would need corn."

Matt Sabre walked out on the street. He was wearing dark jeans and a gray wool shirt. His black hat was pulled low, and he merged well with the shadows. He'd see Pepito first and then look around a bit. He wanted Camp Gordon.

Thinking of that, he turned back into the stable.

"Saddle Gordon's horse, too. He'll be going back with me."

"Him?" Simpson stared. "Man, he's dead drunk and has been for days!"

"Saddle his horse. He'll be with me when I'm back, and if you know another one or two good hands who would use a gun if need be, let them know I'm hiring and there's money to pay them. Fighting wages if they want."

In the back office of the Yellowjacket, three men sat over Galusha Reed's desk. There was Reed himself, Sid Trumbull and Prince McCarran.

"Do you think Tony can take him?" Reed asked. "You've seen the man draw, Prince."

"He'll take him. But it will be close—too close. I think what we'd better do is have Sid posted somewhere close by."

"Leave me out of it." Sid looked up from under his thick eyebrows. "I want no more of the man. Let Tony have him."

"You won't be in sight," McCarran said dryly, "or in danger. You'll be upstairs over the hotel, with a Winchester."

Trumbull looked up and touched his thick lips with his tongue. Killing was not new to him, yet the way this man accepted it always appalled him a little.

"All right," he agreed. "Like I say, I've no love for him."

"We'll have him so you'll get a flanking shot. Make it count and make it the first time. But wait until the shooting starts."

The door opened softly, and Sikes stepped in. He was a lithe, dark-skinned man who moved like an animal. He had graceful hands, restless hands. He wore a white buckskin vest worked with red quills and beads. "Boss, he's in town. Sabre's here." He had heard them.

113

Reed let his chair legs down, leaning forward. "*Here?* In town?"

"That's right. I just saw him outside the Yellow-jacket." Sikes started to build a cigarette. "He's got nerve. Plenty of it."

The door sounded with a light tap, and at a word, Keys entered. He was a slight man with gray hair and a quiet, scholar's face.

"I remember him now, Prince," he said. "Matt Sabre. I'd been trying to place the name. He was marshal of Mobeetie for a while. He's killed eight or nine men."

"That's right!" Trumbull looked up sharply. "Mobeetie! Why didn't I remember that? They say Wes Hardin rode out of town once when Sabre sent him word he wasn't wanted."

Sikes turned his eyes on McCarran. "You want him now?"

McCarran hesitated, studying the polished toe of his boot. Sabre's handling of Trumbull had made friends in town, and also his championing of the cause of Jenny Curtin. Whatever happened must be seemingly aboveboard and in the clear, and he wanted to be where he could be seen at the time, and Reed, also.

"No, not now. We'll wait." He smiled. "One thing about a man of his courage and background, if you send for him, he'll always come to you."

"But how will he come?" Keys asked softly. "That's the question."

McCarran looked around irritably. He had forgotten Keys was in the room and had said far more than he had intended. "Thanks, Keys. That will be all. And remember—nothing will be said about anything you've heard here."

"Certainly not." Keys smiled and walked to the door and out of the room.

Reed stared after him. "I don't like that fellow, Prince. I wouldn't trust him."

"Him? He's interested in nothing but that piano and enough liquor to keep himself mildly embalmed. Don't worry about him."

Fugitive

Matt Sabre turned away from the Yellowjacket after a brief survey of the saloon. Obviously, something was doing elsewhere for none of the men were present in the big room. He hesitated, considering the significance of that, and then turned down a dark alleyway and walked briskly along until he came to an old rail fence.

Following this past rustling cottonwoods and down a rutted road, he turned past a barn and cut across another road toward a 'dobe where the windows glowed with a faint light.

The door opened to his knock, and a dark, Indianlike face showed briefly. In rapid Spanish, he asked for Pepito. After a moment's hesitation, the door widened, and he was invited inside.

The room was large, and at one side, a small fire burned in the blackened fireplace. An oilcloth-covered table with a coal oil light stood in the middle of the room, and on a bed at one side, a man snored peacefully.

A couple of dark-eyed children ceased their playing to look up at him. The woman called out, and a blanket pushed aside, and a slender, dark-faced youth entered the room, pulling his belt tight.

115

"Pepito Fernandez? I am Matt Sabre."

"I have heard of you, señor."

Briefly, he explained why he had come, and Pepito listened, then shook his head. "I do not know, señor. The grant was long ago, and we are no longer rich. My father"—he shrugged—"he liked the spending of money when he was young."

He hesitated, considering that. Then he said carelessly, "I, too, like the spending of money. What else is it for? But no, señor, I do not think there are papers. My father, he told me much of the grant, and I am sure the Sonomas had no strong claim."

"If you remember anything, will you let us know?" Sabre asked. Then a thought occured to him. "You're a *vaquero*? Do you want a job?"

"A job?" Pepito studied him thoughtfully. "At the Señora Curtin's ranch?"

"Yes. As you know, there may be much trouble. I am working there, and tonight I shall take one other man back with me. If you would like the job, it is yours."

Pepito shrugged. "Why not? Señor Curtin, the old one, he gave me my first horse. He gave me a rifle, too. He was a good one, and the son, also."

"Better meet me outside of town where the trail goes between the buttes. You know the place?"

"Si, señor. I will be there."

Keys was idly playing the piano when Matt Sabre opened the door and stepped into the room. His quick eyes placed Keys, Hobbs at the bar, Camp Gordon fast asleep with his head on a table, and a half-dozen other men. Yet as he walked to the bar, a rear door opened, and Tony Sikes stepped into the room.

Sabre had never before seen the man, yet he knew him from Judson's apt and careful description. Sikes was not as tall as Sabre, yet more slender. He had the wiry, stringy build that is made for speed and quick, smooth-flowing fingers. His muscles were relaxed and easy, but knowing such men, Matt recognized danger

116

when he saw it. Sikes had seen him at once, and he moved to the bar nearby.

All eyes were on the two of them, for the story of Matt's whipping of Trumbull and his defiance of Reed had swept the country. Yet Sikes merely smiled and Matt glanced at him. "Have a drink?"

Tony Sikes nodded. "I don't mind if I do." Then he added, his voice low, and his dark, yellowish eyes on Matt's with a faintly sardonic, faintly amused look, "I never mind drinking with a man I'm going to kill."

Sabre shrugged. "Neither do I." He found himself liking Sikes' direct approach. "Although perhaps I have the advantage. I choose my own time to drink and to kill. You wait for orders."

Tony Sikes felt in his vest pocket for cigarette papers and began to roll a smoke. "You will wait for me, *compadre*. I know you're the type."

They drank, and as they drank, the door opened, and Galusha Reed stepped out. His face darkened angrily when he saw the two standing at the bar together, but he was passing without speaking when a thought struck him. He stopped and turned.

"I wonder," he said loudly enough for all in the room to hear, "what Jenny Curtin will say when she finds out her new hand is the man who killed her husband?"

Every head came up, and Sabre's face whitened. Whereas the faces had been friendly or noncomittal, now they were sharp-eyed and attentive. Moreover, he knew that Jenny was well liked, as Curtin had been. Now they would be his enemies.

"I wonder just why you came here, Sabre? After killing the girl's husband, why would you come to her ranch? Was it to profit from your murder? To steal what little she has left? Or is it for the girl herself?"

Matt struggled to keep his temper. After a minute, he said casually, "Reed, it was you ordered her off her ranch today. I'm here for one reason, and one alone. To see that she keeps her ranch and that no yellow-bellied

117

thievin' lot of coyotes ride over and take it away from her!"

Reed stood flat-footed, facing Sabre. He was furious, and Matt could feel the force of his rage. It was almost a physical thing pushing against him. Close beside him was Sikes. If Reed chose to go for a gun, Sikes could grab Matt's left arm and jerk him off balance. Yet Matt was ready even for that, and again that black force was rising within him, that driving urge toward violence.

He spoke again, and his voice was soft and almost purring. "Make up your mind, Reed. If you want to die, you can right here. You make another remark to me and I'll drive every word of it back down that fat throat of yours! Reach and I'll kill you. If Sikes wants in on this, he's welcome!"

Tony Sikes spoke softly, too. "I'm out of it, Sabre. I only fight my own battles. When I come after you, I'll be alone."

Galusha Reed hesitated. For an instant, counting on Sikes, he had been tempted. Now he hesitated, then turned abruptly and left the room.

Ignoring Sikes, Sabre downed his drink and crossed to Camp Gordon. He shook him. "Come on, Camp. I'm puttin' you to bed."

Gordon did not move. Sabre stooped and slipped an arm around the big Englishman's shoulders and, hoisting him to his feet, started for the door. At the door, he turned. "I'll be seeing you, Sikes!"

Tony lifted his glass, his hat pushed back, "Sure," he said. "And I'll be alone."

It was not until after he had said it that he remembered Sid Trumbull and the plans made in the back room. His face darkened a little, and his liquor suddenly tasted bad. He put his glass down carefully on the bar and turned, walking through the back door.

Prince McCarran was alone, idly riffling the cards and smoking. "I won't do it, Prince," Sikes said. "You've got to leave that killing to me and me alone."

118

Matt Sabre, with Camp Gordon lashed to the saddle of a led horse, met Pepito in the darkness of the space between the buttes. Pepito spoke softly, and Sabre called back to him. As the Mexican rode out, he glanced once at Gordon, and then the three rode on together. It was late the following morning when they reached the Pivotrock. All was quiet—too quiet.

Camp Gordon was sober and swearing, "Shanghaied!" His voice exploded with violence. "You've a nerve, Sabre. Turn me loose so I can start back. I'm having no part of this."

Gordon was tied to his horse so he would not fall off, but Matt only grinned. "Sure, I'll turn you loose. But you said you ought to get out of town awhile, and this was the best way. I've brought you here," he said gravely, but his eyes were twinkling, "for your own good. It's time you had some fresh, mountain air, some cold milk, some—"

"*Milk?*" Gordon exploded. "Milk, you say? I'll not touch the stuff! Turn me loose and give me a gun and I'll have your hide!"

"And leave this ranch for Reed to take? Reed and McCarran?"

Gordon stared at him from bloodshot eyes, eyes that were suddenly attentive. "Did you say McCarran? What's he got to do with this?"

"I wish I knew. But I've a hunch he's in up to his ears. I think he has strings on Reed."

Gordon considered that. "He may have." He watched Sabre undoing the knots. "It's a point I hadn't considered. But why?"

"You've known him longer than I have. Somebody had two men follow Curtin out of the country to kill him, and I don't believe Reed did it. Does that make sense?"

"No." Gordon swung stiffly to the ground. He swayed a bit, clinging to the stirrup leather. He glanced sheepishly at Matt. "I guess I'm a mess." A surprised look

119

crossed his face. "Say, I'm hungry! I haven't been hungry in weeks."

With four hands besides himself, work went on swiftly. Yet Matt Sabre's mind would not rest. The five thousand dollars was a problem, and also there was the grant. Night after night, he led Pepito to talk of the memories of his father and grandfather, and little by little, he began to know the men. An idea was shaping in his mind, but as yet there was little on which to build.

In all this time, there was no sign of Reed. On two occasions, riders had been seen, apparently scouting. Cattle had been swept from the rim edge and pushed back, accounting for all or nearly all the strays he had seen on his ride to Yellowjacket.

Matt was restless, sure that when trouble came, it would come with a rush. It was like Reed to do things that way. By now he was certainly aware that Camp Gordon and Pepito Fernandez had been added to the roster of hands at Pivotrock.

"Spotted a few head over near Baker Butte," Camp said one morning. "How'd it be if I drifted that way and looked them over?"

"We'll go together," Matt replied. "I've been wanting to look around there, and there's been no chance."

The morning was bright, and they rode swiftly, putting miles behind them, alert to all the sights and sounds of the high country above the rim. Careful as they were, they were no more than a hundred yards from the riders when they saw them. There were five men, and in the lead rode Sid Trumbull and a white-mustached stranger.

There was no possibility of escaping unnoticed. They pushed on toward the advancing riders, who drew up and waited. Sid Trumbull's face was sharp with triumph when he saw Sabre.

"Here's your man, marshal!" he said with satisfaction. "The one with the black hat is Sabre."

ALL YOURS FREE!

**ONE DOZEN BEAUTIFUL FOUR-COLOR
SCENES FROM THE OLD WEST IN THE**

LOUIS L'AMOUR
WALL CALENDAR

(An $8.99 value in stores)

SPECIAL • SPECIAL • SPECIAL

The best-selling novel:
SACKETT for only $4.⁹⁵
in the hardbound Collector's Edition!

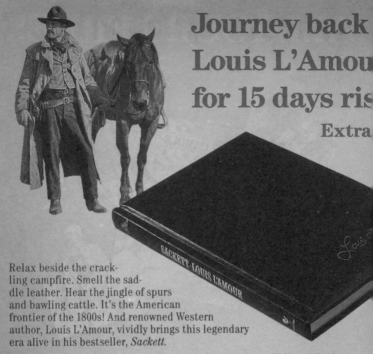

e Old West with
ompelling novel, *Sackett*,
ee!

l: You may keep *Sackett* for only $4.95!*

*plus shipping and handling, and sales tax in NY and Canada.

In Addition to the Free Louis L'Amour Calendar

. . . your risk-free preview volume of *Sackett* will introduce you to these outstanding qualities of the bookbinder's art—

- Each volume is bound in rich, rugged sierra-brown simulated leather.

- The bindings are sewn, not just glued, to last a lifetime. And the pages are printed on high-quality paper that is acid-free and will not yellow with age.

- The title and Louis L'Amour's signature are golden embossed on the spine and front cover of each volume.

"What's this all about?" Matt asked quietly. He had already noticed the badge the man wore. But he noticed something else. The man looked to be a competent, upstanding officer.

"You're wanted in El Paso. I'm Rafe Collins, deputy United States marshal. We're making an inquiry into the killing of Bill Curtin."

Camp's lips tightened, and he looked sharply at Sabre. When Reed had brought out this fact in the saloon, Gordon had been dead drunk.

"That was a fair shooting, marshal. Curtin picked the fight and drew on me."

"You expect us to believe that?" Trumbull was contemptuous. "Why, he hadn't the courage of a mouse! He backed down from Sikes only a few days before. He wouldn't draw on any man with two hands!"

"He drew on me." Matt Sabre realized he was fighting two battles here—one to keep from being arrested, the other to keep Gordon's respect and assistance. "My idea is that he only backed out of a fight with Sikes because he had a job to do and knew Sikes would kill him."

"That's a likely yarn!" Trumbull nodded to him. "There's your man. It's your job, marshal."

Collins was obviously irritated. That he entertained no great liking for Trumbull was obvious. Yet he had his duty to do. Before he could speak, Sabre spoke again.

"Marshal, I've reason to believe that some influence has been brought to bear to discredit me and to get me out of the country for a while. Can't I give you my word that I'll report to El Paso when things are straightened out? My word is good, and that there are many in El Paso who know that."

"Sorry." Collins was regretful. "I've my duty and my orders."

"I understand that," Sabre replied. "I also have my duty. It is to see that Jenny Curtin is protected from those who are trying to force her off her range. I intend to do exactly that."

"Your duty?" Collins eyed him coldly but curiously. "After killing her husband?"

"That's reason enough, sir!" Sabre replied flatly. "The fight was not my choice. Curtin pushed it, and he was excited, worried, and overwrought. Yet he asked me on his deathbed to deliver a package to his wife and to see that she was protected. That duty, sir"—his eyes met those of Collins—"comes first."

"I'd like to respect that," Collins admitted. "You seem like a gentleman, sir, and it's a quality that's too rare. Unfortunately, I have my orders. However, it should not take long to straighten this out if it was a fair shooting."

"All these rats need," Sabre replied, "is a few days!" He knew there was no use arguing. His horse was fast, and dense pines bordered the road. He needed a minute, and that badly.

As if divining his thought, Camp Gordon suddenly pushed his gray between Matt and the marshal, and almost at once Matt lashed out with his toe and booted Trumbull's horse in the ribs. The bronc went to bucking furiously. Whipping his horse around, Matt slapped the spurs to his ribs, and in two startled jumps he was off and deep into the pines, running like a startled deer.

Behind him a shot rang out, and then another. Both cut the brush over his head, but the horse was running now, and he was mounted well. He had started into the trees at right angles but swung his horse immediately and headed back toward the Pivotrock. Corduroy Wash opened off to his left, and he turned the black and pushed rapidly into the mouth of the wash.

Following it for almost a mile, he came out and paused briefly in the clump of trees that crowned a small ridge. He stared back.

A string of riders stretched out on his back trail, but they were scattered out, hunting for tracks. A lone horseman sat not far from them, obviously watching. Matt grinned; that would be Gordon, and he was all right.

Turning his horse, Matt followed a shelf of rock until it ran out, rode off it into thick sand, and then into the pines with their soft bed of needles that left almost no tracks.

Cinch Hook Butte was off to his left, and nearer, on his right, Twenty-Nine-Mile Butte. Keeping his horse headed between them, but bearing steadily northwest, he headed for the broken country around Horsetank Wash. Descending into the canyon, he rode northwest, then circled back south and entered the even deeper Calfpen Canyon.

Here, in a nest of boulders, he staked out his horse on a patch of grass. Rifle across his knees, he rested. After an hour, he worked his way to the ledge at the top of the canyon, but nowhere could he see any sign of pursuit. Nor could he hear the sound of hoofs.

There was water in the bottom of Calfpen, not far from where he had left his horse. Food was something else again. He shucked a handful of chia seeds and ate a handful of them, along with the nuts of a piñon.

Obviously, the attempted arrest had been brought about by either the influence of Galusha Reed or Prince McCarran. In either case, he was now a fugitive. If they went on to the ranch, Rafe Collins would have a chance to talk to Jenny Curtin. Matt felt sick when he thought of the marshal telling her that it was he who had killed her husband. That she must find out sooner or later, he knew, but he wanted to tell her himself, in his own good time.

Bushwhack Bait

When dusk had fallen, he mounted the black and worked his way down Calfpen toward Fossil Springs. As he rode, he was considering his best course. Whether taken by Collins or not, he was not now at the ranch and they might choose this time to strike. With some reason, they might believe he had left the country. Indeed, there was every chance that Reed actually believed he had come there with some plan of his own to get the Curtin ranch.

Finally, he bedded down for the night in a draw above Fossil Springs and slept soundly until daylight brought a sun that crept over the rocks and shone upon his eyes. He was up, made a light breakfast of coffee and jerked beef, and then saddled up.

Wherever he went now, he could expect hostility. Doubt or downright suspicion would have developed as a result of Reed's accusation in Yellowjacket, and the country would know the U.S. Marshal was looking for him.

Debating his best course, Matt Sabre headed west through the mountains. By nightfall the following day, he was camped in the ominous shadow of Turret Butte where only a few years before, Major Randall had ascended the peak in darkness to surprise a camp of Apaches.

Awakening at the break of dawn, Matt scouted the vicinity of Yellowjacket with care.

There was some movement in town—more than usual

at that hour. He observed a long line of saddled horses at the hitch rails. He puzzled over this, studying it narrow eyed from the crest of a ridge through his glasses. Marshal Collins could not yet have returned, hence this must be some other movement. That it was organized was obvious.

He was still watching when a man wearing a faded red shirt left the back door of a building near the saloon, went to a horse carefully hidden in the rear, and mounted. At this distance, there was no way of seeing who he was. The man rode strangely. Studying him through the glasses—a relic of Sabre's military years— Matt suddenly realized why the rider seemed strange. He was riding eastern fashion!

This was no westerner, slouched and lazy in the saddle, nor yet sitting upright as a cavalryman might. This man rode forward on his horse, a poor practice for the hard miles of desert or mountain riding. Yet it was his surreptitious manner rather than his riding style that intrigued Matt. It required but a few minutes for Matt to see that the route the rider was taking away from town would bring him by near the base of the promontory where he watched.

Reluctant as he was to give over watching the saddled horses, Sabre was sure this strange rider held some clue to his problems. Sliding back on his belly well into the brush, Matt got to his feet and descended the steep trail and took up his place among the boulders beside the trail.

It was very hot there out of the breeze, yet he had waited only a minute until he heard the sound of the approaching horse. He cleared his gun from its holster and moved to the very edge of the road. Then the rider appeared. It was Keys.

Matt's gun stopped him. "Where you ridin', Keys?" Matt asked quietly. "What's this all about?"

"I'm riding to intercept the marshal," Keys said sincerely. "McCarran and Reed plan to send out a posse of their own men to hunt you; then, under cover of capturing you, they intend to take the Pivotrock and hold it."

Sabre nodded. That would be it, of course, and he should have guessed it before. "What about the marshal? They'll run into him on the trail."

"No, they're going to swing south of his trail. They know how he's riding because Reed is guiding him."

"What's your stake in this? Why ride all the way out there to tell the marshal?"

"It's because of Jenny Curtin," he said frankly. "She's a fine girl, and Bill was a good boy. Both of them treated me fine, as their father did before them. It's little enough to do, and I know too much about the plotting of that devil McCarran."

"Then it is McCarran. Where does Reed stand in this?"

"He's stupid!" Keys said contemptuously. "McCarran is using him, and he hasn't the wit to see it. He believes they are partners, but Prince will get rid of him like he does anyone who gets in his way. He'll be rid of Trumbull, too."

"And Sikes?"

"Perhaps. Sikes is a good tool, to a point."

Matt Sabre shoved his hat back on his head. "Keys," he said suddenly, "I want you to have a little faith in me. Believe me, I'm doing what I can to help Jenny Curtin. I did kill her husband, but he was a total stranger who was edgy and started a fight.

"I'd no way of knowing who or what he was, and the gun of a stranger kills as easy as the gun of a known man. But he trusted me. He asked me to come here, to bring his wife five thousand and to help her."

"Five thousand?" Keys stared. "Where did he get that amount of money?"

"I'd like to know," Sabre admitted. Another idea occurred to him. "Keys, you know more about what's going on in this town than anyone else. What do you know about the Sonoma Grant?"

Keys hesitated, then said slowly: "Sabre, I know very little about that. I think the only one who has the true facts is Prince McCarran. I think he gathered all the available papers on both grants and is sure that no matter what his claim, the grant cannot be substantiated. Nobody knows but McCarran."

"Then I'll go to McCarran," Sabre replied harshly. "I'm going to straighten this out if it's the last thing I do."

"You go to McCarran and it will be the last thing you do. The man's deadly. He's smooth talking and treacherous. And then there's Sikes."

"Yes," Sabre admitted. "There's Sikes."

He studied the situation, then looked up. "Look, don't you bother the marshal. Leave him to me. Every man he's got with him is an enemy to Jenny Curtin, and they would never let you talk. You circle them and ride on to Pivotrock. You tell Camp Gordon what's happening. Tell him of this outfit that's saddled up. I'll do my job here, and then I'll start back."

Long after Keys had departed, Sabre watched. Evidently, the posse was awaiting some word from Reed. Would McCarran ride with them? He was too careful. He would wait in Yellowjacket. He would be, as always, an innocent bystander. . . .

Keys, riding up the trail some miles distant, drew up suddenly. He had forgotten to tell Sabre of Prince McCarran's plan to have Sid Trumbull cut him down when he tangled with Sikes. For a long moment, Keys sat his horse, staring worriedly and scowling. To go back now would lose time; moreover, there was small chance that Sabre would be there. Matt Sabre would have to take his own chances.

Regretfully, Keys pushed on into the rough country ahead. . . .

Tony Sikes found McCarran seated in the back room

at the saloon. McCarran glanced up quickly as he came in, and then nodded.

"Glad to see you, Sikes. I want you close by. I think we'll have visitors today or tomorrow."

"Visitors?" Sikes searched McCarran's face.

"A visitor, I should say. I think we'll see Matt Sabre."

Tony Sikes considered that, turning it over in his mind. Yes, Prince was right. Sabre would not surrender. It would be like him to head for town, hunting Reed. Aside from three or four men, nobody knew of McCarran's connection with the Pivotrock affair. Reed or Trumbull were fronting for him.

Trumbull, Reed, Sikes, and Keys. Keys was a shrewd man. He might be a drunk and a piano player, but he had a head on his shoulders.

Sikes's mind leaped suddenly. Keys was not around. This was the first time in weeks that he had not encountered Keys in the bar.

Keys was gone.

Where would he go—to warn Jenny Curtin of the posse? So what? He had nothing against Jenny Curtin. He was a man who fought for hire. Maybe he was on the wrong side in this. Even as he thought of that, he remembered Matt Sabre. The man was sharp as a steel blade—trim, fast. Now that it had been recalled to his mind, he remembered all that he had heard of him as marshal of Mobeetie.

There was in Tony Sikes a drive that forbade him to admit any man was his fighting superior. Sabre's draw against Trumbull was still the talk of the town—talk that irked Sikes, for folks were beginning to compare the two of them. Many thought Sabre might be faster. That rankled.

He would meet Sabre first and then drift.

"Don't you think he'll get here?" McCarran asked, looking up at Tony.

Sikes nodded. "He'll get here, all right. He thinks too fast for Trumbull or Reed. Even for that marshal."

Sikes would have Sabre to himself. Sid Trumbull was out of town. Tony Sikes wanted to do his own killing.

Matt Sabre watched the saddled horses. He had that quality of patience so long associated with the Indian. He knew how to wait and how to relax. He waited now, letting all his muscles rest. With all his old alertness for danger—his sixth sense that warned him of climaxes—he knew this situation had reached the explosion point.

The marshal would be returning. Reed and Trumbull would be sure that he did not encounter the posse. And that body of riders, most of whom were henchmen or cronies of Galusha Reed, would sweep down on the Pivotrock and capture it, killing all who were there under the pretense of searching for Matt Sabre.

Keys would warn them, and in time. Once they knew of the danger, Camp Gordon and the others would be wise enough to take the necessary precautions. The marshal was one tentacle, but there in Yellowjacket was the heart of the trouble.

If Prince McCarran and Tony Sikes were removed, the tentacles would shrivel and die. Despite the danger out at Pivotrock, high behind the Mogollon Rim, the decisive blow must be struck right here in Yellowjacket.

He rolled over on his stomach and lifted the glasses. Men were coming from the Yellowjacket Saloon and mounting up. Lying at his ease, he watched them go. There were at least thirty, possibly more. When they had gone, he got to his feet and brushed off his clothes. Then he walked slowly down to his horse and mounted.

He rode quietly, one hand lying on his thigh, his eyes alert, his brain relaxed and ready for impressions.

Marshal Rafe Collins was a just man. He was a frontiersman, a man who knew the West and the men it bred. He was no fool—shrewd and careful, rigid in his enforcement of the law, yet wise in the ways of men. Moreover, he was southern in the oldest of southern traditions, and being so, he understood what Matt Sabre meant when he said it was because he had killed her husband that he must protect Jenny Curtin.

Matt Sabre left his horse at the livery stable. Simpson looked up sharply when he saw him.

"You better watch yourself," he warned. "The whole country's after you, an' they are huntin' blood!"

"I know. What about Sikes? Is he in town?"

"Sure! He never leaves McCarran." Simpson searched his face. "Sikes is no man to tangle with, Sabre. He's chain lightnin'."

"I know." Sabre watched his horse led into a shadowed stall. Then he turned to Simpson. "You've been friendly, Simpson. I like that. After today, there's goin' to be a new order of things around here, but today I could use some help. What do you know about the Pivotrock deal?"

The man hesitated, chewing slowly. Finally, he spat and looked up. "There was nobody to tell until now," he said, "but two things I know. That grant was Curtin's, all right, an' he wasn't killed by accident. He was murdered."

"Murdered?"

"Yeah." Simpson's expression was wry. "Like you he liked fancy drinkin' liquor when he could get it. McCarran was right friendly. He asked Curtin to have a drink with him that day, an' Curtin did.

"On'y a few minutes after that, he came in here an' got a team to drive back, leavin' his horse in here because it had gone lame. I watched him climb into that rig, an' he missed the step an' almost fell on his face. Then he finally managed to climb in."

"Drunk?" Sabre's eyes were alert and interested.

"Him?" Simpson snorted. "That old coot could stow away more liquor than a turkey could corn. He had only *one* drink, yet he could hardly walk."

"Doped, then?" Sabre nodded. That sounded like McCarran. "And then what?"

"When the team was brought back after they ran

away with him, an' after Curtin was found dead, I found a bullet graze on the hip of one of those broncs."

So that was how it had been. A doped man, a skittish team of horses, and a bullet to burn the horse just enough to start it running. Prince McCarran was a thorough man.

"You said you knew that Curtin really owned that grant. How?"

Simpson shrugged. "Because he had that other claim investigated. He must have heard rumors of trouble. There'd been no talk of it that I heard, an' here a man hears everythin'!

"Anyway, he had all the papers with him when he started back to the ranch that day. He showed 'em to me earlier. All the proof."

"And he was murdered that day? Who found the body?"

"Sid Trumbull. He was ridin' that way, sort of accidentallike."

The proof Jenny needed was in the hands of Prince McCarran. By all means, he must call on Prince.

"Stand Up—and Die!"

Matt Sabre walked to the door and stood there, waiting a moment in the shadow before emerging into the sunlight.

The street was dusty and curiously empty. The rough-fronted gray buildings of unpainted lumber or sand-colored adobe faced him blankly from across and up the street. The hitch rail was deserted; the water trough overflowed a little, making a darkening stain under one end.

Somewhere up the street but behind the buildings, a hen began proclaiming her egg to the hemispheres. A single white cloud hung lazily in the blue sky. Matt stepped out. Hitching his gun belts a little, he looked up the street.

Sikes would be in the Yellowjacket. To see McCarran, he must see Sikes first. That was the way he wanted it. One thing at a time.

He was curiously quiet. He thought of other times when he had faced such situations—of Mobeetie, of that first day out on the plains hunting buffalo, of the first time he had killed a man, of a charge the Riffs made on a small desert patrol out of Taudeni long ago.

A faint breeze stirred an old sack that lay near the boardwalk, and farther up the street, near the water trough, a long gray rat slipped out from under a store and headed toward the drip of water from the trough. Matt Sabre started to walk, moving up the street.

It was not far, as distance goes, but there is no walk as long as the gunman's walk, no pause as long as the pause before gunfire. On this day, Sikes would know, instantly, what his presence here presaged. McCarran would know too.

Prince McCarran was not a gambler. He would scarcely trust all to Tony Sikes no matter how confident he might be. It always paid to have something to back up a facing card. Trust Prince to keep his hole card well covered. But on this occasion, he would not be bluffing. He would have a hole card, but where? How? What? And when?

The last was not hard. When—the moment of the gun battle.

He had walked no more than thirty yards when a door creaked and a man stepped into the street. He did not look down toward Sabre but walked briskly to the center of the street, then faced about sharply like a man on a parade ground.

Tony Sikes.

He wore this day a faded blue shirt that stretched tight over his broad, bony shoulders and fell slack in front where his chest was hollow and his stomach flat. It was too far yet to see his eyes, but Matt Sabre knew what they looked like.

The thin, angular face, the mustache, the high cheekbones, and the long, restless fingers. The man's hips were narrow, and there was little enough to his body. Tony Sikes lifted his eyes and stared down the street. His lips were dry, but he felt ready. There was a curious lightness within him, but he liked it so, and he liked the setup. At that moment, he felt almost an affection for Sabre.

The man knew so well the rules of the game. He was coming as he should come, and there was something about him—an edged quality, a poised and alert strength.

No sound penetrated the clear globe of stillness. The warm air hung still, with even the wind poised, arrested by the drama in the street. Matt Sabre felt a slow trickle of sweat start from under his hatband. He walked carefully, putting each foot down with care and distinction of purpose. It was Tony Sikes who stopped first, some sixty yards away.

"Well, Matt, here it is. We both knew it was coming."

"Sure." Matt paused, too, feet wide apart, hands swinging wide. "You tied up with the wrong outfit, Sikes."

"We'd have met, anyway," Sikes looked along the street at the tall man standing there, looked and saw his bronzed face, hard and ready. It was not in Sikes to feel fear of a man with guns. Yet this was how he would die. It was in the cards. He smiled suddenly. Yes, he would die by the gun—but not now.

His hands stirred, and as if their movement was a signal to his muscles, they flashed in a draw. Before him, the dark, tall figure flashed suddenly. It was no more than that, a blur of movement and a lifted gun, a movement suddenly stilled, and the black sullen muzzle of a six-gun that steadied on him even as he cleared his gun from his open top holster.

He had been beaten—*beaten to the draw*.

The shock of it triggered Sikes's gun, and he knew even as the gun bucked in his hand that he had missed, and then suddenly, Matt Sabre was running! Running toward him, gun lifted, but not firing!

In a panic, Sikes saw the distance closing and he fired as fast as he could pull the trigger, three times in a thundering cascade of sound. And even as the hammer fell for the fourth shot, he heard another gun bellow.

But where? There had been no stab of flame from Sabre's gun. Sabre was running, a rapidly moving target, and Sikes had fired too fast, upset by the sudden rush, by the panic of realizing he had been beaten to the draw.

He lifted his right-hand gun, dropped the muzzle in a careful arc, and saw Sabre's skull over the barrel. Then Sabre skidded to a halt, and his gun hammered bullets.

Flame leaped from the muzzle, stabbing at Sikes, burning him along the side, making his body twitch and the bullet go wild. He switched guns, and then something slugged him in the wind, and the next he knew, he was on the ground.

Matt Sabre had heard that strange shot, but that was another thing. He could not wait now; he could not turn his attention. He saw Sikes go down, but only to his knees, and the gunman had five bullets and the range now was only fifteen yards.

Sikes's gun swung up, and Matt fired again. Sikes lunged to his feet, and then his features writhed with agony and breathlessness, and he went down, hard to the ground, twisting in the dust.

Then another bullet bellowed, and a shot kicked up dust at his feet. Matt swung his gun and blasted at an open window, then started for the saloon door. He stopped, hearing a loud cry behind him.

"*Matt!* Sabre?"

It was Sikes, his eyes flared wide. Sabre hesitated, glanced swiftly around, then dropped to his knees in the silent street.

"What is it, Tony? Anything I can do for you?"

"Behind—behind—the desk—you—you—" His faltering voice faded; then strength seemed to flood back, and he looked up. "Good man! Too—too fast!"

And then he was dead, gone just like that, and Matt Sabre was striding into the Yellowjacket.

The upstairs room was empty; the stairs were empty; there was no one in sight. Only Hobbs stood behind the bar when he came down. Hobbs, his face set and pale.

Sabre looked at him, eyes steady and cold. "Who came down those stairs?"

Hobbs licked his lips. He choked, then whispered hoarsely. "Nobody—but there's—there's a back stairs."

Sabre wheeled and walked back in quick strides, thumbing shells into his gun. The office door was open, and Prince McCarran looked up as he framed himself in the door.

He was writing, and the desk was rumpled with papers, the desk of a busy man. Nearby was a bottle and a full glass.

McCarran lay down his pen. "So? You beat him? I thought you might."

"Did you?" Sabre's gaze was cold. If this man had been running, as he must have run, he gave no evidence of it now. "You should hire them faster, Prince."

"Well"—McCarran shrugged—"he was fast enough until now. But this wasn't my job, anyway. He was workin' for Reed."

Sabre took a step inside the door, away from the wall, keeping his hands free. His eyes were on those of

Prince McCarran, and Prince watched him, alert, interested.

"That won't ride with me," Matt said. "Reed's a stooge, a perfect stooge. He'll be lucky if he comes back alive from this trip. A lot of that posse you sent out won't come back, either."

McCarran's eyelids tightened at the mention of the posse. "Forget it." He waved his hand. "Sit down and have a drink. After all, we're not fools, Sabre. We're grown men, and we can talk. I never liked killing, anyway."

"Unless you do it or have it done." Sabre's hands remained where they were. "What's the matter, Prince? Yellow? Afraid to do your own killin'?"

McCarran's face was still, and his eyes were wide now. "You shouldn't have said that. You shouldn't have called me yellow."

"Then get on your feet. I hate to shoot a sittin' man."

"Have a drink and let's talk."

"Sure." Sabre was elaborately casual. "You have one, too." He reached his hand for the glass that had already been poured, but McCarran's eyes were steady. Sabre switched his hand and grasped the other glass, and then, like a striking snake, Prince McCarran grasped his right hand and jerked him forward, off balance.

At the same time, McCarran's left flashed back to the holster high on his left side, butt forward, and the gun jerked up and free. Matt Sabre, instead of trying to jerk his right hand free, let his weight go forward, following and hurling himself against McCarran. The chair went over with a crash, and Prince tried to straighten, but Matt was riding him back. He crashed into the wall, and Sabre broke free.

Prince swung his gun up, and Sabre's left palm slapped down, knocking the gun aside and gripping the hand across the thumb. His right hand came up under the gun barrel, twisting it back over and out of McCarran's hands. Then he shoved him back and dropped the gun, slapping him across the mouth with his open palm.

It was a free swing, and it cracked like a pistol shot. McCarran's face went white from the blow, and he rushed, swinging, but Sabre brought up his knee in the charging man's groin. Then he smashed him in the face with his elbow, pushing him over and back. McCarran dove past him, blood streaming from his crushed nose, and grabbed wildly at the papers. His hand came up with a bulldog .41.

Matt saw the hand shoot for the papers, and even as the .41 appeared, his own gun was lifting. He fired first, three times, at a range of four feet.

Prince McCarran stiffened, lifted to his tiptoes, then plunged over on his face and lay still among the litter of papers and broken glass.

Sabre swayed drunkenly. He recalled what Sikes had said about the desk. He caught the edge and jerked it aside, swinging the desk away from the wall. Behind it was a small panel with a knob. It was locked, but a bullet smashed the lock. He jerked it open. A thick wad of bills, a small sack of gold coins, a sheaf of papers.

A glance sufficed. These were the papers Simpson had mentioned. The thick parchment of the original grant, the information on the conflicting Sonoma grant, and then . . . He glanced swiftly through them, then, at a pound of horses' hoofs, he stuffed them inside his shirt. He stopped, stared. His shirt was soaked with blood.

Fumbling, he got the papers into his pocket, then stared down at himself. Sikes had hit him. Funny, he had never felt it. Only a shock, a numbness. Now Reed was coming back.

Catching up a sawed-off express shotgun, he started for the door, weaving like a drunken man. He never even got to the door.

*   *   *

The sound of galloping horses was all he could hear—galloping horses, and then a faint smell of something that reminded him of a time he had been wounded in North Africa. His eyes flickered open, and the first thing he saw was a room's wall with the picture of a man with muttonchop whiskers and spectacles.

He turned his head and saw Jenny Curtin watching him. "So? You've decided to wake up. You're getting lazy, Matt. Mr. Sabre. On the ranch you always were the first one up."

He stared at her. She had never looked half so charming, and that was bad. It was bad because it was time to be out of here and on a horse.

"How long have I been here?"

"Only about a day and a half. You lost a lot of blood."

"What happened at the ranch? Did Keys get there in time?"

"Yes, and I stayed. The others left right away."

"You *stayed*?"

"The others," she said quietly, "went down the road about two miles. There was Camp Gordon, Tom Judson, Pepito, and Keys. And Rado, of course. They went down the road while I stood out in the ranch yard and let them see me. The boys ambushed them."

"Was it much of a fight?"

"None at all. The surprise was so great that they broke and ran. Only three weren't able, and four were badly wounded."

"You found the papers? Including the one about McCarran sending the five thousand in marked bills to El Paso?"

"Yes," she said simply. "We found that. He planned on having Billy arrested and charged with theft. He planned that, and then if he got killed, so much the better. It was only you he didn't count on."

"No." Matt Sabre stared at his hands, strangely white now. "He didn't count on me."

So it was all over now. She had her ranch, she was a

free woman, and people would leave her alone. There was only one thing left. He had to tell her. To tell her that he was the one who had killed her husband.

He turned his head on the pillow. "One thing more," he began. "I—"

"Not now. You need rest."

"Wait. I have to tell you this. It's about—about Billy."

"You mean that you—you were the one who—?"

"Yes, I—" He hesitated, reluctant at last to say it.

"I know. I know you did, Matt. I've known from the beginning, even without all the things you said."

"I talked when I was delirious?"

"A little. But I knew, Matt. Call it intuition, anything you like, but I knew. You see, you told me how his eyes were when he was drawing his gun. Who could have known that but the man who shot him?"

"I see." His face was white. "Then I'd better rest. I've got some traveling to do."

She was standing beside him. "Traveling? Do you have to go on, Matt? From all you said last night, I thought—I thought"— her face flushed—"maybe you—didn't want to travel any more. Stay with us, Matt, if you want to. We would like to have you, and Billy's been asking for you. He wants to know where his spurs are."

After a while, he admitted carefully, "Well, I guess I should stay and see that he gets them. A fellow should always make good on his promises to kids, I reckon."

"You'll stay then? You won't leave?"

Matt stared up at her. "I reckon," he said quietly, "I'll never leave unless you send me away."

She smiled and touched his hair. "Then you'll be here a long time, Mathurin Sabre—a very long time."

Author's Note:
STEIN'S PASS

One night when I was not quite seventeen years old I was put off a freight train at Stein's Pass, New Mexico, high in the mountains near the Arizona/New Mexico border. I'd been at sea on a merchant ship and needed to save what money I had, so I caught a freight to the west. It was a miserably cold night, and when day broke and I saw some stirring of life, I walked from the depot over to the only lunch counter for coffee.

At the counter I started talking to an old cowboy. Stein's Pass, he said, was where it all happened: holdups, Indian fights, and nearby, in Doubtful Canyon, one of the most desperate desert battles, a fight between the Apaches and the passengers of a stagecoach, all of them salty veterans of many a battle. When all were killed, Cochise is reported to have said they were the bravest men he ever knew.

A few years ago, after watching some work being done on a movie of mine near Tuscon, I drove over to the area I was to write about in SHALAKO. I stopped briefly in Stein's Pass. A few buildings remained with empty windows staring blankly across the desert mountains, and a wild burro was wandering around the street. It was a ghost town and properly named. There could be many ghosts around Stein's Pass. The old cowboy told the truth.

Sleeping echoes of many a battle still wait in the shadow of the canyon.

ONE LAST GUN NOTCH

Morgan Clyde studied his face in the mirror. It was an even-featured, pleasant face. Neither the nose nor jaw was too blunt or too long. Now, after his morning shave, his jaw was still faintly blue through the deep tan, and the bronze curls above his face made him look several years younger than his thirty-five.

Carefully, he knotted the black string tie on the soft gray shirt and then slipped on his coat. When he donned the black, flat-crowned hat, he was ready. His appearance was perfect, with just a shade of studied carelessness. For ten years now, Morgan Clyde's morning shave and dressing had been a ritual from which he never deviated.

He slid the two guns from their holsters and checked them carefully. First the right, then the left. On the butt of the right-hand gun there were nine filed notches. On the left, three. He glanced at them thoughtfully, remembering.

That first notch had been for Red Bridges. That was

the year they had run his cattle off. Bridges had come out to the claim when Clyde was away, cut his fence down, run his cattle off, and shot his wife down in cold blood.

Thoughtfully, Morgan Clyde looked back into the mirror. He had changed. In his mind's eye he could see that tall, loose-limbed young man with the bronze hair and boyish face. He had been quiet, peace loving, content with his wife, his homestead, and his few cattle. He had a gift for gun handling, but never thought of it. That is, not until that visit by Bridges.

Returning home with a haunch of antelope across his saddle, he had found his wife and the smoking ruins of his home. He did not have to be told. Bridges had warned him to move, or else. Within him something had burst, and for an instant his eyes were blind with blood. When the moment had passed, he had changed.

He had known, then, what to do. He should have gone to the governor with his story, or to the U.S. Marshal. And he could have gone. But there was something red and ugly inside him that had not been there before. He had swung aboard a little paint pony and headed for Peavey's Mill.

The town's one street had been quiet, dusty. The townspeople knew what had happened, because it had been happening to all homesteaders. Never for a moment did they expect any reaction. Red Bridges was too well known. He had killed too many times.

Then Morgan Clyde rode down the street on his paint pony, saw Bridges, and slid to the ground. Somebody yelled, and Bridges turned. He looked at Morgan Clyde's young, awkward length and laughed. But his hand dropped swiftly for his gun.

But something happened. Morgan Clyde's gun swung up first, spouting fire, and his two shots centered over Bridges's heart. The big man's fingers loosened, and the gun slid into the dust. Little whorls rose slowly from where it landed. Then, his face puzzled, his left hand fumbling at his breast, Red Bridges wilted.

He could have stopped there. Now, Morgan Clyde knew that. He could have stopped there, and *should* have stopped. He could have ridden from town and been left alone. But he knew Bridges was a tool, and the man who used the tool was Erik Pendleton, in the bank. Bridges had been a gunman; Pendleton was not.

The banker looked up from his desk and saw death. It was no mistake. Clyde had walked up the steps, around the teller's cage, and opened the door of Pendleton's office.

The banker opened his mouth to talk, and Morgan Clyde shot him. He had deserved it.

The posse lost him west of the Brazos, and he rode on west into a cattle war. He was wanted then and no longer cared. The banker hadn't rated a notch, but the three men he killed in the streets of Fort Sumner he counted, and the man he shot west of Gallup.

There had been trouble in St. George, and then in Virginia City. After that, he had a reputation.

Morgan Clyde turned and stared at the huge old grandfather's clock. It remained his only permanent possession. It had come over from Scotland years ago, and his family had carried it westward when they went to Ohio, and later to Illinois, and then to Texas. He had intended sending for it when the homestead was going right, and everything was settled. To Diana and himself it had been a symbol of home, of stability.

What could have started him remembering all that? The past, he had decided long ago, was best forgotten.

He rode the big black down the street toward Sherman's office. He knew what was coming. He had been taking money for a long time from men of Sherman's stripe. Men who needed what force could give them but had nothing of force in themselves.

Sherman had several gunmen on his payroll. He kept them hating one another and grew fat on their hatred. Tom Cool was there, and the Earle brothers. Tough and vicious, all of them.

Perhaps it was this case this morning that had started him thinking. Well, that damned fool nester should have known better than to settle on that Red Basin land. It was Sherman's best grazing land, even if he didn't own it. But a kid like that couldn't buck Sherman. The man was a fool to think he could.

The thought of that other young nester came into his mind. He dismissed it with an impatient jerk of his head.

The Earle brothers, Vic and Will, were sitting in the bar as he passed through. The two big men looked up, hate in their eyes.

Sherman was sitting behind the desk in his office and he looked up, smiling, when Morgan Clyde came in. "Sit down, Morg," he said cheerfully. He leaned back in his chair and put his fingertips together. "Well, this is it. When we get this Hallam taken care of, the rest of the nesters will see we mean business. We can have that range clean by spring, an' that means I'll be running the biggest herd west of the Staked Plains."

Tom Cool was sitting in a chair tilted against the wall. He had a thin, hatchet face and narrow eyes. He was rolling a smoke now, and he glanced up as his tongue touched the edge of the yellow paper.

"You got the stomach for it, Morg?" he asked dryly. "Or would you rather I handle this one? I hear you was a nester once yourself."

Morgan Clyde glanced around casually, one brow lifting. "You handle my work?" He looked his contempt. "Cool, you might handle this job. It's just a cold-blooded killing, and more in your line. I'm used to men with guns in their hands."

Cool's eyes narrowed dangerously. "Yeah?" his voice

was a hoarse whisper. "I can fill mine fast enough, Clyde, any time you want to unlimber."

"I don't shoot sitting pigeons," Morgan said quietly.

"Why, you—" Tom Cool's eyes flared with hatred, and his hand dropped away from the cigarette in a streak for his gun.

Morgan Clyde filled his hand without more than a hint of movement. Before a shot could crash, Sherman's voice cut through the hot tensity of the moment with an edge that turned both their heads toward the leader. There was a gun in his hand.

Queerly, Morgan was shocked. He had never thought of Sherman as a fast man with a gun, and he knew that Cool felt the same. Sherman a gunman! It put a new complexion on a lot of things. Clyde glanced at Tom Cool and saw the man's hand coming away from his gun. There had been an instant when both of them could have died. If not by their own guns, by Sherman's. Neither had been watching him.

"You boys better settle down," Sherman said, leaning back in his swivel chair. "Any shooting that's done in my outfit will be done by me."

He looked up at Clyde, and there was something very much like triumph in his eyes. "You're getting slow, Morg," Sherman said. "I could have killed you before you got your gun out."

"Maybe."

Sherman shrugged. "You go see this Hallam, Clyde. I want him killed, see? An' the house burned. What happens to his wife is no business of yours. I got other plans." He grinned, revealing broken teeth. "Yeah, I got other plans for her."

Clyde spun on his heel and walked outside. He was just about to swing into the saddle when Tom Cool drifted up. Cool spoke low and out the corner of his mouth. "Did you see that, Morg? Did you see the way he got that gun into action? That gent's poison. Why's he been keepin' that from us? Somethin' around here smells to high heaven."

He took his belt up a notch. "Morg, let's move in on him together. Let's take this over. There's goin' to be a fortune out there in that valley. You got a head on you. You take care of the business, an' I'll handle the rough stuff. Let's take Sherman out of there. He's framin' to queer both of us."

Morgan Clyde swung into the saddle. "No sale, Tom," he said quietly. "Riding our trail, we ride alone. Anyway, I'm not the type to sell out or double-deal. When I'm through with Sherman I'll tell him so to his face."

"He'll kill you!"

Clyde smiled wearily. "Maybe."

He turned his horse and rode away. So Sherman was a gunman.

Tom Cool was right, there was something very wrong about that. The man hired his fighting done, rarely carried a weapon, and no one had ever suspected he might be fast. That was a powerful weapon in the hands of a double-crosser. A man who was lightning with a gun and unsuspected—

After all, where did he and Cool stand? Sherman owed him ten thousand dollars for dirty work done, for cattle run off, for forcing men to leave, for a couple of shootings. Tom Cool was in the same position. Now, with Hallam out of the way and the nesters gone, he would no longer need either Cool or himself.

Suddenly, Morgan Clyde remembered Sherman's broken teeth, his sly smile, his insinuating manner when he spoke of Hallam's wife. Oddly, for the first time, he began to see himself in a clear light. A hired gun for a man with the instincts of a rat! It wasn't a nice thought. He shook himself angrily, forcing himself to concentrate on the business at hand.

Vic Hallam was young, and he was green. He was,

they said, a fine shot with a rifle, and a fair man with a
gun when he got it out, but by Western standards he
was pitifully slow. He was about twenty-six, his wife a
mere girl of nineteen, and pretty. Despite his youth,
Hallam was outspoken. He had led the resistance against
Sherman, and had sworn to stay in Red Basin as long as
he wished. He had every legal right to the land, and
Sherman had none.

But Morgan Clyde had long ago shelved any regard
for the law. The man with the fastest gun was the law
along the frontier, and so far he had been fastest. If
Sherman wanted the Red Basin, he'd get it. If it was
over Hallam's dead body, then that's how it would be.

He had never backed out on a job yet, and never
would. Hallam would be taken care of.

Morgan rode at a rapid trot, knowing very well what
he had to do. Hallam was a man of a fiery temper, and
it would be easy to goad him into grabbing for a gun.

Clyde shook his head, striving to clear it of upsetting
thoughts. With the ten thousand he had coming, he
could go away. He could find a new country, buy a
ranch, and live quietly somewhere beyond the reach of
his reputation. Yet even as he told himself that, he
knew it was not true. A few years ago he might have
done just that, but now it was too late. Wherever he
went there would be smoking guns, split seconds of
blasting fire and the thunder of shooting. And wherever
he went he would be pointed out as a killer.

The heat waves danced along the valley floor, and he
reined in his horse, moving at a walk. In his mind he
seemed to be back again in the house he had built with
Diana, and he remembered how they had talked of
having the clock.

Then he was riding around the cluster of rocks and
into the ranchyard at Red Basin. Sitting warily, with his
hands loose and ready, he rode toward the house. A
young woman came to the door and threw out some
water. When she looked up, she saw him.

He was close enough then, and her face went deathly pale. Her eyes widened a little. Something inside of him shrank. He knew she recognized him.

"What—what do you want?" she asked.

He looked down at her wide eyes. She was pretty, he decided.

"I wanted to see Mr. Hallam, ma'am."

She hesitated. "Won't you get down and sit on the porch? He's gone out now, but he'll be back soon. He—he saw some antelope over by the Rim Rocks."

Antelope! Morgan Clyde stiffened a little, then relaxed. He had hard work to make believe this was real. The girl—why, she was almost the size of Diana and almost, he admitted, as pretty. And the house—there was the wash bench, the homemade furniture, just like their own place. And now Hallam was after antelope.

It was all the same, even the rifle in the corner. . . . Something in him leaped. The rifle! A moment ago it had stood in the corner, and now it was gone! Instinctively, he threw himself from his chair—a split second before the shot blasted past his head.

Catlike, he came to his feet. He had twisted the rifle from the girl's hands before she could shoot again. Coolly, he ejected the shells from the rifle and dropped them on the table. He looked at the girl, smiling with an odd light of respect in his eyes. He noted there wasn't a sign of fright or tears in hers.

"Nice try," he said quietly.

"You came here to kill my husband," she said. It wasn't an accusation; it was a flat statement.

"Maybe." He shrugged. "Maybe so."

"Why do you want to kill him?" she demanded fiercely. "What did he ever do to you?"

Morgan Clyde looked at her thoughtfully. "Nothing, of course. But this land is needed by someone else. Perhaps you should move off."

"We like it here!" she retorted.

He looked around. "It's nice. I like it too." He pointed

to the corner across the room. "There should be a clock over there, a grandfather's clock."

She looked at him, surprised. "We—we're going to have one. Someday."

He got up and walked over to the newly made shelves and looked at the china. It had blue figures running around the edges, Dutch boys and girls and mills.

He turned toward the window. "I should think you'd have it open on such a nice morning," he said. "More air. And I like to see a curtain stir in a light wind. Don't you?"

"Yes, but the window sticks. Vic was going to fix it, but he's been so busy."

Morgan Clyde picked up the hammer and drew the strips of molding from around the window, then lifted it out. Resting one corner on the table, he slipped his knife from his pocket and carefully shaved the edges. He tried the window twice before it moved easily. Then he replaced it and nailed the molding back in position. He tried it again, sliding the window up. A light breeze stirred the curtain, and the girl laughed. He turned, smiling gravely.

The sunlight fell across the rough-hewn floor, and when he raised his eyes, he could see a man riding down the trail.

Morgan Clyde turned slowly, and looked at the girl. Her eyes widened.

"No!" she gasped. "Please! Not that!"

Morgan Clyde didn't look back. He walked out to the porch and swung into the saddle. He reined the black around and started toward the approaching homesteader.

Before Hallam could speak, Clyde said. "Bad way to carry your rifle. Never can tell when you might need it!"

"Clyde!" Hallam exclaimed sharply. "What—"

"Good morning, Mr. Hallam," Morgan Clyde said, smiling a little. "Nice place you've got here."

He touched his heels to the black and rode away at a

canter. Behind him, the man stared, frowning. . . .

It wasn't until Clyde was riding down the street of the town that he thought of what was coming. *This is it,* he said to himself. *You knew there would have to be an end to this sort of thing, and this is it.*

The Earle brothers were still in the bar. They looked up at him as he passed, their eyes hard. He stepped to the door of the office and opened it. Sherman was seated at the desk, and Tom Cool was tilted back on his chair against the wall. Nothing, apparently, had changed—except himself.

"I'm quitting, Sherman," he said quietly. "You owe me ten thousand dollars. I want it—*now.*"

Sherman's eyes narrowed. "Hallam? What about him?" he demanded.

Morgan Clyde smiled thinly, with amusement in his eyes. "He's taken care of. Very nicely, I think."

"What's this nonsense about quitting?" Sherman demanded.

"That's it, I'm quitting."

"You don't quit until I'm ready," Sherman snapped harshly. "I want to know what happened out there."

Clyde stepped carelessly to one side so that he could face Tom Cool, too. "Nothing happened," he said quietly. "They had a nice place there. A nice couple. I envied them, so I decided to let them stay."

"*You* decided?"

He's faster than I am, Clyde's brain told him, even as he moved. *He'll shoot first, anyway, so—*

Morgan Clyde's gun roared, and the shot caught Tom Cool in the chest, even as the gunman's weapon started to swing up to shoot him. Clyde felt a bullet fan past his own face, but he shot Cool again before he turned. Something struck him hard in the body, and then in one leg. He went down, then staggered up and emptied his gun into Sherman.

Sherman's body sagged, and a slow trickle of blood came from the corner of his mouth.

Turning, Clyde got to the office door, walking very straight. His brain felt light, even a little giddy. He opened the door precisely and stepped out into the barroom. Across the room, the Earles, staring wide-eyed, jerked out their guns.

Through the door behind him they could see Sherman's body sagging in death. They moved as one man. Gritting his teeth, Morgan Clyde triggered his gun. He shot them both. . . .

Morgan Clyde almost made it to his horse before he fell, sprawling his length in the dust. Vaguely he heard a roar of horse's hoofs, and then he felt himself turned over onto his back. Vic Hallam was staring at him.

Morgan Clyde's breath came hoarsely. He looked up, remembering. "My place," he muttered thickly through the blood that frothed his lips. "There's a clock. Put—put it—in the corner."

There was sympathy and a deep understanding in Hallam's face. "Sure, that'd be fine. When you get well, we'll move it over together—on condition that you'll go partners on the homestead. . . . But why didn't you wait, man? I'd have come with you."

"Partners," Morgan Clyde said, and it seemed good to be able to smile. "That'd be fine. Just fine."

Author's Note:
THE MOGOLLON RIM

Also in the Mogollon Rim country is the Double-Circle Ranch, established about 1880. On the ranch are the graves of four train robbers. Hiding from the law, they had taken jobs on the Double-Circle and were trailed to the ranch by a posse accompanied by two Texas Rangers. The outlaws made their fight, and four of them were buried where they fell.

No ranch in the area was safe from Apache raids, and outlaws were numerous. Black Jack Christian operated in the area and had a hideout in a cave in Cole Creek Canyon, about twenty miles from Clifton. Christian was killed not far from the cave.

Not far from the cave is a place known as Murder Camp, where Felix Burress was killed. His murderer was traced to a line cabin in the mountains and captured. He was sentenced to fifteen years in the Yuma prison.

DEATH SONG
OF THE SOMBRERO

Stretch Magoon, six-foot-five in his sock feet and lean as a buggy whip, put his grulla mustang down the bank of the wash, and cut diagonally across it toward the trail up the bank. His long, melancholy face seemed unusually sad.

When the grulla scrambled up the bank, Stretch kept him to a slow-paced walk. The sadness remained in his eyes, but they were more watchful, almost expectant.

The ramshackle house he was approaching was unpainted and dismal. Sadly in need of repair, the grounds around were dirty and unkempt, the corral a patchwork of odds and ends of rails, the shed that did duty for a barn was little more than a roof over some rails where three saddles rode.

Magoon's eyes caught the saddles first, and the hard bronze of his face tightened. He reined up in the space between the shack and the shed. A big man loomed in the door, a bearded man with small, ugly eyes. "Howdy," he said. "Wantin' somethin'?"

157

"Uh-huh." Stretch dug out the makin's and began to build a smoke. "Wantin' t' tell you all somethin'." He finished his job, put the cigarette in his mouth, and struck a match on the side of his jeans. Then he looked up. Two men were there now; the bigger man had stepped outside, and a runty fellow with sandy hair and a freckled, ugly face stood in the door. One hand was out of sight.

"As of this mornin', come daylight," he said, "I'm ramroddin' the Lazy S."

"You're what?" The big man walked two steps closer. "You mean, you're the foreman? What's become of Ketchell?"

Stretch Magoon looked sadly down at the big man. "Why, Weidman, Ketchell did what I knowed he would do sooner or later. He was a victim of bad judgment. Ever' time that man played a hand of poker, I could see it comin'."

"Get t' the point!" Weidman demanded harshly. "What happened?"

"We had us a mite of an argument," Stretch said calmly, "an' Ketchell thought I was bluffin'. He called. We both drawed a new hand an' I led with two aces—right through the heart."

"Y' killed Burn Ketchell?" Weidman demanded incredulously. "I don't believe it!"

"Well"—Stretch dropped his left hand to the reins—"dead or not, they are havin' a buryin'. I reckon if he ain't dead he'll be some sore when he wakes up an' finds all that dirt in his face." He turned the mouse-colored mustang. "Oh yeah! That reminds me. We had the argument over suggestin' t' you that your Sombrero brand could be run mighty easy out of a Lazy S."

"Y' accusin' us o' rustlin'?" Weidman demanded. His eyes flickered for an instant, and Stretch felt a little shiver of relief go through him. He knew where that third man was now. It had had him bothered some. The third man was beside the corner of the corral.

His eyes dropped, and his heart gave a leap. The sun was beyond the corral, and he could see the shadow of that corner on the hard ground. He almost grinned as his eyes caught the flicker of movement.

"I ain't accusin' you o' nothin'. I ain't sure. If I was sure, I wouldn't be settin' here talkin'. I'd be stringin' your thick neck t' a cottonwood. What I'm doin' is givin' you a tip that the fun's over now. You can change your brand or leave the country. I ain't p'tic'lar which."

"Why, you—" Weidman's face was mottled and ugly, but he made the mistake of trusting too much to his dry-gulch attempt, and when Stretch Magoon drew, it was so fast he didn't have a chance to match him. He was depending too much on that shot from the corral corner.

Magoon's eyes had been on the shadow, unnoticed by Weidman. Stretch had seen the rifle come up from past the corner of the corral, had waited it out, waited until it froze. Then he drew and fired in the same instant.

He fired across his body, and too quickly. It had to be a snap shot because he needed to get his gun around and on the other two men. As it was, his bullet struck the man's hand just where his left thumb lay along the rifle barrel.

Very neatly it clipped the tip of the thumb and continued past to cut a furrow in the man's cheek, cut the lobe from his ear, and bury itself in the ground beyond. It had the added effect of a blow behind the ear, and the marksman rolled over on the ground, knocked momentarily unconscious by the blow.

Weidman's gun was only half out, and Red Posner had not even started to draw when Magoon's gun swung back in line. Weidman froze, then, very delicately, spread his fingers and let his gun slip back into its holster. His face was gray under the stubble of beard.

"No hard feelin's," Stretch said quietly, "but I'm repeatin'. Change your brand or git!"

He swung his horse and, watching warily, rode to the wash. Then, instead of following the trail up the other side, he whipped the mustang around and rode rapidly down the wash for a quarter of a mile. There it branched away to the left, and he took the branch. Well back in the cedars, he rode out of the wash and cut across country toward town.

Despite himself, he was disturbed. Something about the recent action had not gone as he had expected. Barker had sent for him two weeks before, when the missing cattle from the Lazy S had begun to mount rapidly in numbers. In those two weeks, Stretch had ascertained two things: first, that Lazy S cattle were being branded, and then, while the brands were still fresh, drifted into the breaks across the range near the Sombrero spread of Lucky Weidman.

Second, he had trailed Burn Ketchell and had actually caught him in the act of venting a brand. The change from a Lazy S to a Sombrero was all too simple for a handy man with a running iron.

It was merely a matter of making an inverted U over the top bend of the Lazy S to make the crown of the Sombrero, and then running a burned line from the top of the S around and down to the lower tip. It was simple, perfectly simple.

Burn Ketchell had been the brains behind the rustling. With Burn out of the way, Stretch had believed the rustling would be ended. Now, because of that attempted killing, he was not so sure.

Lucky Weidman was crooked and he was dirty, but he was no fool. He would never have taken a chance of having Magoon killed on his place after rustling had been discovered, unless he had friends—and friends in places to do him some good.

Tinkerville was an unsightly cowtown sprawled on a flat at the mouth of Tinker Canyon. Recently silver had been discovered up the canyon and the town had experienced a slight boom. With the boom the town had received an overflow of boomers, a number of whom were from the East and new to Western ways. One of these was the tall, precise, gray-mustached man who became sheriff, Ben Rowsey.

Another was the tall, handsome Paul Hartman.

New to the country himself, Stretch Magoon, itinerant range detective, had looked the town over when he arrived. Paul Hartman, only six months a resident of Tinkerville, was the acknowledged big man of the town.

He had loaned money to Sam Tinker, who owned the Tinker House and had founded the town in Indian days. He bought stock in the mining ventures. He grubstaked three prospectors, he started a weekly newspaper, and he bought a controlling interest in the Longhorn Bar.

Another newcomer was Kelly Jarvis, who owned the Lazy S, of which Dean Barker was manager.

Kelly was twenty-one years old, lovely, and fresh from the East. Her father had been a salty old range rider, tough and saddle-worn. He had made a mint of money, and had lavished it on Kelly. She was named for a companion of her father's. A story she told, and no one questioned.

Within two hours after she reached town, Kelly was being shown around by Paul Hartman. He was handsome and agreeable.

Stretch Magoon knew all of this. Tall, sad, and quiet, he got around, listened, and rarely asked a question. When he did, the questions were casual and calculated to start a flow of talk that usually ended in Magoon's learning a lot more than anyone planned to tell him.

He was having a drink in the Longhorn when Ben Rowsey walked up to him. "Magoon," Rowsey demanded sharply, "what's the straight of that shootin' out at the Lazy S?"

Magoon was surprised. In the West, rustling usually ended promptly with either a rope or a bullet. Not a man given to violence himself, he acted according to the code of the country. He had presented evidence of vented brands to Barker, had proved that Ketchell's orders had sent the cattle into the breaks near the Sombrero, and had been riding with Barker and County Galway when he found Ketchell. Ketchell had not seen Barker and Galway, and had tried to shoot it out.

"Nothin' much t' tell. I found him ventin' a brand, an' he went for a gun. He was too slow."

"You'll have to understand, Magoon," Rowsey said sharply, "that gunplay is a thing of the past out here. There's goin' t' be an investigation. You have witnesses?"

"Uh-huh." Magoon was mildly surprised but not alarmed. "Barker an' Galway were comin' up behind me an' saw the whole play."

Rowsey's eyes narrowed. "Galway, is it? His evidence won't be good in this county. He's been mixed up in too many shootin' scrapes himself."

The door opened then, and Paul Hartman came in. "Oh, hello, Magoon. Just the man I was looking for. Miss Jarvis wishes to see you."

Stretch walked outside into the sunlight. Kelly Jarvis, a vision in red hair and dark green riding habit, was sitting a sorrel horse at the door. Hartman and Sheriff Rowsey followed him out.

"You wanted t' see me, ma'am?" He looked sadly up into her violet eyes. They were cold now.

"Yes, I did. I understand you were hired by Dean Barker to find who was rustling on my ranch. Also, that you killed my foreman. I don't want hired killers on my property. You're fired."

"Fired?" Magoon's long, melancholy face did not change. "I was hired by Barker, ma'am. I reckon I'll let him fire me."

"Barker," Kelly Jarvis said crisply, "has already been fired!"

Magoon looked up at her; then he pushed his battered hat back on his head. "I reckon," he said sadly, "that's all the reward a feller can expect after givin' the best years o' his life t' that ranch like Barker done. I reckon that's all anybody can expect from a girl who was named for a mule!"

Kelly's face turned crimson with embarrassment. "Who told you that?" she flared angrily.

Paul Hartman stepped up abruptly. "That's enough out of you!" he said sharply. "Get going!" He put a hand on Stretch Magoon's shoulder and shoved.

It was an unfortunate thing. Even an unhappy thing. Paul Hartman was a widely experienced young man, not unacquainted with the rough and seamy side of life. Yet when his shoulder blades hit the dust of the street a good six feet off the boardwalk, he was jarred from head to heel, jarred as he had never been before.

"Here!" Rowsey interrupted sharply. "Y' can't—"

Chicken Livers, the town loafer was smiling. "The dude put his hand on him," he said dryly. "He shouldn't a done it."

Hartman got up, brushing off his clothes. Then, quietly, he removed his coat. "I'm going to teach you something!" he snapped, his eyes blazing. "It's about time some of you hicks learned how to talk to a gentleman!"

Hartman had boxed a good deal, but they had been polite boxing matches, between friends. Stretch Magoon had learned his fighting by extensive application, and while a good deal of boxing skill was included, none of it had been politely learned. The left jab that made a bloody puffball of Paul Hartman's lips wasn't in the least polite, and the right uppercut that lifted into Hartman's solar plexus and picked his feet clear of the boardwalk was crude, to say the least. Even a little vulgar.

Sheriff Ben Rowsey was unaccustomed to Western ways. He had been appointed by a board of which Hartman was the chairman and the directing voice. He was, however, something of a fighting man himself. He helped pick Hartman up from the street and dust him off. Aloud, he voiced his sadness at the unfortunate affair. Mentally, he acknowledged it had been months, years even, since he had seen two nicer punches. For the first time, and without adequate reason, he began to wonder about Paul Hartman.

Kelly Jarvis was an angry young lady. Her red hair and Irish ancestry, and perhaps something of the nature that had caused her father to name her for his favorite mule, helped to make her angry.

It took her something over an hour to find that she was much less angry at Stretch Magoon for knocking Hartman into the middle of the street than she was at Hartman for allowing himself to be disposed of so thoroughly. Heroes live by doing, and Paul Hartman had not done.

"The way I figger it," Stretch was saying to Galway, "is this Paul Hartman has been talking to her. She ain't been here long, an' he is the hombre that knows it all. So she listens."

"But what's the idea?" Galway asked. "What's his ante?"

"That," Magoon admitted, "is the point. Maybe he is just a smart lad tryin' t' take over a pretty filly, an' maybe there's something more behind it. I aim t' see."

He was not the only one who was doing some thinking. Kelly was sitting at lunch, and for the first time since coming West, she was using her own pretty red head.

New to the West, she had let Paul Hartman advise her. Now she was wondering. After all, Dean Barker had worked for her since her father had died when she was but fourteen. His reports, poorly written, but always legible, had been coming with regularity, and somehow, she recalled, the ranch had always shown a profit. Now, on the strength of a new friend's advice, she had discharged him, and had discharged the man Barker hired to investigate the rustling of her cattle.

It was true Stretch Magoon had killed her foreman. Hartman had told her Magoon was a professional killer.

But was he? She recalled then that her father had once killed two men trying to rustle his cattle. Another thing came up to irritate her: How had Magoon known that her father had named her for a mule?

It was irritating that he did know. It was also puzzling.

After lunch, Kelly Jarvis mounted her horse and took to the hills. The green riding habit and hat were left behind in the room at Tinker House. She wore a pair of jeans, boots, a boy's shirt, and a hat. And for the first time since she was fourteen, when her father had let her ride alone, she was carrying a pistol.

It had been seven years since she had been West, but she found as she rode that her knowledge had not been lost. She had grown up on the back of a cow pony, and she could use a rope and could ride as well as many a cowhand.

She rode into the breaks that divided her range from that of the new Sombrero outfit. Once, dismounting at a spring to get a drink, she drew a Lazy S in the mud with a stick, then performed the two simple movements essential to change it to a Sombrero. She had to admit that Stretch Magoon had a point. If Lucky Weidman was honest, as Hartman maintained, it was mighty funny he had chosen the Sombrero for a brand.

Red Posner, Weidman's right-hand man, had a face like a horned toad and a disposition like a burro with the colic. He left thinking to his betters, collected his money, drank it up, then rustled more cattle to get more money to buy more whiskey. He was very busy venting a brand on a Lazy S steer when Kelly Jarvis rode down into the clearing.

They saw each other at the same instant, but Red, having a guilty conscience, had the quickest reaction. He hauled iron and threw down on the girl. In a matter of minutes she was on her back in the dust, roped and hogtied with Red's piggin' strings.

When he had her, he paused. There she was, roped and tied. But what now? What to do with her? That he

165

had a lot of ideas on the subject went without saying, but Red Posner had learned that doing things without Lucky Weidman's say-so was very apt to lead to trouble. He tied the girl in her saddle and rode back to the shack on the dry wash.

From Lucky Weidman's viewpoint, it could not have been worse. Had Red Posner come to him and told him he had the girl, he would have instantly framed a rescue and rushed her back to town, to become the hero of the hour—even if he had to shoot Red. Which, as he considered it, was not a bad idea anyway.

Red, however, being simple even if crooked, had ridden right up to Lucky and started telling what had happened. There was no question but what the girl knew they were working together. There was no chance to saddle this on Magoon. Moreover, this was something Hartman could never fix. Rustling cows was one thing; capturing and holding a girl was another.

While Lucky puzzled over the situation, Stretch Magoon was thinking.

Long and lean and unhappy looking, Stretch had a memory as long as his stretch of limb. As an itinerant range detective and law officer, he had a mind filled with odds and ends of lore, and with a veritable mass of data on wanted men and stolen goods. He was thinking as he whittled, and he sat beside Chicken, asking frequent questions and fitting it into the jigsaw of information in his mind.

Chicken Livers had a little mining claim. From time to time he washed out a bit of color. It kept him in food and liquor and free of the awful entangling bonds of labor. Chicken was a philosopher, a dreamer, a man who observed his fellow men with painstaking care. He was no moralist. He was no gossip. He observed and he remembered.

If Livers had observed a murder, he might have been interested in the method and the motive. He would never have dreamed of reporting it. It was a world in

166

which people did strange things. If murder was one of them, it was no business of his.

On this day, however, drawn by the companion whittling of the long-legged range detective and the fact that someone was actually interested in him, Chicken Livers was giving forth.

He remembered, for instance, the very day Paul Hartman had come to town. "Alone, was he?" No. Not alone, but the other man had left him on the outskirts. "Plenty of money?" Uh-huh, plenty. All in twenty-dollar bills. Spankin' new ones, too. "Any friends?" Not right away. Talked with Sam Tinker. Then one day got in a confab with Lucky Weidman, sort of by accident. Only maybe it was not an accident. Weidman had stood around a good deal, like he was waiting.

"Could Weidman have been the man he left on the edge o' town?" Could be. Big feller. 'Bout the size o' Weidman.

After a while Magoon got up and sauntered down to the Longhorn, where Sheriff Ben Rowsey was having a drink. Magoon bought one, then looked at Ben. "I take it," Magoon said, "that you're an honest man?"

"I aim t' be!" Rowsey said.

"I take it that if'n you knew a man was a crook, you'd lay hand on him, no matter who he was?"

"That's right!" Rowsey was sincere. "If it was my own brother!"

"Then," Magoon said, "suppose y' wire El Paso for a description o' the teller an' two gunmen who robbed the bank at Forsyth last May; then check up a little."

With that, Stretch Magoon walked out to his horse and swung aboard. Sheriff Ben stood there with his drink, puckering his brows over it, then tossed it off, straightened up, and walked down to the stage station where they'd just put in one of these telegraph outfits.

The grulla was a trail-liking mustang, and he took to the hills. Magoon had no love for towns and he liked to get out and go. He skirted the plain near the Lazy S headquarters and then turned into the hills, keeping to the high slopes among the cedar and studying terrain with eyes like a hawk's. So it was that after an hour of riding in the hills he noted the thin wisp of smoke from the dying fire where Red Posner had done his work.

In twenty minutes he was on the scene, puzzling over the second set of tracks. Finally, he found, in the welter of dust and tracks, a partly trampled-out boot print made by a small boot.

There were some marks of ropes on the ground. A tight coil had been turned three times around something. That mark, too, had been partly erased, not by intention, but just by the hoofprints of horses. Then one horse had gone off, and from the way the other followed, always the same distance and never farther behind, it was a led horse.

When two horsemen came into a clearing from opposite directions and go out like that, one of the riders is dead, hurt, or a prisoner.

Stretch Magoon started down the trail made by those tracks. He had a fair idea where they had gone, and about how long before. He followed them because he was afraid they might stop before they reached the Sombrero ranch house. He was pretty certain who the first rider was, and that small boot print could only mean that the prisoner was Kelly Jarvis.

Lucky Weidman was mad. He was mad clear through, but he was also worried. Until now his tracks had been well covered, or fairly well covered, with Hartman's help. The disappearance of the girl would set the country on its ears.

He cursed Posner for branding cattle when he should have remained quiet, forgetting that he had told him to go ahead. He cursed Hartman for not keeping the girl in town, cursed Posner for not killing her on the spot, and cursed Stretch Magoon most of all.

Tinny Curtis was going around with a bandage around his neck under his ear, and a bandage on his hand. The wound had been slight, but the missing earlobe was painful in more ways than one. In the West, a man shot through the ear was branded a coward. He was everybody's dog. Curtis realized that he was cursed for life, and was trembling with fury and aching to kill somebody—anybody.

Posner sat on the steps, his face heavy with sullen rage. Lucky had given him a cursing, and he didn't like it.

Kelly Jarvis was inside, a bundle of girl dropped on a dirty bed that smelled of Weidman's huge bulk. Bitterly, she regretted ever knowing Paul Hartman or discharging Magoon.

Out in front, on the hard-packed dirt, the three men stared at each other, hating themselves and everybody else.

There was, of course, just one thing to do. Take the girl up into the mountains, drop her into a deserted mine shaft, and then act innocent. And that wasn't going to be simple.

Into that circle of hell and hatred walked Stretch Magoon.

He had left the grulla in the wash and crept up on foot, knowing the advantage of surprise. He glimpsed the girl on the bed, and she glimpsed him. He had no heroic ideas about slipping in, untying her, and making a break for it. He knew he couldn't get through the window and across the room without making some noise. He had one chance, and he was a man who believed in direct methods.

Stretch Magoon stepped around the corner. "Hello, boys," he said, and went for his gun.

There was no heroism in him. He was a man with a job to do. It was characteristic of the West to give a

man a break, but even men of the West found it conven-
ient to ignore that principle on occasion. And when
one man faces three is not a time to start giving
breaks.

The three of them, seething with hatred as they
were, didn't lag far behind. Magoon's first shot was for
Posner. He didn't want the coyotes yapping at his heels
trying to hamstring him when he went after the old
grizzly.

Red Posner hopped around like the horned toad he
resembled, but his gun never got into action, he took a
bullet through the teeth, and it was immediately apparent that he found the lead indigestible.

Tinny Curtis was sitting down, nursing his jaw and his
hatred. He never got to his feet. The bullet that got
him took him right in the brisket and went right out
through his spine.

Lucky Weidman *was* lucky; he was also careful. He
got his gun out, but Magoon was thin, and his first shot
missed; the second knocked Magoon back into the wall
of the shack, and then Magoon swung his gun onto
Weidman and let one bullet chase another one through
his big stomach. His fifth and last shot, Magoon missed
completely. Then he threw the gun and, with Weidman
firing, went into him swinging wildly. He saw the red
blaze of the gun, felt the heat on his face, and he felt
his fists smashing into that big face. Weidman went
down, and Magoon lit just past him, on his knees, then
he slid forward into the dust.

A half-hour later he was still lying there, more dead
than alive, when Sheriff Ben Rowsey rode in with a
warrant for the arrest of Weidman and Posner. With
him rode Sam Tinker, Chicken Livers, and a scattering
of townspeople, including that unwilling convert to living in towns, County Galway.

When Magoon was able to talk, Rowsey told him,
"Hartman's in jail. You were right about figuring he was

that missin' teller. Weidman an' Posner were the other two."

Kelly was bending over him. He looked at her sadly and she said, "Hurry up and get well. I've put Dean Barker back on the job. I've got some plans for you too, when you get up."

"I reckon," Magoon said woefully, "that I know better than t' argue with a girl who was named for a mule!"

Her face flushed. "Who told you that?" she demanded.

"Your pa," he said. "I rode for him three years steady, after you left!"

There were not as many black cowboys as some recent writers maintain, and in the photos of the old trail drivers they are present but rare. Nonetheless, numbered among them were some of the West's greatest riders.

My favorite, I believe, was Bose Ikard, right-hand man to the great trail driver, Charlie Goodnight. Bose was born a slave in Mississippi in 1847, came west when not yet six years old to a ranch just west of Weatherford, Texas. Perhaps one should not have favorites among people, but in a lot of research I've never heard or found a bad word about Bose. He was a gentleman, an excellent horseman, a good cow-country cook, an excellent night herder, and a good fighting man. Above all, he was responsible and trustworthy. Time and again he carried all of Goodnight's money.

He died in 1929 and is buried in Weatherford. The epitaph Goodnight put on the marker he erected for Bose read:

BOSE IKARD

Served with me four years on the Goodnight-Loving Trail, never shirked a duty or disobeyed an order, rode with me in many stampedes, participated in three engagements with Comanches, splendid behavior.

This is a far greater tribute than the words suggest, for Goodnight was himself among the greatest trail drivers and a man who demanded and got the best men that could be found. He blazed the Goodnight-Loving Trail, ranched the Palo Duro Canyon and opened up some very rough country.

THE GUNS TALK LOUD

He rode into town on a brown mule and swung down from the saddle in front of the Chuck Wagon. He wore a high Mexican hat and a pair of tight Mex pants that flared over his boots. Shorty Duval started to open his mouth to hurrah this stranger when the hombre turned around.

Shorty Duval's mouth snapped shut like a steel trap, and you could almost see the sweat break out on his forehead.

One look was all anybody needed. Shorty was tough, but nobody was buying any trouble from the drifter in the high-crowned hat.

He had a lean brown face and a beak of a nose that had been broken some time or other. There was a scar along his cheekbone that showed white against the leather brown of his face. But it was his eyes that gave you the chills. They were green and brown, but there was something in the way they looked at you that would make a strong man back up and think it over.

175

He was wearing two guns and crossed belts. They were not Peacemakers, but the older Colt, the baby cannon known as the Walker Colt. Too heavy for most men, they would shoot pretty accurate for well over a hundred yards, which wasn't bad for a rifle.

He wore one of them short Mex jackets, too, and when we looked from his queer getup to that brown mule that was all legs we couldn't figure him one little bit.

Not many strangers rode into White Hills. I'd been there all of two months, and I was the last one to come. This hombre showed he knowed the kind of a town he was in when he didn't look too long at anybody. In fact, he didn't even seem to notice us. He just pushed through the doors and bellied up to the bar.

Bill Riding was in there, and some four or five others. Being a right curious hombre, I walked in myself. If this gent did any talkin', I aimed to be where I could listen. I saw Riding look around when I come in. His eyes got mean. From the first day I hit town, we'd no use for each other.

Partly it was because of Jackie Belton's cur dog. Belton was a kid of fourteen who lived with his sister, Ruth, on a nice cattle spread six or seven miles out of White Hills. That dog ran across in front of Riding one day and come durned near trippin' him. He was a hot-tempered hombre, and when he drawed iron, I did, too.

Before he could shoot, I said, and I was standin' behind him, "You kill that dog, Riding, and I'll kill you!"

His face got red, and then white. His back was half toward me, and he knowed he didn't have a chance. "Someday," he said, his voice ugly, "you'll butt in at the wrong time!"

Jackie saw me, and so did his sister, and after the way they thanked me, I figgered it would have been cheap even if I'd had to kill Riding.

White Hills was an outlaw town. Most of the men in town were wanted somewheres, and while it wasn't doin' any deputy much good to come in here, the town was restless now. That was because the bank over to Pierce had been stuck up and ever'body in White Hills figgered the rangers would come here lookin' for him. That was why they'd looked so suspicious when I rode into town.

It didn't take no fortune-teller to guess that Harvey Kinsella had put Bill Riding to watchin' me. Kinsella was the boss o' that town, and he knowed everythin' that went on around.

Riding wasn't the only one had an eye on me, I knowed that. Kinsella had posted two or three other hombres for the same reason. Still, I stuck around. And part of the reason I stayed was Ruthie Belton.

The hombre with the high-crowned sombrero leaned against the bar and let those slow green eyes of his take in the place. They settled on Riding, swung past Shorty Duval, and finally settled on me.

They stayed there the longest, and I wasn't surprised none. We were the two biggest men in the place, me and him. Maybe I was a mite the bigger, but that hat made him look just as tall. His eyes didn't show what he was thinkin', but knowin' how a man on the dodge feels, I knowed what it was.

He had me sized up like I had him. Me, I growed up under the Tonto Rim, and when I wanted to ride the cattle trails, I had to ride east to git to 'em. I'd punched cows and dealt monte in Sonora, and I ain't braggin' none when I say that when I rode through New Mexico and hung around Lincoln and Fort Sumner and Sante Fe, not Billy the Kid nor Jesse Evans wanted any part of what I had to give. Not that I wanted them, either.

There wasn't no high Mex hat on me. Mine was flat crowned and flat brimmed, but my guns was tied down, and had been for more than a little while. My boots was some down at the heel, and I needed a shave, but no man in that place had the power in his shoulders I had, and no man there but me could bust a leather belt with his chest expansion.

He didn't need no second sight to tell him I was ridin' a lone trail, either. They never cut my hide to fit no Kinsella frame. Anyway, he looked at me, and then he says, "I'll buy you a drink!" An' the way he laid that "you" in there was like layin' a whip across the face of ever' other man in the saloon.

Bill Riding jerked like he'd been bee-stung, but Kinsella wasn't there, and Bill sat tight.

Me, I walks over to the bar and bellies up to it. *Amigo*, it done me good to look in that long mirror and see the two of us standin' there. Y' can ride for miles and never find two such big men together. Maybe I was a mite thicker'n him through the chest, but he was big, *amigo*, and he was mean.

"They call me Sonora," he said, lookin' at the rye in his glass.

"Me, I'm Dan Ketrel," I said, but I was thinkin' of what the descriptions of the bandit who robbed the bank at Pierce said. A big man, the descriptions said, a very big man, wearin' two guns.

Sonora was a big man, and he wore two guns. For that matter, I did, too. There was even another big man in town who wore two guns. The boss, it was, Harvey Kinsella.

We looked at each other right then, and neither of us was fooled a mite. He knowed what I was here for, and I knowed what he was here for, and neither of us was in friendly country.

Bill Riding didn't like me bein' here. It was chokin' up in him like a thunderstorm chokin' up a canyon with cloud. It was gittin' in his throat, the meanness of him, and I could see trouble was headin' our way.

For that matter, I'd knowed it was comin', soon or late. I knowed it was comin' because I knowed I was goin' to butt into somethin' that wasn't rightly my business. It had been buildin' for days, ever since I got the lay of the land, hereabouts.

I was goin' to tear down the fence that kept Ruth Belton's cows from grazin' in Reefer Canyon, where the good grass was.

You'd think, maybe, that tearin' down one fence wouldn't do no good. You'd think maybe they'd put it right up again. You'd be wrong.

If'n I tore down that fence once, it was goin' to stay down, because after I tore it down, I'd have to kill Harvey Kinsella and Bill Riding.

They was the ones out to break Ruthie Belton. When her old man was alive, they left him strictly alone. He was old, but he was a ring-tailed wolf on the prowl, and they knowed it. Then he got throwed from a bad hoss, and they started to move in on the Bar B.

It wasn't none of my business. Me, I was up here for a purpose, and rightly I shouldn't think of anythin' else, but sometimes a man stumbles into a place where, if he's a man, he's got to show it. And me, I was a fixin' to tear down that fence.

It would mean shootin', and Kinsella was poison mean, and Riding damn' near as bad. That was sayin' nothin' o' the rest of that outfit. But I had me a plan now, and that plan was buildin' around a certain tall hombre in a high-crowned hat, a man that rode a brown-legged mule and packed two Walker Colts.

Bill Riding got up and walked over to the bar. He was spoilin' for trouble. As big a man as Kinsella in weight, he was a mite shorter than either of us, but nearly as broad as me. A big-handed man, and a dirty fighter in a rough and tumble.

"Stranger," he says, starin' at Sonora, "y' seem kind of limitin' in your offer of a drink. Maybe y' think you're too durned good to drink with us!"

Sonora had his elbows on the bar right then, and he didn't straighten; he just turned his head and let those cold eyes take in Riding, head to foot; then he looked back at his drink.

Riding's face flamed up, and I saw his lips tighten. His hand shot out, and he grabbed Sonora by the shoulder. Bill just had to be top dog, he just had to have ever'body believin' he was a bad hombre, but he done the wrong thing when he laid a hand on Sonora.

The man in the high-crowned hat back-handed his fist into Bill's unprotected midsection. It caught Bill unsuspectin', and he staggered, gaspin' for breath. Then Sonora turned and slugged him. Bill went back into a table, upset it, and then he crawled out of the poker chips with a grunt and started for Sonora.

Just then Harvey Kinsella stepped into the room, and me, I slid back two quick steps and palmed a six-gun. "Hold it!" I said, hardlike. "Anybody butts into this scrap gets a bellyful of lead!"

Kinsella looked at me then, the first time he ever seemed to see me. "If you didn't have that gun out," he said, "I'd kill you!"

Me, I laughed. If'n it hadn't been for Sonora, who was goin' to town on Riding, I'd have called him.

Bein' around like I have, I've seen some men take a whippin', but I never saw any man get a more artistic shellackin' than Sonora give Bill Riding. He started in on him, and he used both hands. He cut him like you'd chop beef. He sliced his face like he had a knife edge across his knuckles.

Me, Dan Ketrel, I slug 'em, and Pap always said I had the biggest fists he ever seen on a man, but Sonora, he went to work like a doc. He raised bumps all over Riding and then lanced ever' one o' them with his knuckles. Riding wanted to drop, but Sonora wouldn't let him fall. He just kept him on his feet until he got so bloody, even I couldn't take it. Then Sonora hooked one, high and hard, and Bill Riding went down into the sawdust.

Sonora looked over at me, standin' with a gun in my

fist. "Thanks," he said, grinnin' a little. We understood each other, him and me.

Harvey Kinsella looked at Riding lying on the floor; then he looked from Sonora to me. "I'll give you until sundown," he said. Then he turned to go.

"I like it here," I said.

"I've told you," he replied.

Sonora and me walked outside. Me, I figgered it was time to talk. "There's been talk," I said, "of a ranger comin' in here after that hombre what done that Pierce bank job. Don't let it worry you none. Not for right now.

"Down the road a piece there's a girl, name of Ruth Belton. Her old man was a he-wolf. He's dead. This here Kinsella, he's tryin' to run her off her range. Scared to tackle it when the old man was alive. He's done put up a fence to keep her cows from the good grass. I aim to cut that fence."

He stood there, his big thumbs in his belt, listenin'. Me, I finished rollin' my smoke. "When I cut that fence, there's goin' to be some shootin', but I aim to cut it and aim to kill Harvey Kinsella. He's got word out that ary a hand on that fence and his guns talk loud.

"I aim to cut it. I aim to kill him so's he won't never put it up again. But he's got a sight of boys ridin' for him. One or two, I might git, but I don't want nothin' botherin' me when I go after Kinsella."

"Where's the fence?" he asked quietly.

"Down the road a piece." I struck a match on my pants. "I reckon if'n we was to ride that way, Ruthie would fix us a bait o' grub. She's quite some shakes with a skillet."

Me, I walked out and swung onto the hurricane deck of that big blue horse o' mine. Sonora lit his own shuck and then boarded his mule. He went down the street and took the trail for Ruthie Belton's place.

Neither of us said no words all the way until we got

up to Ruthie's place and could see the flowers around her door, and Ruthie waterin' 'em down.

"I reckon," Sonora said then, "that ranger could hold off doin' what he has to do till a job like this was over. Don't reckon he'd wait much longer, though, would he?"

"Don't reckon so," I said grimly. "A man's got his duty. Still," I added, "maybe this ranger never seen the hombre he's lookin' for. Maybe he ain't sure when he does see him, so maybe he rides back without him?"

"Wouldn't do no good," Sonora objected. "Too many others lookin', and he'd be follered wherever he'd go."

Ruth looked up when she heard our horses and then turned to face us, smiling. She looked up at me, and when I looked down into those blue eyes, I figgered what a fool a man was to go lookin' into guns when there was eyes, soft like that.

"You're the man," she declared, "who protected Shep!"

Me, I got red around the gills. I ain't used to palaverin' with no womenfolk. "I reckon," I said.

"Won't you get down and come in? We were just about to eat."

We got down, and Sonora sweeps off that high-crowned hat and smiles. "I've heard some powerful nice things about the food you cook, ma'am," he said, "and thank you for a chance to try it."

We went inside, and pretty soon Jack come in. He smiled, but I could see he was plumb worried. It didn't take no mind reader to figger why. Those cows we'd seen was lookin' mighty poor. It wouldn't take much time for them to start dyin' off, eatin' only the skimpy dry, brown grass.

When she had the food on the table, Ruthie looked at me, and I could feel my thick neck gettin' red again. "You boys just riding, or are you going some particular place?"

Sonora looked over a forkful of fried spuds. "Dan here, he figgered there was a fence up here needed cuttin', and he 'lows as how he'll cut it. I'm just sort of ridin' along, in case."

Her face whitened. "Oh no! You mustn't! Harvey Kinsella will kill anybody who touches that fence—he warned us!"

"Uh-huh." I picked up my coffee cup. "We ain't got much time here, ma'am. I got a little job to do, and I reckon Sonora has, too. We sort of figgered we'd take care o' this and Kinsella, too. Then when we rode off up the trail, you'd be all right."

When we finished, I tipped back in my chair. It was right homey feelin', the sort of feelin' I ain't had since I was a kid, me bein' a roamin' man and all. I got up after a bit and saw Sonora look at me. That mule-ridin' man never had a hand far from a gun when we were together. For that matter, neither did I.

It wasn't that we didn't trust each other. We both had a job to do, him and me, but we were the cautious type.

I walked over and picked up the water bucket, then went to the spring and filled it. When I come back, I split a couple of armsful of wood and packed it inside. Sonora, he sat there on the porch, sleepylike, just a-watchin' me.

The door had a loose hinge, and I got me a hammer and fixed it, sort of like I used to when I was a kid, and like my pa used to do. It gives a man a sort of homey feelin', to be fixin' around. Once I looked up and saw Ruthie lookin' at me, a sort of funny look in her eyes.

Then I picked up my hat. "Reckon," I said, "we better be ridin' up to that fence. It's 'most two miles from here."

Ruthie, she come to the door, her eyes wide and her face pale. "Stop by," she said, "on your way back. I'll be takin' a cake out of the oven."

"Sure thing," Sonora said, grinning. "I always did like fresh cake."

That was a real woman. Not tellin' y' to be careful, not tellin' us we shouldn't. That was her, standin' there shadin' her eyes again' the sun as we rode off up the trail, me loungin' sideways in the saddle, a six-gun under my hand.

"You'd make a family man," Sonora said half a mile farther along. "Y' sure would. Ought to have a little spread o' your own."

That made me look up, it cut so close to the trail o' my own thoughts. "That's what I always figgered on," I told him. "Me, I'm through ridin' rough country."

We rode on quietlike. Both of us knowed what was comin'. If'n we came out of this with a whole skin, there was still the main show. I should say, the big showdown. We both knowed it, and neither of us liked it.

In those few hours we'd come to find we was the same kind of hombre, the same kind of man, and we fought the same way. We were two big men, and when we rode that last mile up there to the fence, I was thinkin' that here, at last, was a man to ride through hell with. And then I had to do to him what I had to do because it was the job I had.

The fence was there, tight and strong. "Give me some cover," I suggested to Sonora. "I'm goin' to ride up and cut her—but good!"

The air was clear, and my voice carried, and then I saw Bill Riding step down from the junipers, a rifle holdin' easy in his hands. His voice rang loud in the draw. "Y' ain't cuttin' nothin', neither of you!"

Me, I sat there with my hands down. My rifle was in my saddle boot, and he was out of six-gun range. I could see the slow smile on his face as that rifle came up.

That moro o' mine never lost a rider no quicker in his life. I went off, feet first, and hit the ground gun in hand. I'd no more than hit it before somethin' bellowed like a young cannon, and out of the tail o' my eye I saw Sonora had unlimbered those big Walker Colts.

My six-shooter was out, but I wasn't lookin' at Riding. He was beyond my reach, but there was a movement in the junipers close down, on our side of the fence, and I turned and saw Harvey Kinsella there behind us. He had a smile on his face, and I could almost see his lips tighten as he squeezed off his first shot.

When I started burnin' powder I don't know. Somethin' hit Kinsella, and he went back on his heels, his face lookin' sick, and then I started walkin' in on him. It helped me keep my mind on business to walk into a man while I was shootin'.

Somebody blazed at me from the brush, and when I tried a snapshot that way, I heard a whinin' cry and a rifle rattled on the rocks. But I was walkin' right at Kinsella, and his guns were goin'. I could see flame stabbin' at me from their muzzles, but when I figgered I had four shots left, I kept walkin' in and holdin' my fire.

Behind me them Walkers was blastin' like a couple of cannon from the war atween the states. I wasn't worried about Sonora takin' out on me. He was an hombre to ride the river with. Besides, we each had us a job to do.

Then Kinsella was down on his face, the back o' his fancy coat stainin' red. Two other hombres were down, too, and I could hear the rattle of racin' hoofs as some others took off through the brush.

Then I turned, thumbin' shells into my guns, and Sonora was there, leanin' on a fence post, one o' those big guns danglin' from his fist.

Me, I walked over to the fence, haulin' the wire cutters from my belt, the pair I picked up at the girl's ranch. My head was drummin' somethin' awful, like maybe there was still more shootin'. But it wasn't that—it was deathly still. Y' couldn't hear a sound but the loud click o' my cutters.

When I finished, I turned toward Sonora. He was slumped over the fence then, and there was blood comin' from somewhere high up on his chest. I took the gun out of his fingers and stuck it in his holster. Then I hoisted him on my shoulder and started for his mule.

That mule wasn't noways skittish. I got Sonora aboard and then crawled up on the moro. When I was in the saddle again, I looked around.

Riding was dead, anybody could see that. He'd been hit more than once, and half his head was blowed off. There was another hombre close beside him, and he was dead, too.

As for Kinsella, I didn't have to look at him. I knowed when I was shootin' that I was killin' him, but I walked over to him.

Three times on my way back to Ruthie's I had to stop and straighten Sonora in the saddle, even with his wrists tied to the horn.

Before I got through the gate, Ruthie was runnin' down toward us, and Jack, too. Then I must've passed out.

When my eyes cracked to light again, it was lamplight, and the room wasn't very bright. Ruthie was sittin' by my bed, sewin'.

"Sonora?" I asked.

"He'll be all right. He'd been shot twice. You men! You're both so *big*! I don't see how any bullet could ever kill you!"

Me, I was thinkin' it might not take a bullet, but a rope.

Kinsella got me once, low down on the side. Just a flesh wound, but from what Jack told me, it must've bled like all get-out.

When it was later, Ruthie got up and put her sewin' away; then she went into another room and to sleep. I give her an hour, as close as I could figger. Then I rolled back the blanket and got my feet under me. I was some weak, but it takes a lot of lead to ballast down an hombre big as me.

Softly, I opened the door. Ruthie was lyin' on a pallet, asleep. Me, I blushes, seein' her that way, her hair all over the pillow like a lot of golden web caught in the moonlight.

Easy as could be, I slipped by. Sonora's door was open, and he was lyin' in Jack's bed, a chair under his feet to make it long enough.

Well, there he was, the hombre that meant my ranch to me. I'd strapped on my guns, but as I stood there lookin' down, I figgered it was a wonder he hadn't shot it out already. That reward was dead or alive.

Suddenly, I almost jumped out of my skin. Only one o' them big Walker Colts was in its holster! Why, that durned coyote! Lyin' there with a gun under the blanket, and the chances was he was awake that minute.

Hell! I'd go back to bed! It never did a man no good to run from the law, not even in the wild country! Soon or late, she always caught up with him.

In the mornin', I'd just finished splashin' water on my face when I looked up and he was leanin' again' the door post. "Howdy," he said, grinnin'. "Sleep well?"

My face burned. "Well as you did, y' durned possum-playin' maverick!"

He grinned. "Man in my place can't be too careful." He looked at me. "Ready to ride, or is it a showdown?"

Sonora had his guns on, and there was a quizzical light in those funny eyes o' his'n.

He was a big man, big as me, and the only man I ever saw I'd ride with. "Hell," I said, "ain't y' goin' to eat breaf'st? I'll ride with you because you're too good a man to kill!"

Ruthie was puttin' food on the table, and she looked at us queerly. "What's between you two?" she asked quicklike.

"Why, Ruthie," I said, "this here hombre's a Texas

ranger. He figgers I'm the hombre what robbed that bank over to Pierce!"

She stared at me. "Then—you're a prisoner?"

"Ma'am," Sonora said, gulpin' a big swaller o' hot coffee, "don't you fret none. I reckon he ain't no crook. Just had a minute or two o' bein' a durned fool! I reckon that bank's plumb anxious to git their money back, and I know this hombre's got it on him because last night"—he grinned—"when he was asleep, I had me a look at his money belt!"

Before I could bust out and say anythin', he adds, "I figger that bank's goin' to be so durned anxious to git their money back, they won't fret too much when I suggest this hombre be sent back here, sort of on good behavior. I'd say he'd make a good hand around a layout like this."

Then I bust in. "Y' got this all wrong, Sonora," I told him. "Y' been trailin' the wrong man! Rather, y' trailed the right man, and then when y' walked into the Chuck Wagon, y' took too much for granted.

"I didn't rob no bank. I'll admit I got to thinkin' about ownin' a ranch, and I rode into town with the money in mind. Then I heard the shootin' and lit out. The man who robbed the bank," I said, "was Harvey Kinsella. I took the money belt off him. His name's marked on it!"

He stared at me. "Well, I'll be durned!" he said.

Ruthie was lookin' at me, her eyes all bright and happy. "Man," I was sayin', "I figgered you fer the bandit, first off. I was figgerin' on gittin' you fer the reward, needin' that money like I was fer a ranch."

"An' I was tryin' to decide if I should take y' in or let y' go!" Sonora shook his head.

Ruthie smiled at me and then at him. "I'm going to try and fix it, Sonora," she said, "so he'll stay here. I think he'd be a good man around a ranch—some place where he could take a personal interest in things!"

There was a tint o' color in her skin.

"Just what I think, ma'am," Sonora shoved back his

chair. I got up and handed him the money belt. "And Ruthie," he continued, "if I was to ride by, y' reckon it'd be all right to stop in?"

She smiled as she filled my cup. "Of course, Sonora, and we'll be mighty glad to see you!"

Author's Note:
DEADWOOD DICK

Among black riders famous for their skills were Matthew (Bones) Hooks, Nigger Add, Bronco Sam Stewart, and, of course, in later days, Bill Pickett, who invented bulldogging.

There has been much talk about Deadwood Dick, but there was no such person. He was a creation of a writer of dime novels, Edward L. Wheeler, who wrote for Beadle & Adams. Many men claimed to be the original Deadwood Dick, and Richard Clarke, of Deadwood, South Dakota, was selected by the city fathers to play the part. Bert Bell, a publicity man prepared the stories and found the outfit of clothes Clarke was to wear. He was sent east to invite Calvin Coolidge, then president, to Deadwood. Clarke succeeded so well that he never gave up the role of Deadwood Dick.

In 1927, when Clarke was selected to play the part, there were few horses on the streets of Deadwood and a great many cars. There is no evidence that Richard Clarke ever fired a rifle or pistol in his life, but suddenly, through Bell's efforts, he became a celebrity. There were free drinks, free meals, and a much better life than he'd known, and Clarke was wise enough to accept what the gods—and Bert Bell—had given. He played Deadwood Dick until his death.

CUB LINE RIDE

GRUB LINE RIDER

There was good grass in these high meadows, Kim Sartain reflected, and it was a wonder they were not in use. Down below in the flatland the cattle looked scrawny and half-starved. He had come up a narrow, little-used trail from the level country and was heading across the divide when he ran into the series of green, tree-bordered meadows scattered among the ridges.

Wind rippled the grass in long waves across the meadow, and the sun lay upon it like a caress. Across the meadow and among the trees he heard a vague sound of falling water, and turned the zebra dun toward it. As he did so, three horsemen rode out of the trees, drawing up sharply when they saw him.

He rode on, walking the dun, and the three wheeled their mounts and came toward him at a canter. A tall man rode a gray horse in the van. The other two were obviously cowhands, and all wore guns. The tall man had a lean, hard face with a knife scar across the cheek. "You there!" he roared, reining in. "What you doin' ridin' here?"

Kim Sartain drew up, his lithe, trail-hardened body easy in the saddle. "Why, I'm ridin' through," he said quietly, "and in no particular hurry. You got this country fenced against travel?"

"Well, it ain't no trail!" The big man's eyes were gray and hostile. "You just turn around and ride back the way you come! The trail goes around through Ryerson."

"That's twenty miles out of my way," Kim objected, "and this here's a nice ride. I reckon I'll keep on the way I'm goin'."

The man's eyes hardened. "Did Monaghan put you up to this?" he demanded. "Well, if he did, it's time he was taught a lesson! We'll send you back to him fixed up proper! *Take him, boys!*"

The men started, then froze. The six-shooter in Kim's hand wasn't a hallucination. "Come on," Kim invited mildly. "Take me!"

The men swallowed, and stood still. The tall man's face grew red with fury. "So? A gunslinger, is it? Two can play at that game! I'll have Clay Tanner out here before the day is over!"

Kim Sartain felt his pulse jump. Clay Tanner? Why, the man was an outlaw, a vicious killer, wanted in a dozen places! "Listen, Big Eye," he said harshly, "I don't know you and I never heard of Monaghan, but if he dislikes you, that's one credit for him. Anybody who would hire or have anything to do with the likes of Clay Tanner is a coyote!"

The man's face purpled and his eyes turned mean. "I'll tell Clay that!" he blustered. "He'll be mighty glad to hear it! That will be all he needs to come after you!"

Sartain calmly returned his gun to its holster, keeping his eyes on the men before him without hiding his contempt. "If you hombres feel lucky," he said, "try and drag iron. I'd as soon blast you out of your saddles as not.

"As for you"—Kim's eyes turned on the tall man—
"you'd best learn now as later how to treat strangers.
This country ain't fenced, and from the look of it, ain't
used. You've no right to keep anybody out of here, and
when I want to ride through, I'll ride through! Get
me?"

One of the hands broke in, his voice edged. "Stranger,
after talkin' that way to Jim Targ, you'd better light a
shuck out of this country! He *runs* it!"

Kim shoved his hat back on his head and looked from
the cowhand to his boss. He was a quiet-mannered
young drifter who liked few things better than a fight.
Never deliberately picking trouble, he nevertheless
had a reckless liking for it and never sidestepped any
that came his way.

"He don't run me," he commented cheerfully, "and
personally, I think he's a mighty small pebble in a mighty
big box! He rattles a lot, but for a man who runs this
country, he fits mighty loose!"

Taking out his tobacco, he calmly began to roll a
smoke, his half smile daring the men to draw. "Just
what," he asked, "gave you the idea you did run this
country? And just who is this Monaghan?"

Targ's eyes narrowed. "You know durned well who
he is!" he declared angrily. "He's nothin' but a two-by-
twice would-be cattleman who's hornin' in on my range!"

"Such as this?" Kim waved a hand around him. "I'd
say there ain't been a critter on this in months! What are
you tryin' to do? Claim all the grass in the country?"

"It's my grass!" Targ declared belligerently. "Mine!
Just because I ain't built a trail into it yet is no reason
why . . ."

"So that's it!" Sartain studied them thoughtfully. "All
right, Targ, you an' your boys turn around and head
right out of here. I think I'll homestead this piece!"

"You'll *what*?" Targ bellowed. Then he cursed bitterly.

"Careful, Beetle Puss!" Kim warned, grinning. "Don't
make me pull your ears!"

With another foul name, Targ's hand flashed for his gun, but no more had his fist grabbed the butt than he was looking into the muzzle of Kim's six-shooter.

"I'm not *anxious* to kill you, Targ, so don't force it on me," he said quietly. The cattleman's face was gray, realizing his narrow escape. Slowly, yet reluctantly, his hand left his gun.

"This ain't over!" Targ declared harshly. "You ride out of here, or we'll ride you out!"

As the three drifted away, Kim watched them go, then shrugged. "What the devil, Pard," he said to the dun, "we weren't really goin' no place particular. Let's have a look around and then go see this Monaghan."

While the sun was hiding its face behind the western pines, Kim Sartain cantered the dun down into the cuplike valley that held the ranch buildings of the Y7. They were solidly built buildings, and everything looked sharp and clean. It was no rawhide outfit, this one of Tom Monaghan's. And there was nothing rawhide about the slim, attractive girl with red hair who came out of the ranchhouse and shaded her eyes at him.

He drew rein and shoved his hat back. "Ma'am," he said, "I rode in here huntin' Tom Monaghan, but I reckon I was huntin' the wrong person. You'd likely be the boss of any spread you're on. I always notice," he added, "that redheaded women are apt to be bossy!"

"And I notice," she said sharply, "that drifting, no-good cowhands are apt to be smart! Too smart! Before you ask any questions, we don't need any hands! Not even top hands, if you call yourself that!

"If you're ridin' the grub line, just sit around until you hear grub call, then light in. We'd feed anybody, stray dogs or no-account saddle bums not barred!"

Kim grinned at her. "All right, Rusty. I'll stick around for chuck. Meanwhile, we'd better round up Tom Monaghan, because I want to make him a little deal on some cattle."

"You? Buy cattle?" Her voice was scornful. "You're

just a big-talking drifter!" Her eyes flashed at him, but he noticed there was lively curiosity in her blue eyes.

"Goin' to need some cows," he said, curling a leg around the saddle horn. "Aim to homestead up there in the high meadows."

The girl had started to turn away, now she stopped and her eyes went wide. "You aim to *what*?"

Neither had noticed the man with iron-gray hair who had stopped at the corner of the house. His eyes were riveted on Sartain. "Yes," he said. "Repeat that again, will you? You plan to homestead up in the mountains?"

"Uh-huh, I sure do." Kim Sartain looked over at Tom Monaghan and liked what he saw. "I've got just sixty dollars in money, a good horse, a rope, and a will. I aim to get three hundred head of cows from you and a couple of horses, two pack mules, and some grub."

Rusty opened her mouth to explode, but Tom held up his hand. "And just how, young man, do you propose to pay for all that with sixty dollars?"

Kim smiled. "Why, Mr. Monaghan, I figure I can fatten my stock right fast on that upland grass, sell off enough to pay interest and a down payment on the principal. Next year I could do better. Of course," he added, "six hundred head of stock would let me make out faster, and that grass up there would handle them, plumb easy. Better, too," he added, "if I had somebody to cook for me, and mend my socks. How's about it, Rusty?"

"Why, you insufferable, egotistical upstart!"

"From what you say, I'd guess you've been up there in the meadows," Monaghan said thoughtfully, "but did you see anyone there?"

"Uh-huh. Three hombres was wastin' around. One of them had a scar on his face. I think they called him Jim Targ."

* * *

Sartain was enjoying himself now. He had seen the girl's eyes widen at the mention of the men, and especially of Jim Targ. He kept his dark face inscrutable.

"They didn't say anything to you?" Monaghan was unbelieving. "Nothing at all?"

"Oh, yeah! This here Targ, he seemed right put out at my ridin' through the country. Ordered me to go around by Ryerson. Right about then I started lookin' that grass over, and sort of made up my mind to stay. He seemed to think you'd sent me up there."

"Did you tell him you planned to homestead?"

"Oh, sure! He didn't seem to cotton to the idea very much. Mentioned some hombre named Clay Tanner who would run me off."

"Tanner is a dangerous killer," Monaghan told him grimly.

"Oh, he is? Well, now! *Tsk, tsk, tsk!* This Targ's sort of cuttin' a wide swath, ain't he?"

The boardinghouse triangle opened up suddenly with a deafening clangor, and Kim Sartain, suddenly aware that he had not eaten since breakfast, and little of that, slid off his horse. Without waiting for further comment, he led the dun toward the corral and began stripping the saddle.

"Dad," Rusty moved toward her father, "is he crazy or are we? Do you suppose he really saw Targ?"

Tom Monaghan stared at Sartain thoughtfully, noting the two low-slung guns, the careless, easy swing of Kim's stride. "Rusty, I don't think he's crazy, I think maybe Targ is. I'm going to let him have the cows!"

"Father!" She was aghast. "You wouldn't! Not three hundred!"

"Six hundred," he corrected. "Six hundred can be made to pay. And I think it will be worth it to see what happens. I've an idea more happened up there today than we have heard. I think that somebody tried to walk on this man's toes, and he probably happens to have corns on every one of them!"

When their meal was finished, Monaghan looked over at Kim, who had had little to say during the supper. "How soon would you want that six hundred head?" He paused. "Next week?"

The four cowhands looked up, startled, but Kim failed to turn a hair. "Tomorrow at daylight," Kim said coolly. "I want the nearest cattle you have to the home ranch and the help of your boys. I'm goin' to push cattle on that grass before noon!"

Tom Monaghan's eyes twinkled. "You're sudden, young fellow, plumb sudden. You know Targ's riders will be up there, don't you? He won't take this."

"Targ's riders," Sartain said quietly, "will get there about noon or after. I aim to be there first. Incidentally," he said, "I'll want some tools to throw together a cabin—a good strong one. I plan to build just west of the water," he added.

He turned suddenly toward Rusty, who had also been very quiet. As if she knew he intended speaking to her, she looked up. Her boy's shirt was open at the neck, and he could see the swell of her bosom under the rough material.

"Thought about that cookin' job yet?" he asked. "I sure am fed up on my own cookin'. Why, I'd even marry a cook to get her up there!"

A round-faced cowhand choked suddenly on a big mouthful of food and had to leave the table. The others were grinning at their plates. Rusty Monaghan's face went pale, then crimson. "Are you," she said coolly, "offering me a job, or proposing?"

"Let's make it a job first," Kim said gravely. "I ain't had none of your cookin' yet! If you pass the exams, then we can get down to more serious matters."

Rusty's face was white to the lips. "If you think I'd cook for or marry such a pigheaded windbag as you are, you're wrong! What makes you think I'd marry any broken down, drifting saddle tramp that comes in here? Who do you think you are, anyway?"

Kim got up. "The name, ma'am, is Kim Sartain. As to who I am, I'm the hombre you're goin' to cook for. I'll be leavin' early tomorrow, but I'll drop back the next day, so you fix me an apple pie. I like lots of fruit, real thick pie, and plenty of juice."

Coolly, he strolled outside and walked toward the corral, whistling. Tom Monaghan looked at his daughter, smiling, and the hands finished their supper quickly and hurried outside.

It was daybreak, with the air still crisp when Rusty opened her eyes suddenly to hear the lowing of cattle, and the shrill Texas yells of the hands, driving cattle. Hurriedly, she dressed and stopped on the porch to see the drive lining out for the mountains. Far ahead, her eyes could just pick out a lone horseman, headed toward Gunsight Pass and the mountain meadows.

Her father came in an hour later, his face serious. He glanced at her quickly. "That boy's got nerve!" he said. "Furthermore, he's a hand!"

"But Dad," she protested, "they'll kill him! He's just a boy, and that Tanner is vicious! I've heard about him!"

Monaghan nodded. "I know, but Baldy tells me this Sartain was *segundo* for Ward McQueen, of the Tumbling K when they had that run-in with rustlers a few months back. According to Baldy, Sartain is hell on wheels with a gun!"

She was worried despite herself. "Dad, what do you think?"

He smiled. "Why, honey, if that man is all I think he is, Targ had better light a shuck for Texas, and as for you, you'd better start bakin' that apple pie!"

"Father!" Rusty protested. But her eyes widened a

little, and she stepped farther onto the porch, staring after the distant rider.

Kim Sartain was a rider without illusions. Born and bred in the West, he knew to what extent such a man as Jim Targ could and would go. He knew that with tough, gun-handy riders, he would ordinarily be able to hold all the range he wanted, and that high meadow range was good enough to fight for.

Sartain knew he was asking for trouble, yet there was something in him that resented being pushed around. He had breathed the free air of a free country too long and had the average American's fierce resentment of tyranny. Targ's high-handed manner had got his back up, and his decision had not been a passing fancy. He knew just what he was doing, but no matter what the future held, he was determined to move in on this range and to hold it and fight for it if need be.

There was no time to waste. Targ might take him lightly, and think his declaration had been merely the loud talk of a disgruntled cowhand, but on the other side, the rancher might take him seriously and come riding for trouble. The cattle could come in their own good time, but he intended to be on the ground, and quickly.

The dun was feeling good and Kim let him stretch out in a fast canter. It was no time at all until he was riding up to the pool by the waterfall. He gave a sigh of relief, for he was the first man on the ground.

He jumped down, took a hasty drink, and let the dun drink. Meanwhile he picked the bench for his cabin and put down the ax he had brought with him. Baldy had told him there was a saddle trail that came up the opposite side of the mountain and skirted among the cliffs to end near this pool. Leaving the horse, Kim walked toward it.

Yet before he had gone more than three steps, he heard a quick step behind him. He started to turn, but a slashing blow with a six-gun barrel clipped him on the skull. He staggered and started to fall, glimpsed the hazy outlines of his attacker, and struck out. The blow landed solidly, and then something clipped him again and he fell over into the grass. The earth crumbled beneath him, and he tumbled, over and over, hitting a thick clump of greasewood growing out of the cliff, then hanging up in some manzanita.

The sound of crashing in the brush below him was the first thing he remembered. He was aware that he must have had his eyes open and been half-conscious for some time. His head throbbed abominably, and when he tried to move his leg, it seemed stiff and clumsy. He lay still, recalling what had happened.

He remembered the blows he had taken, and then falling. Below him he heard more thrashing in the brush. Then a voice called, "Must have crawled off, Tanner. He's not down here!"

Somebody swore, and aware of his predicament Kim held himself rigid, waiting for them to go away. Obviously, he was suspended in the clump of manzanita somewhere on the side of the cliff. Above him, he heard the lowing of cattle. The herd had arrived then. What of the boys with it?

It was a long time before the searchers finally went away and he could move. When he could, he got a firm grip on the root of the manzanita and then turned himself easily. His leg was bloody, but seemed unbroken. It was tangled in the brush, however, and his pants were torn. Carefully, he felt for his guns. One of them remained in its holster. The other was gone.

Working with infinite care and as quietly as possible, he lowered himself down the steep face of the rocky bluff, using brush and projections until finally he was standing upright on the ground below. A few minutes search beneath where he had hung in the brush disclosed his other pistol, hanging in the top of a mountain mahogany.

Checking his guns, he limped slowly down into the brush. Here weakness suddenly overcame him, and he slumped to a sitting position. He had hurt his leg badly, and his head was swimming.

He squinted his eyes, squeezing them shut and opening them, trying to clear his brain. The hammering in his skull continued, and he sat very still, his head bulging with pain, his eyes watching a tiny lizard darting among the stones. How long he sat there he did not know, but when he got started moving again, he noticed that the sun was well past the zenith.

Obviously, he had been unconscious for some time in the brush, and had lost more time now. Limping, but moving carefully, he wormed his way along the gully into which he had fallen and slowly managed to mount the steep, tree-covered face of the bluff beyond where he had fallen.

Then, lowering himself to the ground he rested for a few minutes, then dragged himself on. He needed water, and badly. Most of all, he had to know what had happened. Apparently, Targ was still in command of the situation. The herd had come through, but Monaghan's riders must have been driven off. Undoubtedly, Targ had the most men. Bitterly, he thought of his boasts to Rusty and what they had amounted to. He had walked into a trap like any child.

It took him almost an hour of moving and resting to get near the falls. Watching his chance, he slid down to the water and got a drink, and then, crouching in the brush, he examined his leg. As he had suspected, no bones were broken, but the flesh was badly lacerated from falling into the branches, and he must have lost a good deal of blood. Carefully, he bathed the wound in the cold water from the pool, then bound it up as well as he could by tearing his shirt and using his handkerchief.

When he had finished, he crawled into the brush and lay there like a wounded animal, his eyes closed, his body heavy with the pulsing of pain in his leg and the dull ache in his skull.

Somehow, he slept, and when he awakened, he smelled smoke. Lifting his head, he stared around into the darkness. Night had fallen, and there was a heavy bank of clouds overhead, but beyond the pool was the brightness of a fire. Squinting his eyes, he could see several moving figures, and no one sitting down. The pool at this point was no more than twenty feet across, and he could hear their voices clearly and distinctly.

"Might as well clean 'em up now, Targ," somebody was saying in a heavy voice. "He pushed these cattle in here, an' it looks like he was trying to make an issue of it. Let's go down there tonight."

"Not tonight, Tanner." Targ's voice was slower, lighter. "I want to be sure. When we hit them, we've got to wipe them out, leave nobody to make any complaint or push the case. It will be simple enough for us to tell our story and make it stick if they don't have anybody on their side."

"Who rightly owns this range?" Tanner asked.

Targ shrugged. "Anybody who can hold it. Monaghan wanted it, and I told everybody to lay off. Told them how much I wanted it and what would happen if they tried to move in. They said I'd no right to hold range I wasn't usin', an' I told them to start something, an' I'd show 'em my rights with a gun. I like this country, and I mean to hold it. I'll get the cattle later. If any of these piddlin' little ranchers want trouble, I'll give it to 'em."

"Might as well keep these cows and get the rest of what that Irishman's got," Tanner said. "We've got the guns. If they are wiped out, we can always say they started it, and who's to say we're wrong?"

"Sure. My idea exactly," Targ agreed. "I want that Monaghan's ranch, anyway." He laughed. "And that ain't all he's got that I want."

"Why not tonight? He's only got four hands, and one

of them is bad hurt or dead. At least one more is wounded a mite."

"Uh-uh. I want that Sartain first. He's around somewhere, you can bet on that! He's hurt and hurt bad, but we didn't find him at the foot of that cliff, so he must have got away somehow! I want to pin his ears back, good!"

Kim eased himself deeper into the brush and tried to think his way out. His rifle was on his horse, and what had become of the dun he did not know. Obviously, the Monaghan riders had returned to the Y7, but it was he who had led Tom Monaghan into this fight, and it was up to him to get him out. But how?

The zebra dun, he knew, was no easy horse for a stranger to lay hands on. The chances were that the horse was somewhere out on the meadow, and his rifle with him. Across near the fire there were at least six men, and no doubt another one or two would be watching the trail down to the Y7.

It began to look as if he had taken a bigger bite than he could handle. Maybe Rusty was right after all, and he was just a loud-talking drifting saddle bum who could get into trouble but not out of it. The thought stirred him to action. He eased back away from the edge of the pool, taking his time and moving soundlessly. Whatever was done must be done soon.

The situation was simple enough. Obviously, Monaghan and some of the small flatland ranchers needed this upper range, but Targ, while not using it himself, was keeping them off. Now he obviously intended to do more. Kim Sartain had started something that seemed about to destroy the people he called his friends. And the girl too.

He swallowed that one. Maybe he wasn't the type for double harness, but if he was, Rusty Monaghan was the girl. And why shouldn't he be? Ward McQueen had been the same sort of hombre as himself, and Ward was marrying his boss—as pretty a girl as ever owned a ranch.

While he had decided to homestead this place simply because of Targ's high-handed manner, he could see that it was an excellent piece of range. From talk at the Y7 he knew there were more of these mountain meadows, and some of the other ranchers from below could move their stock up. His sudden decision, while based on pure deviltry, was actually a splendid idea.

His cattle were on the range, even if they still wore Monaghan's brand. That was tantamount to possession if he could make it stick, and Kim Sartain was not a man given to backing down when his bluff was called. The camp across the pool was growing quiet, for one after another of the men was turning in. A heavy-bodied, bearded man sat near the fire, half dozing. He was the one man on guard.

Quietly, Kim began to inch around the pool, and by the time an hour had passed and the riders were snoring loudly, he had completed the circuit to a point where he was almost within arm's length of the nearest sleeper. En route he had acquired something else—a long forked stick.

With infinite care, he reached out and lifted the belt and holster of the nearest rider, then, using the stick, retrieved those of the man beyond. Working his way around the camp, he succeeded in getting all the guns but those of the watcher, and those of Clyde Tanner. These last he deliberately left behind. Twice, he had to lift guns from under the edges of blankets, but only once did a man stir and look around, but as all was quiet and he could see the guard by the fire, the man returned to his sleep.

Now, Kim got to his feet. His bad leg was stiff, and he had to shift it with care, but he moved to a point opposite the guard. Now came the risky part, and the necessity for taking chances. His Colt level at the guard, he tossed a pebble against the man's chest. The fellow stirred, but did not look up. The next one caught him on the neck, and the guard looked up to see Kim Sartain, a finger across his lips for silence, the six-shooter to lend authority.

The guard gulped loudly, then his lips slackened and his eyes bulged. The heavy cheeks looked sick and flabby. With a motion of the gun, Kim indicated the man was to rise. Clumsily, the fellow got to his feet and at Sartain's gesture, approached him. Then Sartain turned the man around, and was about to tie his hands when the fellow's wits seemed to return. With more courage than wisdom, he suddenly bellowed, *"Targ! Tanner! It's him!"*

Kim Sartain's pistol barrel clipped him a ringing blow on the skull, and the big guard went down in a heap. Looking across his body, Kim Sartain stood with both hands filled with lead pushers. "You boys sit right still," he said, smiling. "I don't aim to kill anybody unless I have to. Now all of you but Tanner get up and move to the left."

He watched them with cat's eyes as they moved, alert for any wrong move. When they were lined up opposite him, all either barefooted or in sock feet, he motioned to Tanner. "You get up, Clyde. Now belt on your guns, but careful! Real careful!"

The gunman got shakily to his feet, his eyes murderous. He had been awakened from a sound sleep to look into Sartain's guns and see the hard blaze of the eyes beyond them. Nor did it pass unnoticed that all the guns had been taken but his, and his eyes narrowed, liking that implication not a bit.

"Targ," Kim said coldly, "you and your boys listen to me! I was ridin' through this country a perfect stranger until you tried to get mean! I don't like to have nobody ridin' me, see? So I went to see Monaghan, whom I'd never heard about until you mentioned him. I made a deal for cows, and I'm in these meadows to stay. You bit off more than you could chew.

"Moreover, you brought this yellow-streaked, coyote-killin' Tanner in here to do your gunslinging for you. I hear he's right good at it! And I hear he was huntin' me!

"The rest of you boys are mostly cowhands. You know the right and wrong of this as well as I do! Well, right here and now we're goin' to settle my claim on this land! I left Tanner his guns after takin' all yours because I figured he really wanted me. Now he'll get his chance; afterwards if any of the rest of you want me, you can buy in, one at a time! When the shootin's over here tonight, the fight's over."

His eyes riveted on Targ. "You hear that, Jim Targ? Tanner gets his chance, then you do, if you want it. But you make no trouble for Tom Monaghan, and no trouble for me. You're just a little man in a big country, you can keep your spread and run it small, or you can leave the country!"

As he finished speaking, he turned back to Tanner. "Now, you killer for pay, you've got your guns. I'm going to holster mine." His eyes swung to the waiting cowhands. "You," he indicated an oldish man with cold blue eyes and drooping gray mustaches, "give the word!"

With a flick of his hand, his gun dropped into its holster, and his hands to their sides. Jim Targ's eyes narrowed, but his cowhands were all attention. Kim Sartain knew his Western men. Even outlaws like a man with nerve and would see him get a break.

"Now!" The gray-mustached man yelled. "Go for 'em!"

Tanner spread his hands wide. "No! No!" he screamed the words. "Don't shoot!"

He was unused to meeting men face to face with an even break. The very fact that Sartain had left his guns for him, a taunt and a dare as well as an indication of Sartain's confidence, had wrecked what nerve the killer had.

Now he stepped back, his face gray. With death imminent, all the courage went out of him. "I ain't got no grudge agin you!" he protested. "It was that Targ! He set me on to you!"

The man who had given the signal exploded with anger. "Well, of all the yellow, two-bit, four-flushin' windbags!" His words failed him. "And you're supposed to be tough!" he said contemptuously.

Targ stared at Tanner, then shifted his eyes to Sartain. "That was a good play!" he said. "But I made no promises! Just because that coyote has yellow down his spine is no reason I forfeit this range!"

"I said," Sartain commented calmly, "the fighting ends here." Stooping, he picked up one of the gun belts and tossed it to Targ's feet. "There's your chance, if you want a quick slide into the grave!"

Targ's face worked with fury. He had plenty of courage, but he was remembering that lightning draw of the day before, and knew he could never match it, not even approach it. "I'm no gunfighter!" he said furiously. "But I won't quit! This here range belongs to me!"

"My cattle are on it," Kim said coolly. "I hold it. You set foot on it even once in the next year, and I'll hunt you down wherever you are and shoot you like a dog!"

Jim Targ was a study in anger and futility. His big hands opened and closed, and he muttered an oath. Whatever he was about to say was cut off short, for the gray-mustached hand yelled suddenly, "Look out!"

Kim wheeled, crouched and drawing as he turned. Tanner, his enemy's attention distracted, had taken the chance he was afraid to take with Sartain's eyes upon him. His gun was out and lifting, but Kim's speed was as the dart of a snake's head, a blur of motion, then a stab of red flame. Tanner's shot plowed dust at his feet. Then the killer wilted at the knees, turned halfway around, and fell into the dust beside the fire.

Sartain's gun swung back, but Targ had not moved, nor had the others. For an instant, the tableau held, and then Kim Sartain holstered his gun.

"Targ," he said, "you've made your play, and I've called you. Looks to me like you've drawn to a pair of deuces."

For just a minute the cattleman hesitated. He had his faults, but foolishness was not one of them. He knew when he was whipped. "I guess I have," he said ruefully. "Anyway, that trail would have been pure misery, a buildin'. Saves us a sight of work."

He turned away, and the hands bunched around him. All but the man with the gray mustache. His eyes twinkled.

"Looks like you'll be needin' some help, Sartain. Are you hirin'?"

"Sure!" Sartain grinned suddenly. "First thing, catch my horse—I've got me a game leg—and then take charge until I get back here!"

The boardinghouse triangle at the Y7 was clanging loudly when the dun cantered into the yard.

Kim dismounted stiffly and limped up the steps.

Tom Monaghan came to his feet, his eyes widened. The hands stared. Kim noted with relief that all were there. One man had a bandage around his head, another had his arm in a sling, his left arm, so he could still eat.

"Sort of wound things up," Sartain explained. "There won't be any trouble with Targ in the high meadows. Figured to drop down and have some breakfast."

Kim avoided Rusty's eyes but ate in silence. He was on his second cup of coffee when he felt her beside him. Then, clearing a space on the table, she put down a pie, its top golden brown and bulging with the promise of fruit underneath.

He looked up quickly. "I knew you'd be back," she said simply.

Author's Note:
RATTLESNAKE JACK FALLON

Western towns were inclined to be tolerant of rambunctious cowhands, but their mood could change with really bad men if the lead got to flying around promiscuously.

Rattlesnake Jack Fallon and Ed (Longhair) Owen rode into Lewistown, Montana, on July 4, 1884, in a disgruntled mood and, after beating up a citizen or two, took to shooting up the town. The two were known to be horse thieves and that coupled with a growing lack of patience brought out the citizens of Lewistown with Winchesters at the ready.

The two had been drinking, but when they saw the citizens forting up they started out of town. Their decision came too late. Longhair went down, Rattlesnake Jack fought his way back to his side, and the two cashed in their chips, firing until neither could pull a trigger any longer.

This led to a cleanup of rustlers in general, an action headed by Theodore Roosevelt and the Marquis de Mores, both ranching at the time in eastern Montana and North Dakota.

THE MARSHAL OF
PAINTED ROCK

Late as it was, the street of Painted Rock was ablaze with light. Saddled horses lined the hitch rails, and the stage was unloading down at the Empire House. Bearded men hustled by in the streets, some of them with packs, some hurrying to get packs. Word of the strike had gone out, and the town was emptying swiftly.

Matt Sabre stood against the wall of the Empire House and watched it absently. This he had seen many times before, this hurry and bustle. He had seen it over cattle, over land, over silver and gold. Wherever it seemed that money might quickly be had, there men thronged.

Good men, many of them. The strong, the brave, the true. But they were not alone, for here also were the scum. The cheats, the gamblers, the good-for-nothings. The men who robbed, who killed, who lived by deceit or treachery. And here also were those who felt that strength or gun skill made them the law—their own law. And these were often the most dangerous. And it was for these that he was here.

Two days now Matt Sabre had been marshal of Painted Rock. Yet the job was not new to him, for he had been marshal before in other towns. And this town was no different. Even the faces were the same. It was strange, he thought, how little difference there was in people. When one traveled, got around to many towns, one soon realized there were just so many types, and one found them in every town. Names were different, and expressions, but it was like many casts playing the same roles in a drama. The parts remained the same; only the names of the cast had changed.

Darius Gilbert, who owned the gambling house, for example. And Owen Cobb, the banker. Or tall, immaculate Nat Falley, with mining interests. The three were partners in the general store, and they ran the town. They were the council, and they had hired Matt Sabre as town marshal. A tough man for a tough job.

His eyes veiled as he watched the dismounting stage passengers, considering the three men, and most of all Nat Falley. Gilbert and Cobb were good men, upright men, but not fighters. If he was to get help or hindrance, it would come from Falley. In this town or any other, a man like Falley was a man to consider.

A girl was getting down from the stage, a girl dressed in gray. Her cheekbones were high yet delicate, her mouth too wide for true beauty, yet it added to her perfection. She stepped up to the walk, stared at by all, and then asked a question. A man gestured toward Matt Sabre. At once, her eyes turned to him, and he felt their impact. He took a step forward, removing his hat.

"You were looking for me? I'm the town marshal."

She smiled at him, a quick, woman's smile that told him she found him attractive, and also that she wanted something from him . . . and she could see that he believed her beautiful.

This was a woman to quicken the blood in a man, Sabre thought. As he stepped toward her, he saw Falley come from the Empire House and look down the street toward them. Strange, until then he had not noticed. Falley never seemed to carry a gun.

The girl in gray held out her hand to him. Her eyes were clear and very, very lovely.

"I am Claire Gallatin. I came as quickly as I could, but I've been afraid I'd be too late."

"Too late?"

"To see about your prisoner, about my brother."

Matt Sabre returned his hat to his head, and when his hand returned to his side, his eyes were again quiet. "I see. Your brother is a prisoner of mine? Under another name perhaps?"

"Yes. He was known here as Rafe Berry."

Matt Sabre somehow knew he had expected this. And yet he showed nothing in his face. "I am sorry, Miss Gallatin, sorry for you and your family. It is most unfortunate, but you see, Rafe Berry is to be hanged the day after tomorrow."

"Oh, no!" Her fingers touched his arm. "He mustn't be! It's all a dreadful mistake! Rafe couldn't have done what they accuse him of doing! I just know it!"

Her face was agonized, showing the shock and pain she must be feeling. He glanced around at the curious gathering about them. None listened obviously, yet all were attentive.

"We'd better go inside. We can talk in the dining room," he said quietly.

When they were seated at a table over coffee, she looked across the table at him; her eyes were very large. She leaned toward him, her hand resting on his sleeve. The touch was light yet intimate, and Matt found that he liked it. "Rafe wasn't a bad boy," she said quickly, "although he was reckless. But he never did hurt anybody, and I am sure he would not. There's been some dreadful mistake."

"The evidence was quite conclusive," Matt said quietly. "And in any event, I am only the marshal. I arrested

215

him, but I did not try him. Nor could I free him."

She ignored this. Her voice was low and persuasive as she talked, telling him of their Louisiana home, of her ailing mother, of how they needed Rafe at home. "I'm sure," she added, "that if he were home again, he would never come back here." And she talked on, her voice low. She was, he decided, just exactly what one would expect a cultured lady of Louisiana to be like.

He shook his head slowly. "Unfortunately, ma'am," he said gently, "Rafe has already been sentenced. There's nothing I, or anyone, could do."

She bit her lip. "No," she said, lifting her handkerchief, "I suppose not, but if there is anything—just anything—I could do, no matter how much it costs, would you let me know? After all, what will be gained by his death? If he goes away and is never seen again, wouldn't that be just as good?"

"I'm afraid folks wouldn't think so, ma'am. You see, the jury sentenced Rafe for murder, but it wasn't only that that they had in mind. This is to be an example, ma'am. There have been a lot of murders around here lately. They have to stop."

She left him then and went to her room, and Matt Sabre returned to the street. It was quiet that night, more quiet than usual. It was almost as if the whole town were waiting to see Rafe Berry hanged and if he was hanged on schedule . . . if not, the whole lid might blow off.

The lawless element had been running Painted Rock with complete immunity, and the first blow at this immunity had been struck by the arrest of Rafe Berry and his sentencing. For Sabre had demanded an immediate trial for Berry, and before anybody had time to cool off and before his friends had a chance to frighten the jury, Rafe Berry was tried and convicted and sentenced to hang.

The first attempt to save him had followed the trial when a note was found by Matt Sabre lying on his bed.

The note told him to see that Berry escaped or die. He not only ignored the note's warning but took added precautions. He double-locked the cell door and carried one key himself.

On the street, he paused, lighting a cigarette and letting his eyes travel slowly along the loafers who were beginning to gather with the ending of day. His eyes hesitated slightly as they reached the walk before Gilbert's Palace. Burt Breidenhart was standing there leaning against an awning post.

He bulked big standing there, and he bulked big in Painted Rock, too. Sabre watched with cold, knowing eyes as men turned across the street to avoid the man. And some of them were tough men. Breidenhart was cruel, vindictive, and dangerous. A brute with his fists, he was also a gunman of sorts. Yet it was his willingness to fight and kill that worried more peaceful men. And Breidenhart had trailed with Rafe Berry.

Matt Sabre turned from his place and walked slowly down the street, purposely walking close to Breidenhart. The big man turned slowly as he neared, and he smiled, his hard eyes dancing with a reckless light. "Hello, marshal!" He said it softly, yet with a certain lifting challenge in his voice. "Hope you ain't all set for that hangin'."

Sabre paused. "It doesn't really matter whether I am or not, Burt," he said quietly. "The hanging is scheduled and it will go off on schedule."

"Don't bet on it," Breidenhart said, hitching up his jeans. "Just don't you bet on it."

"It would be a safe bet," Sabre said quietly. And then he walked on, feeling Breidenhart's eyes following him. Other eyes followed him too. And then he felt a queer little start. Across the street were three horses, and he knew those horses and knew their riders. Johnny Call was in town!

Darius Gilbert came out of the Emporium with Cobb and Falley. They stopped when they saw him, and

Cobb said worriedly, "Matt, things don't look so good. Maybe we made a bad bet."

His eyes strayed from one to the other of them and rested finally on Nat Falley. "You boys getting the wind up? Nothing to worry about."

"Breidenhart's in town, spoiling for trouble." Gilbert looked over his cigar at Sabre. "You know he doesn't bluff. If he came in, he won't leave without starting something."

"I'll handle it."

"It isn't that easy," Falley said suddenly, irritably. "We've property to consider. Rafe Berry has fifty friends in this town right now, and they are all armed and ready for trouble. People will be killed and property damaged. If we go through with this hanging, they'll tear the town to pieces."

"And if we don't, they've got us whipped, and they'll know it. They'll bleed the town white. Sorry, but you've got to make a stand somewhere. We've got to show our teeth."

Gilbert cleared his throat and then nodded worriedly. "I suppose you're right, but still—"

"The jury found him guilty; the judge sentenced him." Matt Sabre let his eyes wander off up the street. "Sorry, gentlemen, but that's the way it stands."

"That's easy for you to say!" Cobb burst out. "What about us? What about our property?"

"You'll be protected," Sabre replied shortly. "I'm sorry, gentlemen, but there is something more than your property at stake. I refer to the welfare of the community. We are making a decision here today whether this community is to be ruled by justice and by law or by force and crime." Sabre took a step back. "Good evening, gentlemen!"

Yet as he turned away, he was uneasy. He needed support; one man alone could not stand before a mob. And these three were the town's wealth and power. Among them, they owned everything but the homes of the workers in the mines and small claims. Men with wives and families, but with little property and no power.

And Johnny Call was in town. Never forget that, Matt Sabre, he told himself. If you forget that, you die.

Johnny Call was a killer. Scarcely nineteen, utterly vicious, with nine killings behind him. His friends bragged that he was faster than Billy the Kid, that by the time he was twenty-one, he would have more killings chalked up and would still be alive.

Johnny Call had been a friend of Rafe Berry's too. Not that it mattered. Johnny had been hunting an excuse to tackle him, Matt knew. Yet the Johnny Calls of the West were an old story to Matt Sabre of Mobeetie. Matt Sabre of the cattle drives, Matt Sabre who had been Major Sabre and Colonel Sabre in more than one army.

He stopped at the corner, glanced both ways, then turned and started back, taking his time. Suddenly, he cut across the street. Long ago, he had practiced these sudden deviations from the way he appeared to be taking, and to it he probably owed his life on more than one occasion.

He was a tall man, lean in the body and wide in the shoulder. He wore a .44 Russian in the holster on his leg and had another, invisible to the casual eye, thrust behind his waistband under the edge of his coat.

He had known Johnny Call before. He had seen him before and watched his climb up the ladder of gunslinging fame. Johnny was not yet nineteen, and he had done most of his killing in two years. Four of the dead men had been town marshals, the last one had been the marshal of Painted Rock, who preceded Matt Sabre.

Lights were out now, and the street that had been crowded was about empty. With a curious sense of loss, he realized the men who had voted to hang Rafe Berry were gone on this gold rush. He considered that. . . . Suppose it had been a ruse?

No matter what the reason, they were gone, and what came he must face alone. He walked down to the Empire House and entered. It was the quietest night he had known.

Forcing the jail would not be easy. Jeb Cannon was jailer, and Jeb was a man who knew no compromise with duty. The building was strongly built, carved, in fact, from solid rock. It could be got at only from in front, and Jeb was inside with several rifles, two shotguns, and plenty of ammunition.

Still Breidenhart had seemed very sure of himself. Sabre thought that over and decided he did not like it. The big man would stop at nothing, but the place was invulnerable . . . unless they had a cannon. If a shell exploded against the door . . . Sabre felt a queer sense of premonition go through him, a subtle warning from his subconscious.

Blasting powder!

Quickly, over a cup of coffee, he surveyed the possible places where they might secure it. The store . . . he would have to see Falley and the others and block that. Or one of the claims. That could not be blocked, but there was probably little around. Those on the rush had probably taken their supplies with them.

Mentally, he reviewed the case against Rafe Berry. The man had shot and killed Plato Zappas, a Greek prospector, and had stolen his poke and his equipment. He had been seen on the road before Zappas's death, and he had been caught trying to sell Zappas's horse and pack mules.

It was given in evidence that he had also sold a horse once known to belong to Ryan, an Irish miner recently murdered. He was utterly vicious. He had laughed when they arrested him. He had laughed at the trial. He had said he had friends, that he would be set free. He had seemed very sure.

Breidenhart? Somehow Matt Sabre did not find that logical. Nor Johnny Call. To set him free against the will of the town would not be easy. It meant somebody of influence.

He shook his head. He was imagining things. Suddenly, he looked up to see Claire Gallatin beside him. "May I join you?" She smiled widely, then sat down. "I'm still hoping to persuade you to help us, you know." Her purse had fallen open, facing him. There was a fat sheaf of bills visible. "I must free my brother."

Matt shook his head. "Sorry. The answer is the same as before."

Her eyes searched his. "You're a strange man, Matt. Tell me about yourself."

"Nothing much to tell." His eyes were faintly humorous as he looked across the table. "I'm past thirty, single, and own a ranch south of here. I've covered a lot of countries and places." He smiled as he said this. "And I've known a lot of women, in Paris, in London, in Vienna and Florence. Twice women got things from me that I shouldn't have given them. Both times were before I was eighteen."

Her eyes chilled a little. "You mean you can't be persuaded now? Is it so wonderful to be hard? To be cold? Do you find it so admirable to be able to refuse a girl who wants to help her only brother to escape death? Is that something of which to be proud?" Her lips trembled. Her chin lifted proudly. "I'll admit, I had little hope, but I'd heard that western men were gallant and that if . . . if they lacked gallantry, they might . . . they might be persuaded by other means." She touched the packet of bills.

"And if that failed?"

"Matt Sabre," she said, her voice low and pleading, "can't you see? I am offering all that I have! Everything! I know it is very little, but—"

He smiled at her, his eyes twinkling faintly. "Very little? I think it is quite a lot. There must be two thousand dollars in that sheaf of bills!"

"Three thousand."

"And you . . . you're very lovely, very exciting, and you play your role even better than you did when I saw you play in *East Lynne*. That was last year, in El Paso."

Her face stiffened with anger. "You've been laughing at me! Why, you—"

Matt Sabre got up quickly and stepped back. "Laughing at you? Of course not! But this performance has been preposterous. Two days ago, I became marshal. My first official act was to arrest Rafe Berry and bring him to trial. He was convicted. Almost at once you appear and claim to be his sister."

"I was close by! I am his sister!" Her face was hard, and her lips had thinned, yet she was still, he admitted, beautiful.

"His sister? And you haven't even asked to see him?" Matt chuckled. "But don't be angry. I've enjoyed it. Only"—he leaned over the table—"who paid you to come here?"

She rose and walked away from him, walking rapidly toward the steps. He watched her, frowning thoughtfully.

Three thousand dollars was a lot to protect Rafe Berry. Or was it to protect somebody else? Somebody who could afford three thousand dollars to keep him quiet?

Nat Falley had come in, and he watched the girl up the stairs. "You're lucky," he said dryly. "She's very beautiful."

Sabre nodded. "Yes," he agreed, regretfully, "but maybe too expensive for me. For some things, the price is always too high."

Falley watched him go out the door, frowning thoughtfully. He looked up the steps, hesitated, then shrugged and walked away.

Back at the jail, Jeb opened the door for Sabre. "Town's full up," Jeb commented, "with mighty tough hombres. Reckon there'll be trouble?"

"Could be." Matt took a worn ledger from the desk.

In this ledger, arrests and dispositions were entered. Jeb eyed him dyspeptically as he opened it.

"Ain't much in there," he said. "What you huntin'?"

"I don't know exactly," Sabre admitted, "but Berry isn't the only man here who deserves hanging. And there's somebody behind this."

Jeb said nothing, watching the big man loitering across the street. Others were coming. They were beginning to close in. "You all right here?" Sabre asked him.

"Yep." Jeb turned his head. "Better'n you'll be out there. You better stay until day comes."

"I've work to do. I'll be able to do more outside, anyway. Keep back from the door. I've an idea they'll use blasting powder."

"They'd have to throw it," Jeb replied. "That won't be easy."

He closed the door behind Matt Sabre, and the marshal strolled forward; men faded back into the shadows, but anxious to avoid precipitating trouble, he seemed unaware of them. Yet he knew he must hurry. There was little time.

Darius Gilbert, one of the owners of the general store, was seated in the big buffalo-hide chair. He looked pale and worried. His usually florid cheeks had lost color, and his brows were drawn in. As Matt entered the Empire House, he got hurriedly to his feet and thrust a note into his hands. Matt glanced at it, the same cheap paper, the penciled words: *Call off your marshal or we'll burn you out*. It was unsigned.

"They won't." Sabre folded the note and put it in his pocket. It was not, he realized, an entire sheet. It had been torn from a larger sheet, as had his own warning note. Each had been written on the bottom of a page. Hence, if he found that tablet and these torn sheets fitted . . . "Where's Owen Cobb?" he asked.

"At the store. He's worried about it. He's sittin' over there with a rifle."

223

Sabre tapped his pocket. "You sell paper like that note?"

"I don't know. Cobb does the buyin' an' sellin'. I've just got money invested, like Nat Falley."

Matt Sabre sat down and opened the ledger he had brought with him. Time and again, the same names. Most were simple drunk and disorderly charges, yet there were a number of arrests for robbery, most of them released for lack of evidence.

"Did you ever stop to think, Gilbert, that somebody has been protecting the crooks around here?"

Gilbert turned his big head and stared at Sabre. His eyes blinked. "You mean somebody is behind 'em? That I doubt."

"Look at this: Berry bailed out three times. No evidence to bring him to trial at any time. And this man Dickert. His fines paid, witnesses that won't talk, some of them bribed and some frightened."

Sabre tapped the book as Falley joined them. "Checking this book and the one I examined last night, I find Breidenhart bailed some of these men out and paid fines for others. It figures to be more than a thousand dollars in the past three months."

Gilbert rubbed his jaw. "That's a lot of money."

"It is. And did Breidenhart ever impress you as a philanthropist? Where does he get that kind of money? To my notion, he's the middleman, and somebody else is behind all this, taking the major portion of the loot for protection and tipoffs."

Sabre tapped a folded paper. "Here's a list of robbed men. All had money. In the very nature of things, thieves would make an occasional bad guess, but not these fellows. That means they were told who carried money and who did not."

"What do you plan to do?" Falley asked.

Sabre got to his feet. He looked at Nat Falley and shrugged. "The answer is obvious. Get the leader and your crime will drop to nothing at all. He's the man we want. And I may ask you gentlemen for help."

He must see Owen Cobb. He walked swiftly along the street, noting the increasing number of men who loitered about. But there was time. He found Cobb in his room, one shoe off. "Yes," Cobb admitted, "I did sell some powder today. Sold it to that man Dickert."

Sabre got to his feet. "Thanks. Just what I wanted to know."

Cobb looked up, rubbing his foot. "Matt, you forget it. This is too big for us. Let Berry go. If we don't let him go, there'll be hell to pay. I been settin' here wonderin' if I dare go to bed."

"You go to bed." Sabre's face was somber in the reflected lamplight. "This is my problem."

At the door he hesitated, considering again the problem before him. He must talk to Nat Falley. It was just a hunch, but Falley would know about the mining claims.

Outside, he paused, listening. There was subdued movement, and he knew his time was growing short. So far, they were still gathering; then they would bunch and talk before moving against the jail. He turned into a dark alleyway and walked swiftly along it.

There was a cabin a block off the main street, and a light was showing. Sabre's step quickened, and he dropped a hand to his gun to make sure it was ready. At the cabin, he did not knock or stop; he lifted the latch and stepped in.

Dickert was sitting at the table cutting a short piece of fuse still shorter. A can of powder was on the floor near him. As he saw Sabre, he started to his feet, clawing for a gun. Matt struck swiftly, and Dickert toppled back, knocking the table over. Yet the miner was a burly man, and rugged. He came up swiftly and swung. Matt, overly eager, stepped in and caught the punch on the cheekbone. Springing after him, Dickert

stepped into a wicked, lifting right uppercut to the
brisket. He gulped and stepped back and, grabbing his
stomach, turned sideways. Sabre struck swiftly and without mercy, smashing the man behind the ear with his fist.

Dickert hit the floor on his face and lay still. Swiftly,
Matt Sabre bound him. Then he picked up the powder,
and dabbing at the cut on his cheekbone, he left the
cabin.

When he again reached the street, he moved quietly
up to the gathering of men. One man hung on the edge
of the crowd, and Matt tapped him gently on the
shoulder, then drew him to one side. In the vague light
from a window, he recognized the man as a tough
miner he had seen about. "Hello, Jack," he said quietly.
"Kind of late for you to be around, isn't it?"

Uneasily, the miner shifted his feet. That he had not
expected Sabre was obvious, and also that he had planned
to shield his own identity in the anonymous shadow of
the crowd. Now he was suddenly recognized and in the
open. He had no liking for it. "You know, Jack," Sabre
suggested, "I've never found you in trouble so far, but
I'm here to stay, Jack, and if there's trouble, I'll know
one man to arrest. You want to be the goat?"

"Now, look Matt," Jack protested, "I'm just lookin'
on. I ain't done a thing!"

"Then why not go home and keep out of it?" Sabre
suggested.

The miner shrugged. "Reckon you're right. See you."
He turned and walked quickly away.

Sabre watched him go, searching for Breidenhart. No
sign of him yet. Knowing much of the psychology of
mobs, Sabre circulated through the crowd, staring long
into this face and that, occasionally making a suggestion.
Here and there, a man slipped away and vanished into
darkness. Mobs, he reflected, must be anonymous. Most
men who make up mobs act only under influence of the
crowd. Singled out and suddenly alone, they become
uncertain and uneasy. Deliberately, he let them know

that he knew them. Deliberately, he walked among them, making each man feel known, cut off.

Returning to the shadows, Sabre unlocked a door and picked up a bundle of tied-up man. He cut loose the ropes around his ankles. "Just walk along with me and you'll have no trouble."

"You can't get away with this!" Dickert protested. "I ain't done nothin'!"

"And you aren't going to. You've been arrested and the powder confiscated until things quiet down. I'm keeping you out of trouble."

As they moved into the light beside the jail door, there was a shout from the crowd. Men surged forward. "There's Dickert! What's up? Why's he arrested?"

Sabre glanced at them, then said, "Prisoner, Jeb." He shoved Dickert inside, then turned to the angry crowd. He singled out their angry stares one by one, nodding at each recognition. "I arrested Dickert to keep him out of trouble. There's been some fool talk about blowing the jail, and he had possession of some powder. He'll stay inside until he's safe."

Sabre smiled. "I suppose you boys are down here to be sure the prisoner isn't taken away. Well, he's in safe hands. You'll have your hanging, all right. No need to worry." His eyes settled on the face of one man. "Hello, Bill. I noticed on the jail books that you're out on bond. Don't leave town as I'll pick you up in a day or two. There are eight or ten of you here tonight who are due for trial within the next few weeks. I'm going to clean the books fast. I know you don't want to have to wait for trial.

"Those of you"—he spoke louder—"who deserve hanging will get it. Any attempt at mob violence here tonight will be punished by hanging. I've a man who will talk to save his own skin, so there will be evidence enough."

Inwardly, his stomach was tight, his mouth dry. He stood in the full light, outwardly calm and confident, aware that he must break their shell of mob thinking and force each man to think of his own plight and the consequences to himself. He must make each man sure he was recognized, known. As a mass, thinking with one mind, they were dangerous, but if each began to worry . . . "Glad to see you, Shroyer. I'll be picking you up tomorrow. And you, Swede. No more protection, boys; that's over."

There was a sudden stir in the crowd, and Breidenhart pushed his way through. He grinned at Sabre. "All right, boys! Let's bust this jail open and turn Rafe loose!"

Breidenhart half turned his head to speak to the crowd, and Matt took a swift step forward and grabbed him by the back of the shirt collar, jerking him backward, off balance. As the big man toppled, Sabre took a quick turn on the collar, tightening it to a strangling grip. His other hand held a quickly drawn .44 Russian. "Stand back! Let's have no trouble now!"

Breidenhart struggled furiously, kicking and thrashing while his face turned dark.

"He's stranglin'," Shroyer protested.

"That's too bad," Sabre replied shortly. "A man who hunts trouble usually gets it."

"Take him!" a voice shouted from the rear. "Rush him, you fools! He's only one man! Don't let him get away with this!"

The voice was strangely familiar. Sabre strained his eyes over the heads of the crowd as they surged forward. Shroyer was in the lead, not altogether of his own volition. Sabre dropped Breidenhart and kicked him away with his foot. Then he shot Shroyer through the knee. The man screamed and fell, and that scream stopped the crowd.

"The next shot is to kill," Sabre said loudly. "If that man in the rear wants trouble, send him up. He's mighty anxious to get you killed, but I don't see him up in front!"

Behind him, Jeb Cannon's voice drawled lazily from the barred window of the jail door. "Let 'em come, Matt," he said. "I got two barrels of buckshot ready and enough shells laid here on a chair to kill an army. Let 'em come."

Breidenhart was tugging at his collar, still gasping. He started to rise, and with scarcely a glance, Sabre slashed down with his gun barrel, and Breidenhart fell like a dropped log and lay flat. Sabre waited, his gun ready, while Shroyer moaned on the ground.

Men at the back of the crowd slipped quietly away into the darkness, and those in front, feeling the space behind them, glanced around to see the crowd scattered and melting.

When the last of them had drawn back and disappeared, Jeb opened the jail door. He collared Breidenhart and dragged him within. Sabre picked up Shroyer and carried him inside. The bone was shattered, and the wound was bleeding badly. Sabre worked over it swiftly, doing what he could. "I'll get the doctor," he said then.

At breakfast, Matt Sabre looked up to see Claire Gallatin come into the room. He got up quickly and invited her to join him. She hesitated, then crossed the room and sat down opposite him. "What happened last night? I'm dying to know!"

After explaining briefly, he added, "I've nothing against you, but tell me. Who paid you to come here?"

"I have no idea." She drew a letter, written on the already-familiar tablet paper, from her purse. It was an offer of five hundred dollars if she would claim to be the sister of the prisoner and use her wiles on the marshal. If that failed, she was to offer a bribe. "I wasn't much good at it," she told him, "or else you aren't very susceptible."

Sabre chuckled. "I'm susceptible, but you're better in the theater. I've seen you in New Orleans as well as El Paso. In fact, you're very good."

Her smile was brilliant. "I feel better already! But"—

her face became woeful—"what will we do? The company went broke in El Paso, and now I won't get the rest of my money. I'd planned on the pay to get us back East again."

"You still have the bribe money?"

She nodded.

"Then keep it." He shrugged. "After all, to whom could you return it? You just go back to El Paso and get the show on the road."

The door opened before she could protest, and Nat Falley came in with Gilbert and Cobb. Falley smiled quickly, looking from the girl to Sabre. Gilbert looked worried, and Cobb was frowning. When they were seated, Sabre explained about the bribe money. "You agree?" he asked.

Gilbert hesitated, then shrugged. "S'pose so." Cobb added his agreement, and then Falley.

"You seem to have handled a bad situation very well," Falley said. "Who was hurt by that shot?"

"Shroyer. He's in jail with a broken leg."

"You'll try him for that old killing?" Falley demanded.

Sabre shook his head, looking at the mining man again. "No, I promised him immunity."

"What? You'd let him go?" Cobb protested. "But you know he's one of the worst of them!"

"He talked," Sabre said quietly. "He gave me a sworn statement. Since then, I've been gathering evidence."

"Evidence?"

Falley sat up straight. Only Cobb seemed relaxed now. He was watching Sabre, his eyes suddenly attentive. Nat Falley crossed and uncrossed his legs. He started to speak, then stopped. His eyes were on Sabre. Gilbert hitched his chair nearer.

"What evidence?" Gilbert demanded. "What did you find out?"

"All we need now is a jury. We can hold our trial today. That's one blessing," he said grimly, "about mak-

230

ing your own law and having no court calendar to consider."

"But who was it? Who is behind this crime?"

Matt Sabre looked into the tightly drawn face of the man opposite him. "Don't try anything, Falley," he said quietly. "I've had you covered under the table ever since you came in."

To the others, he explained, "There was more behind it than the loot. Falley was trying to grab all the valuable claims by having the owners murdered. Checking over the list, I noticed the apparent coincidence, that the victims not only carried money but in each case owned a valuable claim. The murderers got the money, while Falley moved in and took over the claims. Rafe Berry and Breidenhart were the right hand men."

With his left hand, he drew a tablet from his coat pocket. "Ever see that before?"

Cobb leaned forward. "Why, it's Falley's! Those are his notations on the pages, I'd know them anywhere!"

"Flip the pages to the back and you'll see the note you found, Gilbert, will fit perfectly in one of the torn sheets. The same thing is true with the note that reached me."

Cobb looked at Falley. "Anything to say, Nat? He's got you cold."

"Only that he'll never get out of town alive." Falley's eyes were ugly. "I made sure of that."

Cobb disarmed Falley, and then at a movement near the door, their heads turned. It was Johnny Call.

Matt Sabre nodded to him. "I was hoping you'd come around, Johnny. I wanted to say good-by."

"Good-by?" Johnny blinked stupidly. "What's the idea?"

"Why, you're leaving town, Johnny. You're leaving inside the hour—and you're not coming back."

"Who says so?" Johnny took a sliding step farther into the room. His hands hovered above his guns. "Who says so?"

"Johnny"—Sabre's voice held a great patience—"you'll do all right with guns as long as you shoot up old men and common cowhands, but stay away from the good ones. Don't start anything with Jeff Milton, Bat Masterson, or Luke Short. Any one of them could tell just when you're going to draw by the way you move your feet."

"My feet?" Johnny looked down. Instantly, his eyes came up, only now he was looking into Sabre's .44 Russian.

"That's it, Johnny." Sabre was low-voiced. "You aren't good with a gun; you've just been trailing with slow company. And you think too slow, Johnny. Now unbuckle your belts."

For a long minute, Johnny Call hesitated. He had bragged that he would kill Matt Sabre. He had told Nat Falley he would kill him. But Matt Sabre was a dead shot, and the range was less than twenty feet. Carefully, he unbuckled his belts and let them drop. "Now get out of town, Johnny. If you're here after one hour, I'll kill you." His eyes held Call's. "Remember, it's better to be a live cowhand than a dead gunman."

Call turned and went out the door, and he did not look back. Matt got to his feet. "Let's go, Falley."

Heavily, the man got to his feet. He glanced at his former friends and started to speak, then walked out ahead of Sabre.

Claire Gallatin looked after Sabre. "He's—he's quite a man, isn't he?" she said, wistfully.

Gilbert nodded slowly. "Any man," he said, "can run a town with killings, if he is fast enough. To clean up a tough town without killing, that takes a *man!*"

Author's Note:
BLOODSUCKING TICKS

Among the parasites that afflicted cattle on the western range, bloodsucking ticks were the worst. They fattened on the blood of ranchers' cattle, but there is no record of a tick ever raising a cow itself.

The following story, "Trap of Gold" has already been collected in WAR PARTY. I'm only including it as an extra story in this volume as well because the unauthorized edition of my frontier stories contains the magazine version of this story, and I did not want any of my readers to feel that this authorized edition of LAW OF THE DESERT BORN was "missing" anything.

TRAP OF GOLD

Wetherton had been three months out of Horsehead before he found his first color. At first, it was a few scattered grains taken from the base of an alluvial fan where millions of tons of sand and silt had washed down from a chain of rugged peaks; yet the gold was ragged under the magnifying glass.

Gold that has carried any distance becomes worn and polished by the abrasive action of the accompanying rocks and sand, so this could not have been carried far. With caution born of harsh experience, he seated himself and lit his pipe, yet excitement was strong within him.

A contemplative man by nature, his experience had taught him how a man may be deluded by hope, yet all his instincts told him the source of the gold was somewhere on the mountain above. It could have come down the wash that skirted the base of the mountain, but the ragged condition of the gold made that improbable.

The base of the fan was a half mile across and hundreds of feet thick, built of silt and sand washed down by centuries of erosion among the higher peaks. The point of the wide V of the fan lay between two towering upthrusts of granite, but from where Wetherton sat, he could see that the actual source of the fan lay much higher.

Wetherton made camp near a tiny spring west of the fan, then picketed his burros and began his climb. When he was well over two thousand feet higher, he stopped, resting again, and while resting, he dry-panned some of the silt. Surprisingly, there were more than a few grains of gold even in that first pan, so he continued his climb and passed at last between the towering portals of the granite columns.

Above this natural gate were three smaller alluvial fans that joined at the gate to pour into the greater fan below. Dry-panning two of these brought no results, but the third, even by the relatively poor method of dry-panning, showed a dozen colors, all of good size.

The head of this fan lay in a gigantic crack in a granite upthrust that resembled a fantastic ruin. Pausing to catch his breath, he let his gaze wander along the base of this upthrust, and right before him the crumbling granite was slashed with a vein of quartz that was literally laced with gold!

Struggling nearer through the loose sand, his heart pounding more from excitement than from altitude and exertion, he came to an abrupt stop. The band of quartz was six feet wide, and that six feet was cobwebbed with gold.

It was unbelievable, but there it was.

Yet even in this moment of success, something about the beetling cliff stopped him from going forward. His innate caution took hold, and he drew back to examine it at greater length. Wary of what he saw, he circled the batholith and then climbed to the ridge behind it, from which he could look down upon the roof. What he saw from there left him dry-mouthed and jittery.

The granite upthrust was obviously a part of a much older range, one that had weathered and worn, suffered from shock and twisting, until finally this tower of granite had been violently upthrust, leaving it standing, a shaky ruin among younger and sturdier peaks. In the process, the rock had been shattered and riven by mighty forces until it had become a miner's horror. Wetherton stared, fascinated by the prospect. With enormous wealth there for the taking, every ounce must be taken at the risk of life.

One stick of powder might bring the whole crumbling mass down in a heap, and it loomed all of three hundred feet above its base in the fan. The roof of the batholith was riven with gigantic cracks, literally seamed with breaks like the wall of an ancient building that has remained standing after heavy bombing. Walking back to the base of the tower, Wetherton found he could actually break loose chunks of the quartz with his fingers.

The vein itself lay on the downhill side and at the very base. The outer wall of the upthrust was sharply tilted so that a man working at the vein would be cutting his way into the very foundations of the tower, and any single blow of the pick might bring the whole mass down upon him. Furthermore, if the rock did fall, the vein would be hopelessly buried under thousands of tons of rock and lost without the expenditure of much more capital than he could command. And at this moment, Wetherton's total of money in hand amounted to slightly less than forty dollars.

Thirty yards from the face, he seated himself upon the sand and filled his pipe once more. A man might take tons out of there without trouble, and yet it might collapse at the first blow. Yet he knew he had no choice. He needed money, and it lay there before him. Even if he were at first successful, there were two things he must avoid. The first was tolerance of danger that might bring carelessness; the second, that urge to go back for that "little bit more" that could kill him.

It was well into the afternoon, and he had not eaten, yet he was not hungry. He circled the batholith, studying it from every angle, only to reach the conclusion that his first estimate had been correct. The only way to get to the gold was to go into the very shadow of the leaning wall and attack it at its base, digging it out by main strength. From where he stood, it seemed ridiculous that a mere man with a pick could topple that mass of rock, yet he knew how delicate such a balance could be.

The tower was situated on what might be described as the military crest of the ridge, and the alluvial fan sloped steeply away from its lower side, steeper than a steep stairway. The top of the leaning wall overshadowed the top of the fan, and if it started to crumble and a man had warning, he might run to the north with a bare chance of escape. The soft sand in which he must run would be an impediment, but that could be alleviated by making a walk from flat rocks sunken into the sand.

It was dusk when he returned to his camp. Deliberately, he had not permitted himself to begin work, not by so much as a sample. He must be deliberate in all his actions, and never for a second should he forget the mass that towered above him. A split second of hesitation when the crash came—and he accepted it as inevitable—would mean burial under tons of crumbled rock.

The following morning, he picketed his burros on a small meadow near the spring, cleaned the spring itself, and prepared a lunch. Then he removed his shirt, drew on a pair of gloves, and walked to the face of the cliff. Yet even then he did not begin, knowing that upon this habit of care and deliberation might depend not only his success in the venture but life itself. He gathered flat stones and began building his walk. "When you start moving," he told himself, "you'll have to be fast."

Finally, and with infinite care, he began tapping at the quartz, enlarging cracks with the pick, removing fragments, then prying loose whole chunks. He did not swing the pick but used it as a lever. The quartz was rotten, and a man might obtain a considerable amount by this method of picking or even pulling with the hands. When he had a sack filled with the richest quartz, he carried it over his path to a safe place beyond the shadow of the tower. Returning, he tamped a few more flat rocks into his path and began on the second sack. He worked with greater care than was, perhaps, essential. He was not and had never been a gambling man.

In the present operation, he was taking a carefully calculated risk in which every eventuality had been weighed and judged. He needed the money, and he intended to have it; he had a good idea of his chances of success but knew that his gravest danger was to become too greedy, too much engrossed in his task.

Dragging the two sacks down the hill, he found a flat block of stone and with a single jack proceeded to break up the quartz. It was a slow and hard job, but he had no better means of extracting the gold. After breaking or crushing the quartz, much of the gold could be separated by a knife blade, for it was amazingly concentrated. With water from the spring, Wetherton panned the remainder until it was too dark to see.

Out of his blankets by daybreak, he ate breakfast and completed the extraction of the gold. At a rough estimate, his first day's work would run to four hundred dollars. He made a cache for the gold sack and took the now-empty ore sacks and climbed back to the tower.

The air was clear and fresh, the sun warm after the chill of night, and he liked the feel of the pick in his hands.

Laura and Tommy awaited him back in Horsehead, and if he was killed there, there was small chance they would ever know what had become of him. But he did not intend to be killed. The gold he was extracting from this rock was for them and not for himself.

It would mean an easier life in a larger town, a home of their own, and the things to make the home a woman desires. And it meant an education for Tommy. For himself, all he needed was the thought of that home to return to, his wife and son—and the desert itself. And one was as necessary to him as the other.

The desert would be the death of him. He had been told that many times and did not need to be told, for few men knew the desert as he did. The desert was to him what an orchestra is to a fine conductor, what the human body is to a surgeon. It was his work, his life, and the thing he knew best. He always smiled when he looked first into the desert as he started a new trip. Would this be it?

The morning drew on, and he continued to work with an even-paced swing of the pick, a careful filling of the sack. The gold showed bright and beautiful in the crystalline quartz, which was so much more beautiful than the gold itself. From time to time as the morning drew on, he paused to rest and to breathe deeply of the fresh, clear air. Deliberately, he refused to hurry.

For nineteen days, he worked tirelessly, eight hours a day at first, then lessening his hours to seven and then to six. Wetherton did not explain to himself why he did this, but he realized it was becoming increasingly difficult to stay on the job. Again and again, he would walk away from the rock face on one excuse or another, and each time he would begin to feel his scalp prickle, his steps grow quicker, and each time he returned more reluctantly.

Three times, beginning on the thirteenth, again on the seventeenth, and finally on the nineteenth day, he heard movement within the tower. Whether that whispering in the rock was normal he did not know. Such a natural movement might have been going on for centuries. He only knew that it happened then, and each time it happened, a cold chill went along his spine.

His work had cut a deep notch at the base of the tower, such a notch as a man might make in felling a tree, but wider and deeper. The sacks of gold, too, were increasing. They now numbered seven, and their total would, he believed, amount to more than five thousand dollars—probably nearer to six thousand. As he cut deeper into the rock, the vein was growing richer.

He worked on his knees now. The vein had slanted downward as he cut into the base of the tower, and he was all of nine feet into the rock with the great mass of it above him. If that rock gave way while he was working, he would be crushed in an instant, with no chance of escape. Nevertheless, he continued.

The change in the rock tower was not the only change, for he had lost weight, and he no longer slept well. On the night of the twentieth day, he decided he had six thousand dollars and his goal would be ten thousand. And the following day, the rock was the richest ever! As if to tantalize him into working on and on, the deeper he cut, the richer the ore became. By nightfall of that day, he had taken out more than a thousand dollars.

Now the lust of the gold was getting into him, taking him by the throat. He was fascinated by the danger of the tower as well as the desire for the gold. Three more days to go—could he leave it then? He looked again at the tower and felt a peculiar sense of foreboding, a feeling that here he was to die, that he would never escape. Was it his imagination, or had the outer wall leaned a little more?

On the morning of the twenty-second day, he climbed the fan over a path that use had built into a series of continuous steps. He had never counted those steps, but there must have been over a thousand of them. Dropping his canteen into a shaded hollow and pick in hand, he started for the tower.

The forward tilt *did* seem somewhat more than before.

Or was it the light? The crack that ran behind the outer wall seemed to have widened, and when he examined it more closely, he found a small pile of freshly run silt near the bottom of the crack. So it had moved!

Wetherton hesitated, staring at the rock with wary attention. He was a fool to go back in there again. Seven thousand dollars was more than he had ever had in his life before, yet in the next few hours he could take out at least a thousand dollars more, and in the next three days he could easily have the ten thousand he had set for his goal.

He walked to the opening, dropped to his knees, and crawled into the narrowing, flat-roofed hole. No sooner was he inside than fear climbed up into his throat. He felt trapped, stifled, but he fought down the mounting panic and began to work. His first blows were so frightened and feeble that nothing came loose. Yet when he did get started, he began to work with a feverish intensity that was wholly unlike him.

When he slowed and then stopped to fill his sack, he was gasping for breath, but despite his hurry, the sack was not quite full. Reluctantly, he lifted his pick again, but before he could strike a blow, the gigantic mass above him seemed to creak like something tired and old. A deep shudder went through the colossal pile, and then a deep grinding that turned him sick with horror. All his plans for instant flight were frozen, and it was not until the groaning ceased that he realized he was lying on his back, breathless with fear and expectancy. Slowly, he edged his way into the air and walked, fighting the desire to run, away from the rock.

When he stopped near his canteen, he was wringing with cold sweat and trembling in every muscle. He sat down on the rock and fought for control. It was not until some twenty minutes had passed that he could trust himself to get to his feet.

Despite his experience, he knew that if he did not go back now, he would never go. He had out but one sack for the day and wanted another. Circling the batholith, he examined the widening crack, endeavoring again, for the third time, to find another means of access to the vein.

The tilt of the outer wall was obvious, and it could stand no more without toppling. It was possible that by cutting into the wall of the column and striking down, he might tap the vein at a safer point. Yet this added blow at the foundation would bring the tower nearer to collapse and render his other hole untenable. Even this new attempt would not be safe, although immeasurably more secure than the hole he had left. Hesitating, he looked back at the hole.

Once more? The ore was now fabulously rich, and the few pounds he needed to complete the sack he could get in just a little while. He stared at the black and undoubtedly narrower hole, then looked up at the leaning wall. He picked up his pick and, his mouth dry, started back, drawn by a fascination that was beyond all reason.

His heart pounding, he dropped to his knees at the tunnel face. The air seemed stifling, and he could feel his scalp tingling, but once he started to crawl, it was better. The face where he now worked was at least sixteen feet from the tunnel mouth. Pick in hand, he began to wedge chunks from their seat. The going seemed harder now, and the chunks did not come loose so easily. Above him, the tower made no sound. The crushing weight was now something tangible. He could almost feel it growing, increasing with every move of his. The mountain seemed resting on his shoulder, crushing the air from his lungs.

Suddenly, he stopped. His sack almost full, he stopped and lay very still, staring up at the bulk of the rock above him.

No.

He would go no farther. Now he would quit. Not another sackful. Not another pound. He would go out now. He would go down the mountain without a backward look, and he would keep going. His wife waiting at home, little Tommy, who would run gladly to meet him—these were too much to gamble.

With the decision came peace, came certainty. He sighed deeply and relaxed, and then it seemed to him that every muscle in his body had been knotted with strain. He turned on his side and with great deliberation gathered his lantern, his sack, his hand pick.

He had won. He had defeated the crumbling tower, he had defeated his own greed. He backed easily, without the caution that had marked his earlier movements in the cave. His blind, trusting foot found the projecting rock, a piece of quartz that stuck out from the rough-hewn wall.

The blow was too weak, too feeble to have brought forth the reaction that followed. The rock seemed to quiver like the flesh of a beast when stabbed; a queer vibration went through that ancient rock, then a deep, gasping sigh.

He had waited too long!

Fear came swiftly in upon him, crowding him, while his body twisted, contracting into the smallest possible space. He tried to will his muscles to move beneath the growing sounds that vibrated through the passage. The whispers of the rock grew into a terrifying groan, and there was a rattle of pebbles. Then silence.

The silence was more horrifying than the sound. Somehow he was crawling, even as he expected the avalanche of gold to bury him. Abruptly, his feet were in the open. He was out.

He ran without stopping, but behind him he heard a growing roar that he couldn't outrace. When he knew from the slope of the land that he must be safe from falling rock, he fell to his knees. He turned and looked back. The muted, roaring sound, like thunder beyond mountains, continued, but there was no visible change in the tower. Suddenly, as he watched, the whole rock formation seemed to shift and tip. The movement lasted only seconds, but before the tons of rock had found their new equilibrium, his tunnel and the area around it had utterly vanished from sight.

When he could finally stand, Wetherton gathered up his sack of ore and his canteen. The wind was cool upon his face as he walked away, and he did not look back again.

About Louis L'Amour

"I think of myself in the oral tradition—as a troubadour, a village taleteller, the man in the shadows of the campfire. That's the way I'd like to be remembered—as a storyteller. A good storyteller."

It is doubtful that any author could be as at home in the world recreated in his novels as Louis Dearborn L'Amour. Not only could he physically fill the boots of the rugged characters he wrote about, but he literally "walked the land my characters walk." His personal experiences as well as his lifelong devotion to historical research combined to give Mr. L'Amour the unique knowledge and understanding of people, events, and the challenge of the American frontier that became the hallmarks of his popularity.

Of French-Irish descent, Mr. L'Amour could trace his own family in North America back to the early 1600s and follow their steady progression westward, "always on the frontier." As a boy growing up in Jamestown, North Dakota, he absorbed all he could about his family's frontier heritage, including the story of his great-grandfather who was scalped by Sioux warriors.

Spurred by an eager curiosity and desire to broaden his horizons, Mr. L'Amour left home at the age of fifteen and enjoyed a wide variety of jobs including seaman, lumberjack, elephant handler, skinner of dead cattle, assessment miner, and officer on tank destroyers during World War II. During his "yondering" days he also circled the world on a freighter, sailed a dhow on the Red Sea, was shipwrecked in the West Indies and stranded in the Mojave Desert. He won fifty-one of fifty-nine fights as a professional boxer and worked as a journalist and lecturer. He was a voracious reader and collector of rare books. His personal library contained 17,000 volumes.

Mr. L'Amour "wanted to write almost from the time I could talk." After developing a widespread following for his many frontier and adventure stories written for fiction magazines, Mr. L'Amour published his first full-length novel, *Hondo*, in the United States in 1953. Every one of his more than 100 books is in print; there are nearly 230 million copies of his books in print worldwide, making him one of the bestselling authors in modern literary history. His books have been translated into twenty languages, and more than forty-five of his novels and stories have been made into feature films and television movies.

His hardcover bestsellers include *The Lonesome Gods*, *The Walking Drum* (his twelfth-century historical novel) *Jubal Sackett*, *Last of the Breed*, and *The Haunted Mesa*. His memoir, *Education of a Wandering Man*, was a leading bestseller in 1989. Audio dramatizations and adaptations of many L'Amour stories are available on cassette tapes from Bantam Audio Publishing.

The recipient of many great honors and awards, in 1983 Mr. L'Amour became the first novelist ever to be awarded the Congressional Gold Medal by the United States Congress in honor of his life's work. In 1984 he was also awarded the Medal of Freedom by President Reagan.

Louis L'Amour died on June 10, 1988. His wife, Kathy, and their two children, Beau and Angelique, carry the L'Amour tradition forward with new books written by the author during his lifetime to be published by Bantam well into the nineties—among them, four Hopalong Cassidy novels: *The Rustlers of West Fork*, *The Trail to Seven Pines*, *The Riders of High Rock*, and *Trouble Shooter*.